I0666736

Rapture of the Deep

Alan Gill

ISBN: 978-0-6151-8875-1

Publisher: Alan Gill

Rights Owner: Alan Gill

Language: English

Country: United States

Version 4

Thriller—Washington State
Mermaids—Washington State
Scuba diving—Washington State

For my patient wife, Pam

Prologue

The rape was especially violent yet strangely tender at the same time. The beast rumbled out of the sea, and flung her to the wet sand. He entered her from behind, his weight pressing her painfully into the cold ground. She did not cry out. No one would have heard on this deserted expanse of rocky coastline. The clouds scudded overhead. They hovered above the cliff tops and then sent down cold rain to cover up the incriminating evidence.

His body was not clothed, but covered in thick hair that stunk of animal. For a moment she thought her attacker was a sea lion. She could smell his breath, fouled by dead fish, as he gently nibbled her earlobes and the back of her neck. His penis throbbed and pulsated with a mind of its own. The assault continued as he increased the tempo of his thrusts and forced her to accommodate him by lifting her hips to meet his attack. The pain between her legs increased as the rhythm became more violent and she cried out. Her shrill scream, flung into the cold wind, left her gasping as he spent himself inside her and filled her with warm liquid

Afterwards he remained inside her and encompassed her within the folds of his massive body. She never thought to fight because of his overwhelming strength. He warmed her and made her sleepy. Before she drifted into a dreamless sleep; she heard him say, "When the boy-child is one year old, I shall return to claim him and raise him in the sea."

* * *

The woman woke in darkness to the sound of the sea as it crashed upon the sand. She sat up and looked around, fearful her attacker might still be near. She rose from the sand and headed toward the cliff. On the trail leading home she crouched like an old woman limping arthritically up the steep path with her hands clasped between her legs. The pain emanated from her wounded vagina and radiated outward. Her mind still muddled from the brutal assault she thought only of her warm house and her sisters. They would take care of her; heal her, for she was their leader. She was the prophetess Veleda.

The Druid hierarchy concerned that the healing skills practiced by the women were not sanctioned; ordered the women and their black arts eliminated.
The prophetess Veleda and her contingent of twenty-five sisters fought the Druid warriors on the ancient lands until they found surcease on the Isle of Skye. Here they could continue the

studies that had been interrupted by the harassment of their small order and the death of countless followers. The sisters were trained by the Druid hierarchy, as doctors, teachers, and priests. The local fishermen, whose families were in need of such services that the Sisterhood would provide, welcomed them. Here they could rest and regroup, regain their strength, and plan for the future.

Twenty-five women sat together in a circular formation on the cool grass, sheltered beneath the spreading branches of a ring of oak trees. The leaves were the color of new grass. The breeze smelled of spring showers and baby rabbits. The women were clothed in black robes from head to foot, one indistinguishable from the next. Veleda was similarly attired, but in her presence the women sat in rapt attention as their leader stated that a man did not commit this rape.

"It was a Selkie that planted his seed. It is a Selkie that will return in a year to take my baby to the sea. This child will be a daughter of the Sisterhood. She will be strong and holy. We shall invoke all our magic to use the strength of the Selkie and combine it with the will of the Sisterhood. Together we will begin a new chapter that will carry us out of blackness and into the light of the future."

Chapter 1

The dive boat <u>Spirit</u> glided noisily out of Eagle Harbor on Bainbridge Island, in Washington State. The little diesel engine coughed as the captain increased throttle power and stirred the dark waters to life. A cloud settled heavily, enfolded and held us prisoner on the noisy little vessel as shorelines, buoys, and evergreen trees peeked through windows in the fog. The engines vibrations comforted us; a thousand explosions blended into a syncopated staccato, broken only by the captain's lamentations of "Fuckin' divin' on a day like this?"

The captain, like his boat, existed comfortably here. Each was lined and worn from many such trips into the salt air. The captain's hair fell lank and wet, his long heavy mustache, worn like a frown, was stained with tobacco juice. He was a tall man with long legs and arms, his shoulders too broad to fit through the cabin hatch without turning. He wore black canvas trousers, threadbare but clean. A soiled, white windbreaker, buttoned halfway to the top, covered a red and white flannel shirt.

The Captain moved slowly, unaware of the pitch and roll of the little boat. With the autopilot engaged, the captain roamed about the boat tending to pumps and switches, his eyes tuned to anything out of place. He examined our personal gear then moved it to where it belonged.

As we motored to the dive site, the captain carried on a conversation with his boat. He complimented, teased and gave her directions. He answered her demands. "Yeah, I know we need a little more rudder."

Thirty-one feet of cedar planking held together by stout oak ribs, the Spirit was the captain's companion. She was alive, like the captain, and seen many long days on the saltwater. Unlike him, she was clean, dressed in new paint and shiny brass. Her cabin house was snow-white, her hull electric blue. I could hear her heart beat, and when the captain increased throttle, it beat faster, excited to be alive in his world. She was carpeted in black rubber matting on her wet deck to protect her from banging tanks and weight belts. Inside her cabin, stainless steel competed with rich, dark mahogany, which reflected the light that streamed through her portholes. The array of sophisticated navigation electronics seemed out of place in a lady so accustomed to the vagaries of travel in these dark Northwest waters.

Dawn broke and changed the fog from dirty gray to soiled white, maintaining its cotton consistency. The fog thickened and our world grew even smaller. Sounds and smells were accentuated. The aroma of coffee brewing in the galley wafted through the open hatch, inviting us to open ourselves to the dawn.

"Coffee's ready!" The petite dive master bounced through the open hatch with two cups of steaming black coffee balanced in her tiny hands. The dive gear was organized on the aft deck, tanks in racks against the bulkhead, regulators and buoyancy compensators nearby. Our dry suits were hung amidships and gave the impression of three prisoners readied for execution.

As we sipped our coffee the dive master explained.

"These suits will keep you warm and dry in the fifty degree water." She stood like a drill sergeant looking down at her troops. "I know you two are warm water divers, so listen up. The buoyancy compensator looks like the kind you wear in the Caribbean, but is much heavier. We will be carrying more weight in the cold waters, and the buoyancy compensator must be able to keep you neutral underwater, as well as bring you to the surface." Catherine sipped her coffee before she continued. "The air tank connects to the buoyancy compensator the same, as does the regulator with the mouthpiece."

She scurried between sets of gear, a tornado loosed in a small place, meticulously setting up and adjusting our underwater life support systems with one hand, while the other caressed a hot cup of coffee. I could see by the set of her jaw that once the gear was adjusted to her satisfaction, it was not to be tampered with, leastwise by two warm water amateurs like us.

I met with the captain and Catherine, two days prior to the dive to discuss the dive site and dive gear requirements. My partner, Dr. Stephen Hopkins, and I were previously involved in extensive dive operations in tropical waters. Steve's work involved marine ecology and was centered in tropical waters. When I thought of dropping into these cold dark waters, it unnerved me.

"Diving in the Northwest is gear and instrument intensive, and visibility at times drops to as little as twelve inches. You will have to reconcile yourself to this condition and dive your instruments, much like an airline pilot landing on a fog-shrouded strip," Catherine explained. "We have a dive plan, Gentlemen, and we will stick to the plan."

The tone said that there would be no mercy if we varied from the plan.

"If the captain's not lost in the fog we should be at the dive site in fifteen minutes. At that time you will be geared up and ready to hit the water. We will step into the water from the dive step, swim to the anchor line, and descend together. Together, is that clear?"

"The anchor should be set on top of the reef in seventy-five feet of water. We estimate the visibility at between twenty-five and thirty feet. Your camera setting should be four point five and ten feet, strobe on max."

Steve looked at me and smiled. He knew that no one set up my photo shots for me.

I held my tongue and set my camera.

Catherine turned and shouted into the cabin, "Captain, you sober yet?"

We were suited up, our dry suits and forty-five pounds of lead made it difficult to climb over the gunwale. Catherine manhandled the tank and regulator assembly up onto our shoulders. I stood on the dive step and looked around; saw nothing but heavy mist enshrouding our little boat. Foghorns moaned in the distance. I, too, hoped the captain was sober.

"Gil, Steve, do it!" Catherine barked, and we stepped into the dark November water.

The cold water stung my face and after a moment under swirling water, I bobbed to the surface.

Catherine donned in her own tank assembly, quite gracefully stepped up onto the transom and dove headlong into the water. She surfaced and made a final inspection of our gear. After she made an adjustment to my mask she then swam ahead of us, led us to the bow anchor line. The line disappeared, at a forty-five-degree angle into black water. Catherine motioned for us to descend; we dumped the remaining air from our buoyancy

9

compensators and slid silently down the anchor line.

The descent was like nothing I ever encountered. There was no reference in space, and as I dropped, the anchor line and my gauges were all I could see. I kept a close watch on my depth gauge and slowed only to clear pressure from my ears. All was silent except my own breathing, which sounded labored and loud. My companions disappeared into the gloom, the anchor line my only tether. We were to meet at the anchor on the bottom. I gripped the anchor line with all my strength to slow my descent, which gave me the illusion of some control.

The gloom was replaced by huge, monolithic rock formations that resembled a cityscape of skyscrapers leaning at extraordinary angles. Tunnels, fissures, and caves intersected one another leaving me with a sense of demonic architecture hidden from human eyes by ninety feet of water.

The anchor implanted itself neatly between two massive boulders in a small bed of sand. I thought the captain must indeed be sober or extremely lucky. My two dive companions were on there knees and faced one another next to the anchor and conversed in sign language. As they breathed, exhaled bubbles burst from their regulators, and drifted lazily upward. They expanded then burst into thousands of tiny bubbles before they broke the surface. I watched the bubbles ascend for a moment then joined my dive buddies, anxious to heat up my strobe and begin to shoot this shadowy reef. I almost forgot my job was to photograph wolf eels for Steve's research.

Steve had approached me months earlier to see if I were willing to accompany him on this research project. Over a few drinks, he explained, "The Pacific wolf eel is particular to this area and is often hard to find and even harder to photograph. My research deals with studies which indicate that these ferocious sea creatures mate for life and raise their young together."

We were suspended at the top of an underwater city, looking into grottos and caves bisected by rocky apartment buildings that teemed with odd, slow-moving fish. I thought to myself, if I got lost in this city, I'd never find my way out. Catherine led, dropping immediately down a steep canyon wall, and, as on the surface, moved at an alarming pace.

Afraid I would lose sight of her I sped headlong into the dark abyss, focused on the bottom of her yellow fins. I hoped Steve was keeping up with me. The rock walls were painted with thick, green algae broken by cracks and small caves. Some were decorated with red and orange starfish as well as purple sea cucumbers. Fish were abundant, darting out of our way as we plummeted through their neighborhood.

I glanced back at Steve momentarily, and immediately lost sight of our dive master. We slowed and tried to locate her, astonished at the immensity of this underwater city. My depth gauge registered ninety –feet as we continued to descend surrounded by rock walls on three sides. We touched bottom in 110 feet on a rock plateau. Unaware of where our dive master went, we were faced with two directions to swim: one led into an apartment-sized cave, the other through a narrow twisting channel between the rock face. Neither of these were good choices.

Unexpectedly, I was assaulted from above; my head pummeled. I jerked back and raised my hands to protect myself. When I looked up I saw the sweet face of my tormentor, Catherine. She twisted around, pointed and headed up. She then turned left and disappeared into a small opening.

Ascending to 100 feet, Catherine perched on the ledge that led to what I thought to be a deep cavern. Catherine watched the two of us. A giant, orange, starfish was anchored on the black rock wall above the cavity. When Catherine brushed against the creature it contracted like a dead man's hand clenching a precious clue. She then turned and, with her underwater light on full, swam into the cavern.

We entered a dark environment teeming with creatures that brushed against me from overhead. Up or down did not exist as Steve and I followed this madwoman into pitch-blackness. Catherine slowed down, but to follow her proved no easier with only the refracted beam of her light to show me her location but not what was directly in front of me. I extended my arms like a blind man to feel my way forward. The giant barnacles that sprouted from the cavern walls were rough-textured and tore at my gloved hands.

The light at the end of the tunnel was Catherine. She waited for us as we rounded out of the tunnel into a large opening. She waited on bended knees as if in supplication. Would she beg our forgiveness for having lost us? I doubted it.

Indeed not--she bent over a vertical cave two feet in diameter and peered into the den of two of the largest eels I ever encountered. One eel was so dark, it was almost maroon, and the other one a light gray. Their heads were twice the size of mine; their mouths opened and closed, needle-sharp teeth bared, bodies poised as if on coiled steel springs. They looked aggressive and ready to attack. I backed off, ready to retreat. Steve swam up to Catherine and gently nudged her aside to get a better look.

My camera in hand, I began to shoot. The flash illuminated the cave like lightning and exposed the immensity of the cavern. A three-bedroom apartment could have fit within these walls. At each flash, the startled eels ducked their heads. Their mouths opened and closed rapidly, and their teeth reflected the light from my strobe. They became restless and nervous, as they entwined about one another, their slick bodies slithered back and forth.

Catherine signaled me to stop shooting. Then, to my horror, she extended her arms, reached into the wolf eels' den and gently grasped the male wolf eel by the gills and pulled it upward toward her face. The wolf eel was reluctant at first but succumbed to the gentle pressure, then like a cork out of a bottle, popped from its den. Ten feet of slippery eel nudged and rubbed against Catherine before it wrapped itself around her, slid between her legs and nibbled on her ear; teeth hidden behind blue, rubbery lips. The wolf eel's skin moved independently, unattached and oily. Catherine stroked the long body, moving her hands over the skin, further exciting the creature into more rapid movement, and intimate contact. Were these two lovers, unable to keep their affair a secret?

Catherine reached into her goodie bag to retrieve small fish treats, which were immediately devoured by the eel. As soon as the bag was opened, the female wolf eel decided that to be shy was to be hungry and quickly helped herself to the offerings. Steve held the light on the show while I shot off more film.

Time at depth underwater is limited and Catherine signaled for us to return. She swam back into the darkness of the cave as the eels moved back into their den. The cave was still pitch-black, but I was more comfortable knowing this was the way out.

I heard a noise to my left and took a chance, turned my camera and shot. The flash of my strobe was brilliant inside the enclosure and the subject of my photo was at once illuminated and etched into my brain. A woman lay naked; her skin bluish-white, auburn hair floated freely and framed her dead face like a surrealistic eighteenth century painting.

I couldn't believe my eyes. I stopped abruptly and Steve crashed into me. I tried to communicate to him what I had seen, but he did not understand. I checked my air supply. My gauge showed less than 400 pounds, which left me no time to think or explore, only time to swim through the cave and ascend. I had no intention of running out of air in this mysterious underwater tomb.

Our ascent seemed to take forever. We made a safety stop at fifteen feet to allow for off-gassing of the excess nitrogen our bloodstream gathered during our deep dive. We hovered, neutrally buoyant and faced each other and waited a long three minutes as our bodies exhaled the nitrogen bubbles that could cause the bends. I grasped Steve by the straps of his buoyancy compensator and turned him toward me. I signed to him and tried to make him understand what I had seen. He smiled. I shook his harness and planted my faceplate on his and screamed through my mouthpiece. "A dead body!" He shrugged his shoulders and made a small adjustment to his air. Our bubbles gurgled and softly floated to the surface, mixing with the minute particulates that swept by us, pushed by the gentle current.

I reflected on the entire dive as I floated mid-water and wondered what other dark secrets may be hidden in the depths of these cold waters.

We broke the surface into bright sunlight. The fog had dissipated leaving in its place an unsurpassed view of a tiny harbor bordered by tall evergreen trees and pebble beaches. The dive boat offered a safe haven and hot coffee. Catherine stood on the dive step and waited. We swam to the boat.

"Call the Coast Guard! There's a dead woman in that cave!" I shouted.

Catherine smiled and waved for me to board. I unsnapped

my gear and she pulled it aboard. I kicked and climbed up onto the dive step.

"Catherine, I saw a dead woman inside that cave we just exited." I gasped between words trying to make her understand.

"And was she beautiful?" Catherine mocked.

"Look, I know this doesn't sound possible. I heard a noise and that's when I saw a woman with long hair lying naked in that cave."

By now, Steve was on board and all three of them looked at me as if I were crazy. I turned to Steve. "You saw the woman, didn't you?"

Steve shrugged.

"Tell them I'm not crazy. You know I don't make shit up"

The captain shook his head, and mumbled, "The fucker's narcked."

Catherine helped me out of my gear, and quietly intoned, "You know we were at one-hundred-plus feet for some time. The water is cold and dark. Nitrogen narcosis can sneak up on you and make you see things that aren't really there." She smiled and patted my arm. "That's why they call it rapture of the deep. You have a little brain short-circuit that will go away soon."

I shook my head. "I saw what I saw. I can prove what I saw. I have it on film."

"Sorry Gil, there was no naked woman down there. I had my halogen light on full. I would have seen her. If you want we'll take a look on our second dive, after lunch." She smiled and turned away.

The captain stepped out onto the open deck and exclaimed, "No more divin'. Once you're narcked, the divin' is done. Insurance. Pack your shit. We're headin' in."

Steve and I jumped to our feet. "We paid for a two-tank

dive." Steve said.

"The captain doesn't care about the money," explained Catherine. "When the captain says we don't dive, we don't dive."

The diesel engine barked once, belched out black smoke, sputtered and wheezed into life, reluctant to wake and move. I could imagine her timbers stretch as the anchor was hauled aboard and the sputter changed into a throaty whine. The throttle advanced slowly; the whine became a roar. The Spirit was ready to go home.

Steve and I sat on the aft deck and watched our dive master. Catherine reminded me of a dancer, she whirled and stretched, her every motion seemed choreographed as the dive gear was shifted and moved. She never slowed until the aft deck was cleared and all the dive gear stowed. Catherine bounced into the pilothouse slamming the hatch door. She then stood with her arm around the captain.

I looked at Steve and shrugged my shoulders.

He looked back. "Let's not worry about this thing, Gil, until we develop your film."

I smiled sheepishly, already convinced that what I saw was in my own imagination, however real it looked at the time.

As the little boat neared the harbor entrance, houses perched along the hillside sparkled like jewels in the cold November light. The captain brought the boat quickly alongside the public dock where Steve and I jumped ashore.

"Try the Harbor Pub for dinner," cried Catherine as the Spirit swung off the dock and headed home.

Chapter 2

The red jeep moved down the dirt road, four-wheel drive engaged. Its headlights twisted and turned as if searching for the safest track. The wet weather made the drive into a quagmire of mud and the steep descent into the forest, a challenge to the jeeps' traction. The driver shook her mane of red hair from her eyes, and looked at the sky. Black clouds hovered above the tops of the giant fir trees and promised more rain. She wrinkled her nose as the odor of decaying vegetation increased the deeper into the forest she drove. A mist cloaked the jeep, as she turned into the parking area adjacent to the house.

"You would think we would be able to afford covered parking," she growled as she slammed the car door and ran to the front porch. "Hello is anyone home?" Lois called out, and closed the massive oak door behind her.

A tiny voice sang out from somewhere inside the home. "Sister Lois? Is that you?"

"Yes, Trish. Are the other girls here now?"

The tiny voice appeared wearing an equally tiny body. She ran and leaped into Lois' arms. "Did you tell the judge how stupid he is?" She wrapped her slender arms around Lois' neck and grinned.

"You bet I did, Young Lady, and I won the case today."
She tousled the red ringlets and bent down and placed the
youngster on the carpet. "Now, go tell your sisters that it is
almost pool-time. Okay?"

"Yes, Ma'am." She turned and ran down the hallway.

Lois followed slowly. The day had been a long one. Her
fingers fumbled with the buttons on her suit jacket.

"I need to get into the water again," she said out loud. Her
voice echoed off the high ceilings, as she turned into the living
room, tossed her jacket on the leather couch, and poured herself a
glass of single malt from the sideboard. "Yes, this will help."
She drank deeply, then walked to the window facing the beach
and watched a ferryboat make its way, leisurely through Rich
Passage. She had spent some time in the water, earlier, on the
other side of the island, but she craved more.

Lois Ferguson lived in the home in the woods with eleven
other women and five young girls. She was the teacher
scheduled tonight, and her students were not moving fast enough.
"Girls," she called out.

Feet scampered on hardwood floors.

"Let's go, Girls. Get down to the pool now." An outer
door slammed and Lois watched out the window as her five
students skipped down the brick pathway that led to the pool
house on the edge of the beach.

She threw on a raincoat, held it tightly around her, kicked
off her shoes and opened the living room door to the deck.
"More rain," she grumbled and hurried down the steps of the
wooden deck to the pathway below. "Hurry, hurry," she called
out to her charges.

Lois entered the pool house and was pleased to see her
students in their proper places around the table. She smiled as

she watched them swing their skinny legs to unheard music.

"Good afternoon, Sister Lois," the called out together, and then giggled through clenched fists held up in front of their smiles.

Lois walked around the table and patted each child as if they each were her favorite pet. She squatted and ran her hand along the edge of the pool. It's cool water caressed her skin. The lights above were too bright. She turned the rheostat to the left, diminishing the illumination. The pool house was more comfortable in the dark, she thought. She wished she could dull the underwater lights as well.

"I can see a ferryboat," Trisha called out and pointed.

"We're not here to look at ferryboats, are we, Ladies?" Lois turned a stern face to the students. "Why are we here?"

"To protect marine life, and strengthen the sisterhood," they chanted in unison.

A weather cell blew rain against the pool house, and pounded an urgent tattoo upon the steel roof. Lois gazed at the rain and sighed, looked back at the children and nodded. "Good," she whispered.

* * *

Catherine arrived later that afternoon to meet with Lois. They sat opposite one another on the leather couch, their legs folded beneath them. Two glasses of scotch sat on the coffee table, untouched.

Lois said, "I taught them the introduction to the Sisterhood today and explained to them in detail, how we have a covenant to protect marine life."

Catherine picked up her scotch, sipped it, and stood. She stepped away from the couch and turned toward the window.

19

Her reflection stared back into the room as a rain-streaked distortion. She looked at Lois. "Do you think they feel different?"

I think they understand that we are unique and I think they feel special."

Catherine nodded and then said, "We had a charter today, Lois. A special charter." Her eyes glowed like live coals in a winter stove.

"Tell me, what is it?" Lois whispered. "What's wrong?" She stood and moved next to Catherine. She rubbed against her then stroked the other woman's hair with her fingers and purred. "Is there a problem?"

Catherine burned up the moment and gazed deep into the Lois' eyes. "A McCrae, Lois. I smelled him. I touched him. He was the photographer for the Hopkins charter. He doesn't even know who he is." She caught her breath. "He's beautiful, Lois. We can use him."

Lois stepped away, turned and retrieved her drink. She sampled the scotch with the tip of her tongue and with her back to Catherine said gently, "I saw the camera flash. Did he see me?"

"Why were you there, Sister?"

Lois shrugged. She turned and met Catherine's gaze and then looked at the floor. "The captain told me you would be diving the boulder today, and I just--"

"Just what?"

Lois placed her glass down on the coffee table and stepped close. She slid her lips along the silk blouse that covered Catherine's shoulders and whispered, "I wanted to be there with you in the water, Sister. I want to hunt with you."

"We hunt when I say. Do you understand?"

"Yes, Sister. Did he see me?"

"He thinks he did, but he's not so sure anymore. We'll have to be careful." She encircled the younger woman's waist and turned her toward the window, and the storm that brewed beyond the glass.

Lois squirmed in Catherine's embrace and then relaxed. "If I were leader…"

"You're not." Catherine's staccato reprimand discouraged the conversation.

Sheet lightening turned the black night into day and illuminated the crests of waves that boiled under the onslaught of the southerly wind. The giant evergreen firs bent and shivered as the gusts tore at their limbs and sprinkled the steel rooftop of the pool house with black needles. The lights inside the home of the sisterhood blinked twice and then blinked out and left the house in darkness.

The two women held hands and watched the rain rinse out the remainder of the day.

Chapter 3

The red and white houseboat looked much like a barn that had been plucked from a farmer's field and dropped onto a steel barge. The structure was tied up at the end of the dock next to an assortment of floating houses, some partially underwater, and all in various states of disrepair. A wooden plank bridge connected it to shore.

"It's good to be home," Steve said, out of breath."It was only a ten minute walk, Partner. How come you're huffing and puffing?"

"I was thinking on the way over--"

"Thinking makes you tired?"

"Deep thought; something you are unable to comprehend, can be tiring." He tried to clip me on the shoulder, but missed and nearly fell off the dock. "We need to stay here a month, maybe less. It will take time to study the wolf eel and correlate the photos."

"I'll be a prune in a month in this climate." As if on cue, it began to rain gently. "Shit, let's get inside." I grabbed Steve's arm and hurried him along the wooden dock to the front porch.

The front door was ajar. I pushed it open and walked in ahead of Steve. I motioned for him to wait, thinking that someone might have broken in, then searched the house quickly.

"Looks clear, Steve. We must have forgotten to lock up. Close the door, will you? It's freezing in here." The door slammed and I heard Steve mutter something. "Come in the kitchen, so I can hear you."

"I said, you can't complain when National Geographic is paying the bills."

He turned into the kitchen and stumbled on the dive gear bags piled in the center of the kitchen floor. "What the hell--?"

I caught him before he fell and pushed him against the counter. "What the hell is right," I agreed. "Why not leave the gear on the boat?'

"More to the point," Steve said, "why not unload us and the gear, instead of making us walk all of the way down here."

I looked out of the window and thought I could see the stern of the Spirit as it zigzagged its way through the harbor.

"It was only a ten minute walk." I thought it strange but shook the feeling off. "I guess we clean our own gear."

"Clean our own gear?" Steve whined and sat down on a barstool. He removed his glasses, ripped off a piece of paper towel and rubbed at the lens. "Too cold out there to be cleaning gear. I'll just do it in the morning."

"Too cold out there? It's cold in here as well." I grabbed the canvas bags and headed for the door. "I'll make you a deal. You build up a fire and I'll clean the gear. Okay?"

"Roger, thanks, Buddy."

As I rinsed the gear, I looked across the harbor through the gentle rain, unable to tell where the Spirit docked. The harbor was small and enclosed on three sides, but the rain obscured visibility. I suspected that the captain docked near the head of the bay, within walking distance to the nearest tavern. With the dive gear rinsed and hung beneath the eaves of the boathouse, I turned and smiled as I watched my friend though the bay window before I snuck back inside.

Steve sat in front of the wood stove. He unsuccessfully tried to lever a log into the fireplace opening. He turned sideways, scooted closer to the opening, pushed his glasses up onto the bridge of his nose, and managed to arrange the logs in their proper place. He clapped at his success and touched a match to the paper before he closed the stove door.

"Good job, Partner." I stood behind him.

"Jesus Christ! Don't sneak up on me." He spun around and tried to stand.

I gave him a hand up and a pat on his belly. "That thing going to be a girl, or a boy?"

"Stow it, Skinny. Don't you have work to do?" He turned to the kitchen. "I'll make a pot of coffee. Get those photos developed. I want to see that naked lady." He laughed at me. When the coffee pot was filled with water he turned. "Seriously, I'd like to see some great wolf eel shots. So get your ass in gear."

For my lab, I light-proofed the second bedroom with black plastic and duct tape. My processor could produce slides within thirty minutes. I would then scan them onto my computer and print what we needed.

My wolf eel photos were better that I had hoped. "Steve, come in here and look at these." I arranged the photographs on the computer. "Steve, are you there?"

"Hold your water." Steve burst into the room balancing a glass of red wine. "What have you got?" He pushed me aside and scanned the photos. "Good, good. Oh, yes, I like this one." He stared at the groups of photos and chuckled. His feet were doing the tango and the wine threatened to spill.

"Watch the wine." I was as pleased at the good results as I was with the look on Steve's face. Our first photo shoot was a success, or nearly so. "No naked lady."

"What?" He stopped his dance and turned. "What?"

"The naked lady didn't take." I shrugged. Too much backscatter ruined the shot. Goddammit!"

"Naked lady?" He narrowed his eyebrows, "Oh, <u>that</u> naked lady." Steve took a swallow of wine, "Fuck the naked lady. Forget it, Gil. She was never there to begin with." He took another sip and said, "So, where did the back scatter come from anyway?"

"The dive master, she swam ahead of me. Her fins must have kicked up the silt, and when my flash went off, it reflected off the particles. "Look," I pointed. "It shows up as snow on the photos." I turned the computer off and looked at Steve. "She was there, Partner. I saw her."

"The <u>dive master</u> was there, Gil."

"So was the naked lady."

****

Dinner wouldn't be for two hours, so like all obsessive runners with a couple of hours to kill, I decided to find the local runner's hangout. I heard about a park called Battle Point, located mid-island where I could rack up some miles. The park boasted a perimeter track that wound through old growth Douglas fir and ponds filled with ducks and Canada geese.

The track was busy this time of day. I began at a slow pace so that I could relax and reflect on what had occurred at Devil's Boulder today. Pebbled pathways lined by trees that stood naked with the onset of winter reflected in the still water, a few ducks swam leisurely around the perimeter. I increased my pace and runners, young and old, moved to the right as I approached to let me pass. I was in the 'zone'.

I came upon a woman who ran at a slow pace and watched her young lithesome body shimmer in shiny blue shorts. As I passed her I turned for a quick look at her face. My feet froze in their tracks as my body, charged with inertia, propelled itself headlong onto the track directly in front of her. I hit hard. I lay there, flat on my face, not wanting to look up. I knew I would see the face of the dead woman from our dive this morning at Devil's Boulder. I sensed her as she kneeled beside me and felt her cool hand on my shoulder.

"Are you all right, Soldier?" Her voice was deep and almost melancholy.

"I'm not a soldier, and yes, I'm all right." I groaned and turned over, still reluctant to look into her face.

"Let me help you," she purred, and pulled me to a sitting position. She brushed dirt and pebbles from my skinned knees. The small cut on my knee oozed blood and she dabbed at it with her finger. She closed her eyes and lifted the finger to her nose. I watched her inhale deeply. Her lips parted and as I waited for her tongue to touch the tip of the finger, she smiled, opened her eyes and touched my leg, marking a red stripe above my wound. Her eyes were pale blue, almost gray. Her gaze hypnotized me, held me, and strangled me. I was unable to speak

She laughed. "Do we know each other?"

"I think we met earlier today diving, didn't we?" I chanced.

She looked at me for a long moment and winked. "Maybe I'll see you at the pub sometime." She straightened up, and continued her run.

I couldn't move. I watched as the distance grew between

us. Her face was etched in my brain long before I saw her here in the park. I thought, I don't know if I'm going crazy, or not but I know where I'd be having dinner tonight.

Once I made it to my feet, I limped back to my rental car. My mind was a quagmire of unanswered questions. Am I losing my mind? How could this be the same woman? The only logical answer was that she couldn't be, and that I was indeed narcked. I must have seen this woman somewhere and inserted her face into my narcosis-induced hallucination. The logical half of my brain was content with this explanation. The other half was still unsure.

I drove back to the houseboat as the late afternoon sun cast shadows across the roadway. Giant fir trees blocked much of what was left of the afternoon, as dusk came early this time of the year. I had to swerve and brake twice, once for a doe and her fawn, and once for a speeding ball of gray and white fur wearing a robber's mask. The wildlife on the island was as plentiful as life in the waters that surrounded it.

The fire blazed and the place was heated to sauna temperatures when I walked in the houseboat.

"Honey, I'm home." I dropped my jacket on the chair. The keys clattered to the floor.

"Hey," he replied, pointing at my bloody shins. "You look like a little kid that just fell off his new two-wheeler." Steve wore a towel draped around his bulging belly, which threatened any moment to drop to the floor. His wet hair stuck up at odd angles.

"If you were my wife, I'd fire you. And hang on to that towel!" I laughed and pushed past him to the bathroom to wash the blood and mud from my arms and legs.

The bathroom, like the kitchen, was all stainless steel. The compact shower forced me to contort my body in order to soap and clean myself. Steaming water soothed and washed off the earlier saltwater, the blood, and the encounter with the <u>dead woman</u> at the track. Once refreshed and sitting in front of the fire I told Steve what happened and of my conversation with the woman.

He sat against the cushions, wiped off his glasses and stared at me. "What you need is some pussy." He grinned. "You're taking all this too seriously." He slid his glasses back in place. "You couldn't see a dead woman ninety feet under water and then two hours later watch her jog around a track." He stood and hit my leg, "Come on, let's get dressed and try out this famous pub for dinner; I'm starving."

"Okay I'm nuts," I conceded. "but, I'm also hungry."

We dressed and headed out. Thanksgiving was three weeks away and jack-o-lanterns still sat with tiny flames dancing inside on the little houseboats along the dock. Dew on the railings sparkled and foretold of morning fog. The wind rattled through the rigging on nearby boats with a tinkling sound, wavelets slapped against their broadsides; uneasiness filled the night air.

The pub was a ten-minute walk from our houseboat, as we ambled along the harbor causeway we could hear sea lions bark in the harbor, hidden by the evening mist.

A steep, wooden staircase led from the causeway to the entrance of the pub. We could hear raucous laughter from within, mixed with the clatter of glassware being slid across a wooden surface. We opened the door into the cacophony of loud music, and louder storytellers. Waitresses scurried between the tables, dishes of food balanced in their hands. Then everything stopped.

The sensation that we intruded into a private home overwhelmed us. This local hangout obviously did not cater to outsiders very often. Fifty people, some in baseball caps and coveralls, others dressed in their finest, stopped what they were doing and openly stared at us until a familiar voice shouted from the corner.

"Hey, Soldier, get your fuckin' ass in the door, and close it so's we don't all freeze to fuckin' death." The captain stood up, stalked over, grabbed me by the arm and pulled me to his table. Steve stumbled closely behind.

The noisy atmosphere commenced unabated as if it had never been disconnected. The captain pulled us both down hard on to wooden, straight-backed chairs, he then signaled for the waitress. My chair started to topple backward and I struggled to regain my balance. A tiny hand grasped the back of my neck and gently pushed me forward. I turned, and attached to the tiny hand was our dive master.

I would not have recognized Catherine if I walked all through the pub knowing she would be there. Her auburn hair flowed over her shoulders, danced between her shoulder blades and framed her exquisite face and full lips. Her blood red, silk dress barely contained her figure; her large breasts stretched the silky material. The fiery dress flowed down her tiny waist and surged over her hips, then separated and continued to pour down muscular legs, where it stopped just below her knees. Her calves rounded onto tiny, child-size feet. Her eyes looked up at me merrily. "Who were you expecting, Soldier?"

Even her voice changed its timbre. On the boat it rasped and sputtered like the little diesel engine. Here, she sounded soft and sensual, the words rolled off her tongue smooth and silky, like her dress.

I was being manipulated and knew it, but I was still

29

speechless. I finally managed, "Hi Catherine, nice seeing you here." I might as well have stood up, put my hands in my pockets, kicked the floor and said, 'aw shucks'.

Steve grinned in an attempt to cover up his own shock at Catherine's metamorphosis. He leaned toward me. "What's this soldier stuff?"

I shrugged. "Look at her. Who cares?"

Our beers arrived and I drank deeply. The captain entertained us with a story about how he grappled with a giant octopus at twenty fathoms, while Steve tried hard to look like he believed him.

Catherine reached over the table and touched my arm. I looked up.

"I heard you had an accident at the park today."

Was she playing with me or genuinely concerned?

"Yes," I said, "I must have slipped. How did you know?"

"It's a small island," she countered. "Are you all right?"

"You mean, can I dive in the morning? You betcha!" I took her hand off my arm and held it a moment, and in my most charming manner said in a voice only meant for her ears, "I'm sorry I stared, I simply didn't recognize you."

She cocked her head to the side, "You coming on to me soldier?" Then she stood up, grabbed the captain by his ear, "Let's go captain, we've got an early call out in the morning." She looked back at me as she sliced through the crowded room and called, "Try the fish and chips, and don't be late tomorrow." She grabbed two coats from the back of a chair and then disappeared.

I watched her leave with the captain in tow. I looked at Steve and shook my head.

Steve bent close to me and whispered, "The captain called

Catherine his sister and says he lives on an old tugboat in the harbor, while she lives in a condominium next door to the pub. It seems she aims him downhill toward the wharf, and he stumbles into a dinghy and rows out to his boat, then she goes home. Why don't you see if she's still around; you can maybe walk her home."

"No thanks." I sighed. "I think that woman is trouble. There's no good mixing work and play, but she's one woman who could change my mind."

We ordered fish and chips.

The clock above the bar chimed eight-o-clock and the day was wearing long on me. I thought of a warm fire and a cold scotch to end the day.

The walk back to our houseboat was uneventful except that the mist had settled. Foghorns blew and complemented one another. They melded into a symphony out of tune. The mood was oppressive; people silhouetted in the swirling mists passed and didn't acknowledge our presence. They quickened their step to get inside and away from whatever might loom in the fog.

At our houseboat, we knew the fire crackled and would have kept the living room cozy. As we neared, the scent of wood smoke filled the air, punctuated by the familiar acrid odor of seaweed. I went to the door thinking we may have left it open. As I crossed into the living room, I noticed a trail of water led from our front door into the small bedroom. I clicked on the overhead light and saw that the trail of water stopped at the desk and made a pool on the floor. I reached down and dipped my index finger into the puddle. After a tentative smell and suspecting its nature, I tasted it-- seawater.

"Steve, come in here a minute." I looked around, but

nothing seemed out of place.

Steve shuffled in on stocking feet. "Here you go, Boss." He pushed a tumbler of scotch into my hand. "What's up?"

"I checked my negatives, they're all here, but the last two negatives are smudged. Some kind of sticky substance, like a water-based adhesive…kind of salty." I sipped my scotch.

"Let me see." He pushed me aside and handed me his glass. "Looks like water to me." He took an index card from the desk and captured a droplet and then sat in down carefully onto the desktop. "No, it's not water, is it?" He took his drink out of my hand and sipped and then handed it back. "Hmm, get me the magnifying glass, will you?"

I sat Steve's glass down next to him, pulled the magnifying glass from the desk drawer and handed it to him. He picked up the card and the scotch and turned into the living room.

"Let's go in the other room, better light."

I brought my drink with me and followed him. He placed the card on the kitchen counter beneath the cupboard light.

"Here, let me see." He took the magnifying glass and bent over the card. "Looks like developing emulsifier. Were the negatives dry before we went to dinner?"

"Yes, they were dry. I'm positive."

"Hmm, wait a minute." Steve bent his head so that the magnifier nearly touched the small square of film. "Take a look at this, Gil."

I held the film close to the light and looked through the lens. "I don't see--" I squinted my left eye. "Wait a minute. Yes, yes, I think I can see her." The negative had a definite outline of a woman lying, as if suspended in a snowstorm emerged. If I open both eyes, she disappeared. "I knew it. Still think I'm crazy?"

"Maybe crazy like a fox. Do you think you can resolve some of that backscatter and re-print the photo?"

"I can try. You bet I can try."

"Then, we've definitely had a visitor. I don't know what this stuff is." He finished the scotch in a single gulp. "You said it tastes salty. Why are you putting that stuff in your mouth anyway?"

"I don't know. Yeah, sticky seawater." I'd left my drink on the kitchen table and retrieved it. "I need another drink." I swallowed the rest of it and proceeded to make a new one. "I'm getting god dammed tired of people breaking into our house."

"Make me another, will you?" He scraped at the droplet with a toothpick. "I'm going to get some more of this substance and bag it."

"Then what?"

"We need to plan a Seattle trip soon anyway so that I can get a twelve volt hook-up for my laptop, and I know a professor at the University of Washington who may be able to tell us what this stuff is." He turned and looked at me. "Hey, where's my drink?"

* * *

I slept uneasily that night. I listened for footsteps and squeaking door hinges, but instead, heard foghorns and whistles. The fog settled in like pea soup and the wind ceased. Sounds of creatures rummaging through garbage cans and footsteps on the causeway were magnified. A dog barked at the moon or the fog, or possibly something in the water. The hairs on the back of my arm stood up, and I shivered.

I heard a rustle and a splash outside. Was it a sea lion or a wolf eel or was it my imagination? The day's events swirled around my brain and confused my rational thought. I wondered if the deep dive and the nitrogen narcosis were still producing irrational thought processes. Catherine had said that the excess nitrogen would not last long. Maybe I just needed a good nights sleep.

Chapter 4

"Drop your cocks, and grab your socks and saddle up," Steve sang out.

I pulled the blanket over my head. "Where's my coffee?"

Steve was first up and, bless his soul had coffee ready. "Black, no sugar." He pulled my blanket down and set the cup on the nightstand. "Come on, get up. We're going diving, remember?"

I sat up and took a sip, then looked out over the top of my cup at the day breaking through the window. The fog was on the move, a sure sign that it would either get better or worse.

"Looks a little foggy out there." Steve banged around the kitchen and whistled out of tune.

I sat my half empty cup down and fell back into bed, covered my head and tried and drown out the cheery sounds of my roommate. Steve sat on the edge of the bed and I rolled toward him. "Get off the bed."

"Do you know that the sun burns off fog at a rate of fifty feet an hour; starting from the top, then burning down to the surface of the water?" He bounced on the side of the bed. "The changing tide will determine whether that same fog will become thicker, or thinner."

"Okay, I'm up. Quit rambling and get me some more coffee, would you?" I swung my legs over the side of the bed. "You got my gear packed yet, Mother?"

"Checked it and stowed." He walked back into the room with a fresh cup.

"You're dressed and ready? What time is it?"

"Seven-ten, Bucko, so let's drop our--"

"Hey, Gil, our taxi is here," Steve called out.

I gulped down the rest of my coffee, threw on the same clothes I wore the day before and slipped into my sneakers. My foul weather coat hung next to the door, I grabbed it and closed the door.

Spirit was alongside the dock. The fog hid all of her except the top gunwale where Catherine stood quietly and held a line around a cleat. The morning was quiet, save the chug-chug of the diesel engine. Catherine waved for us to come aboard. We clambered over the gunwale and unloaded our dive gear in a pile on the aft deck.

Catherine let go of the line and the Spirit turned into the fog. As the boat moved into the harbor, Catherine took the wheel as the captain bent over the radarscope and called out helm instructions.

"Five degrees right rudder. Okay, now steady up. That's right, ease her up." The captain continued this quiet litany as Catherine obeyed without question. Like a surgeon and his nurse assistant during a delicate operation, each respected the other's expertise and knew full well that their cooperation was the only thing that mattered now. We dare not interrupt, lest the patient die. The captain picked up his coffee cup, then his spit cup. He drank out of one and spat into the other, his eyes never left the small round radarscope. I wondered when he would drink out of the wrong cup.

Catherine tapped her foot impatiently. The fog began to dissipate, blue sky here, a little scrap of beach there.

"Okay Catherine, I got her, thanks." The captain stepped in to take the wheel and nudged Catherine. He kicked the box, that was Catherine's step stool out of his way and it clattered into the corner and then leaned into the steering wheel, ducked his head and peered through the window.

Steve and I sat on benches on the aft deck and leaned against the bulkhead, moving with the boat as she gently rolled on unseen swells. A heater in the cabin kept the aft deck comfortable. My eyes closed as the diesel engine vibrated under my feet and massaged my tired muscles.

The door to the galley swung open with a bang. It was slammed into the bulkhead as the dive master boiled out onto the aft deck with three cups of coffee. "Hot, hot, hot!" Catherine juggled the cups, Steve and I each took one.

She gasped, then shook her hands to try and cool her fingers. "The dive plan, Gentlemen." She wore the same bulky sweater she had worn yesterday, hot pink shorts and a purple baseball cap.

"Today we will visit a wolf eel den in a small, rocky, ballast pile in Rich Pass. Their den is located on the shoreward side of a sunken fishing trawler in about seventy feet of water. Two problems." She took a tentative sip of coffee. "Number one; we must make our way through the bowels of the wreck in order to get to the ballast pile. Number two; the site itself is situated in a high current area with a big exchange today and we have just a small window of time to get in and get out before the current gets us." She looked at each of us in turn, and then cocked her head. "Questions?"

Steve and I glanced at each, looked back at her and nodded our heads.

"Your skills will be tested today. Gil, you have a question?"

"Can I have some more coffee?"

Steve spoke up, "What's an exchange?"

"When I talk about the exchange," she continued, "I'm talking about the difference between high and low tide moving in a certain time frame. The greatest difference between a high and a low water indicates that the current will be exceedingly strong, unless we can confine our time to slack water. That's the time the water is still between tidal changes."

Steve knocked over his cup on the deck between his feet. "Shit…sorry." He picked up the cup and sat it next to him. "What if we still have air left? Can we--?"

"No." Catherine stood and shook her finger in Steve's face. "To deviate from the dive plan will run the risk of getting caught inside the wreck with the running current trapping you." She picked up the cup and sat it next to the stack. "You understand?"

Steve clasped his hands tightly. "Gotcha. We never had to deal with exchanges in the Caribbean. So, uh, this should be fun?"

"We have a window of about thirty-five minutes to get in, do our dive, and get back aboard. The maximum current speed will be two-point-five knots, and will begin right after slack water." She looked at each of us, "This is a great dive, but a serious dive. Don't get down there and rubberneck and fuck up the plan. We'll be in and out before the flood begins." She reached up and pulled her knit cap over her ears.

Steve's head jerked. "Flood?"

"Quit worrying. That's when the tide begins to come in. That's a seaman's term, they call it flooding." She stood, picked Steve's cup next to the stack and reached for mine.

I handed her the cup. "How much time before we jump in, Catherine?" I checked my gear.

"Twenty minutes, and we'll have a live boat, no anchor and no buoy. That means that we will make a free descent and a free ascent upon the completion of the dive." She turned and made her way back into the galley with the three empty cups.

"We better get our shit together today, Steve." I winked. "I think the boss is serious."

Steve removed his glasses and cleaned them with his shirt, put them back on, and then removed them again and laid them on the ledge next to the smokestack. "Can't wear these underwater," he muttered, before he returned to the task of assembling his gear. His hands shook.

"Are you okay, Partner?" I slapped him on the shoulder.

"I'm good."

"You're a good diver. This will be an easy one. Not to worry." I knew Steve was at best, uncomfortable in tricky dive conditions. He was an accomplished diver, but tended to worry.

I could make out a large, red, bell buoy on our starboard side. Perched on the round base was a sea lion, close enough to touch. He raised his head and stared at us.

Catherine appeared from below, pointed and smiled at the large mammal. "The sea lions are back in Puget Sound this time of year, after having spent the summer in mating rituals in Northern waters. They normally stake a claim to a particular area and defend it, even against scuba divers." She winked and said, "Don't worry; I'll take care of you."

The engine noise diminished. At the same time, the gentle

forward movement changed to an agitated motion as we were caught in a vortex of swells and currents.

Catherine called out, "Five minutes, Gentlemen."

Steve and I geared up and stumbled into each another. The violent activity began to make my stomach uneasy. Steve took large gulps of air and tried to stave off seasickness. I was more than ready to jump into the water and begin our dive.

The captain maneuvered the boat as the three of us clambered ungracefully over the transom and onto the dive step.

"There's still some current before the slack water begins," Catherine said "When the captain blows the whistle, it's time for us to jump into the water and descend to the bottom. The current will carry us to the sunken wreck." She turned and looked toward the captain.

When the whistle blew we leaped off the dive step in unison. As we hit the water, we dumped all the residual air from our suits and buoyancy compensators, to facilitate the descent. I immediately felt the tug of the current pushing me sideways as I dropped. There was no visual reference, no anchor line, or reef to guide by, just my gauges that showed depth and decent rate.

I began to experience mid-water disorientation as current-borne organisms drifted by my facemask horizontally as I continued to plunge. I concentrated on my gauges and hoped that at seventy feet I would begin to see bottom.

My fins found the bottom and the rest of my body crashed into the floor. The cocoon of silt, I'd created, was so thick; I could not see my instruments or gauges. I sat quietly and waited for the silt to settle. The current still gently propelled me, to what, I didn't know. Stretched out face down, I pushed my compensator button to inject air into my buoyancy compensator, which lifted me five feet above the bottom. The dim light filtered through the water column. I wouldn't need my dive light.

Ahead of me at a distance of about twenty feet, I could see the distinct outline of a wreck. The vessel was encased in huge white flowers that Catherine told us about earlier, some more than two feet long attached to the hull and sides of the drowned vessel. I heard Catherine's voice in my head, "The flowers you will see are living animals called plumose anemone, similar to the soft corals you see in the South Pacific."

The anemones had thick white trunks, which undulated in time to some unheard orchestra. As I moved closer, I could see that the entire wreck was outlined in a milky cloud, like fog on the surface. Amidships, I saw a gaping hole four feet in diameter with jagged edges as if a torpedo had sunk the craft. Inside the wreck was total blackness. With the current slackening, I was able to hold my position at the base of the dark hull and await my companions.

Alongside the wrecked vessel, ragged boulders were scattered, intermixed with orange sea pens that grew out of the silt like flowers. Crabs danced sideways from rock to rock and skittered across huge sunflower starfish, which waved its twenty or more arms and scrambled for traction.

A blast of air bubbles captured my attention as Catherine came toward me. She swam from the direction of the bow. Her head moved from side to side until she spied me. Steve was behind her and they both flared, like a parachutist before they touch ground, and fell in beside me. Catherine switched on her powerful halogen lantern, directed it into the darkness through the hole in the side of the wreck, and then swam inside. Like two ducklings behind their mother, we followed; afraid she might lose us in the pitch-blackness of the ships hull.

Our heads turned toward the light in whatever direction Catherine directed it, first one side then the other; like spectators at a tennis match. Catherine illuminated the interior of the wreck, which revealed massive timbers, the vessels skeleton. Some were broken and lay at odd angles atop one another. The engine lay on its side, the propeller shaft bent and rusted. Catherine moved the light near the upper left corner of the interior hull, and there, suspended on a corner beam perched a giant Pacific octopus. The beam of light lit the animal from an obtuse angle, leaving most of its mantle in shadow. It stared at us with one immense golden eye. The octopus draped over the beam; its tentacles dangled twenty feet or more to the base of the keel. It did not move. The body of the animal was still, yet the tentacles trembled and waved independently as if they were not connected to the body. The girth in diameter of the tentacles near the base and closest to the body measured at least twelve inches. The animal was nearly the length of the Spirit.

Catherine swam toward the octopus, and once directly beneath the animal, slid between the drooping tentacles and brushed them aside like branches along a wooded trail. As the three of us worked our way through this living obstruction, the suckers, which lined the appendages, adhered to parts of our gear. My heart beat in my ears so loudly, it was doubtful I would have heard a bomb explode, let alone the gentle smacking of the suckers. Catherine swam with her light on full and behind her pitch-blackness filled the void as Steve and I felt our way through the tentacles. They were heavier than they looked. It felt like a swim through live snakes that hung from a tree branch, and it made my skin crawl.

I saw Catherine's light turn to the left as she illuminated another hole near the stern of the vessel. As we swam through the hole, the pitch-blackness changed to semi-dark. We could see a pile of stones that would easily have filled a ten-yard dump truck. The wreck lay alongside the pile of ballast stones so that the uppermost sections of the shipwreck seemed bonded to the pile. On the bottom, a three-foot wide path snaked between the wreck and the rocks and allowed us to swim the length of the pile itself. Halfway there and ten feet from the bottom, two wolf eels poked their heads from holes. They were smaller than the eels from Devil's Boulder, more delicate, but with the same rheumy eyes and grayish skin that shivered when they moved. A younger couple perhaps?

Catherine again reached into the den and pulled out the male wolf eel and began feeding it scraps from her goodie bag. I photographed the event while Steve took notes on an underwater slate. The female remained inside the den with no apparent desire to share in the treats. Near the end of my shoot, both eels retreated so far into the depths of their den. They were spooked, no doubt, from the repeated flash of my strobe. Catherine checked her watch and signaled that it was time to head back to the surface.

Catherine led the way back along the underwater pathway to the hole in the side of the wreck. She swam through the dark opening, her powerful light reflected off the skeletal silhouette of the interior of the hull. We could feel the movement of the flood current. Thousands of tiny, white microorganisms that resembled a swarm of miniature bees reflected in her light and rushed through the wreck, propelled by the flood current. I had two more shots left on the roll of film and decided I would shoot the giant octopus as we swam beneath it--a blind shot, for Catherine would be clear of the wreck by then. The descending tentacles were illuminated as Catherine approached then, darkened to invisibility as she passed through. I turned onto my back in order to swim directly underneath the animal and shoot vertically from the tentacles to the body. As I came into contact with the first tentacle I fired off two quick shots in succession, and then turned over again to swim out the exit. I was blind, any night vision destroyed by the bright flashes from my strobe.

All at once I was engulfed by massive tentacles. I twisted and turned, flailed my arms and legs, and tried desperately to grasp a part of the ship. The embrace became rigid as the octopus increased its pressure and wound me tightly in its clinch. The more I struggled, the more tightly I was held. My mask was ripped from my face when a tentacle wrapped around my head and threatened to pull my regulator from my mouth. I began to suck water through my nostrils. My hands were uselessly pinned against my sides.

The beast pressed against my chest. The mantle pulsated, smooth as silk, and quivered against my face. Giant suckers attached themselves to my body, adhered to my dry suit like a hundred vacuum cleaners that smacked and un-smacked as they moved along my body. It pulled me closer to the huge beak hidden within the folds of the creature's mantle.

Where were my dive buddies? There was no more fight left in me. I remembered basic scuba practices and relaxed my body and concentrated on breathing. In the back of my mind I knew my air would soon run out, and then I would have to resort to plan B. Panic!

A hand touched my face. It stroked and caressed me. I felt pressure released from around my mid-section as the giant tentacles were gently removed from their stranglehold. Catherine discovered my predicament and had come to my rescue. Without my mask, I had to keep my eyes closed and rely completely on

Catherine. I clung to her and grasped at her shoulder straps, her weight belt, anything that would prevent me from losing contact with her. I couldn't find them. My hand became entangled in a chain that hung from her gear; her dive light lanyard? I held on tight, a small connection, but better than nothing. It snapped off in my hand I was near panic, but was convinced that her ease with these giants of the dark would save me from certain death. She propelled me forward through the exit hole, and then pushed me gently upward. I popped to the surface with my tank resonating like a hollow drum, nearly empty. When I opened my eyes, I found myself astern of and practically underneath the dive step. The light lanyard was still in my hand and I stuffed into my dry suit pocket. I reached up and grasped the handholds on the dive step. A hand reached over the side and unhooked my weight belt, and then my buoyancy compensator. I hoisted myself onto the dive step, removed my fins, and stood up. My dive buddy's stood and removed their gear on the wet deck as the captain helped me over the transom.

He looked me over and said, "Where's your fuckin' mask?"

I glanced at the captain and then at Catherine. "Didn't you tell them what just happened down there?"

She raised her eyebrows and tilted her head. "What happened down there, when?"

"With the octopus!"

She looked genuinely surprised. "What are you talking about?"

What the hell is going on? Could it be that oxygen deprivation caused by systematic compression over my entire body could have caused me to hallucinate again? Had that octopus simply tired of me and let go?

45

I brushed the bulge in my pocket. No, Catherine was not the woman who had saved my life after all.

"I saw you shoot off that strobe near the octopus inside the wreck. I should warn you that octopuses are extremely sensitive to light, and you could end up pissing them off." She rambled on as she pulled her head through the neck seal of her dry suit and wiggled out of the arms and legs. She turned and walked into the pilothouse.

"No shit!" I muttered

I stood aft on the wet deck facing out to sea, and I peeled off my dry suit. I removed the lanyard from my pocket and looked at it. It was not a dive light at all. It was a pendant, attached to a heavy, gold chain. The stone was amber colored glass and filled with a clear liquid that pulsed when I endeavored to hold it still. Maybe the vibration of the diesel engine was enough to excite the liquid. I turned the pendant over in my hand and the strangest feeling came over me. I shook my head and dangled the pendant from my fingers. I did not need any more mysteries today.

"What do you have there?" Steve reached for the pendant. "Where did you find this?" He took it from me, picked up his glasses from the dry stack and looked closer. "Wow!"

"Stick it in your pocket, Steve," I said quietly. We'll take a closer look later." I moved between him and the door to the pilothouse while he pocketed the necklace. "Unzip me, will you?"

He turned me around and pulled on the zipper lanyard. "There's slime all over your suit. What did you get into?" He wiped his hands on his pant leg.

"Octopus," I whispered.

"Why are we whispering?" Steve whispered back.

"I'm not sure."

* * *

The captain was also our chef and prided himself on concocting between-dive meals. Spicy tomato soup steamed on the galley stove. Its aroma floated on the still air and settled over the aft deck and made my mouth water. Freshly baked herb bread, still warm from the oven and served up with fresh, sweet cream butter, was placed on the makeshift table secured to the dry stack. The captain brought out hot, mugs of the soup then disappeared back inside his galley. He muttered, and sounded much abused amid loud clanking of pans and crockery. Steve looked concerned over the captain's chagrin. He turned to Catherine and shrugged.

"Something we said?"

"Don't worry yourself over the captain, Doc. He works so hard preparing his soups, he hates to see anyone eat it up, but he'd complain a lot louder if you didn't, so bottoms up," Catherine advised.

The soup was wonderful with spicy pepper that seared my throat, chunks of blood-red tomato, and sweet basil in a hot liquid paste. The herb bread crunched on the outside, but was soft and warm on the inside. It made me think of Catherine. Eating always reminded me how closely food and sex are related.

I must have smiled, for Catherine looked at me as if she could read my mind and said softly, "What's on your mind now, Soldier?"

I blushed and said, "You'll never guess, but it doesn't have anything to do with being a soldier."

* * *

"Catherine, I think I'll stay topside with the captain for the next dive." I sipped at a cup of coffee and leaned against the warm stack.

Catherine strapped the tanks onto the buoyancy compensators. She looked up at me and smiled. "We won't see an octopus on this dive."

"I'm a little tired; besides, I lost my favorite mask on the last dive. So…" In fact, my hands still shook and my insides trembled from the encounter. When I brushed the hair along the top of my arms it sent chills down my spine one moment, then pain along the inside of my elbow a moment later.

She hefted the tank assembly for Steve up onto the bulwarks. "Whatever you say, Gil, it's your money."

Steve was geared up and turned to me. "It's okay, Gil, we don't need photos on this dive anyway. Catherine will take care of me." He looked at her nervously. "You will, won't you?"

She laughed and pushed Steve into the water. "You know I will. Come on Steve, let's go diving." She dropped into the water beside him and they descended.

Steve and Catherine began their dive at noon and expected to be down forty-five to fifty minutes. The sun burned through the gloomy fog and transformed the day into a glistening afternoon. Pockets of wispy fog still hung low to the water, trapped near the head of the little bay where we were anchored. The wind freshened and swept clean those areas exposed to the north; insubstantial remnants of fog hung vertically against the rocky shore.

The sun bore down and warmed us as the captain and I sat on the aft deck and watched the bubble trail from the divers. The

Spirit, her bow pointed into the light wind protected her passengers on the stern. She was relaxed, sleepy, and idle from her difficult trip through the morning fog.

Her captain basked in the late fall sunshine. Shirtless and tanned from the summer on the water, he turned his head and spit over the side. "We have to charge up them old batteries when we can around here," he growled. "Sunshine can be fuckin' hard to find now 'til May." He stretched his arms and reached for the sky like an old tomcat after a nap.

On the near shore, house-sized boulders with barnacles growing like cancer their black skins, marched down into the water, covered by high tides, and glistened as the water receded.

On the opposite side of the bay a four-story, brick and stone house stood amid the otherwise forested hillside. The house could have been transported from the sixteenth century. Turrets bedecked the north and south sides; slotted windows ran up each tower and spires stood like sentinels atop the main roof. The house was shaded on all but the beach side with tall fir trees that lent it an ominous air that even this sunny afternoon could not dispel.

"That's Catherine's ancestral home," muttered the captain, shading his eyes with the flat of his hand. "Awful looking place, ain't it?" He alternated between looking at the house and watching for the diver's telltale bubbles.

"I thought she lived in town."

"Oh, she does," he explained. "She wouldn't live in that fuckin' place. Wintertime, or summertime it's fuckin' damp and moldy. No insulation you know, and the seawater runs right underneath the place, what with all the caves and cracks under its foundation. No, she should knock that place down, put up a decent little house, and cut those god dammed trees down, too."

He shivered despite the sun, stood and spit tobacco juice into the water.

The divers bubble trail had stopped and became more agitated. Concentric rings, which continued to grow in diameter.

"Divers up," barked the captain as he climbed over the transom. He stood on the dive step.

As each diver maneuvered to the dive step, they handed up their weight belt then their tank assembly. The captain slung the gear over the transom and then helped Steve onto the dive step. Catherine simply placed her hands on the gunwale and kicked her way up over the side of the boat. Steve, on the other hand had to be manhandled up to the dive step where, once rested, he took off his fins and laboriously crawled over the transom. He fell onto the wet deck.

"You okay, Partner?" I pulled him to his feet.

"I'm fine, Gil." He smiled at Catherine. "Great dive Catherine, Thanks."

Catherine deposited her tank assembly onto the rubber mat. "I told you I'd take good care of him."

The north wind rippled the waters surface as the dive boat headed back to Eagle Harbor. The sun hung low on the horizon and its brilliant rays struck the water at a forty-five-degree angle. The reflection was so incredible on our port side that we averted our eyes and sought shade under the boat's superstructure. We rounded a second buoy and turned left, which headed us directly into the sun's path, then left around the third buoy and then into the shade of the steep bank that overlooked the harbor. The captain landed the <u>Spirit</u> alongside our houseboat dock. Catherine jumped onto the dock with a line, neatly held the boat in place and Steve and I unloaded our gear.

"What time tomorrow will you pick us up?" I called out as Catherine let go of the line, letting the Spirit drift away from the dock.

"No diving on Friday," she called back. "Did I forget to tell you? The captain plays golf on Friday. See you early Saturday morning."

The little boat was gone.

"Golf my ass," I muttered as I hoisted my dive gear onto one shoulder. "I'll bet the captain doesn't know a golf club from a polo pony. Hey, Steve, can you imagine the captain on a golf course?" I laughed as I tried to imagine the crusty old bastard teeing off with a putter. "Speaking of bastards," I continued, edging my way around the corner of the houseboat, "the captain mentioned that Catherine's ancestral home sits just above where you dove today. But he didn't mention anything about having any financial interest in the house himself. Are you sure that they're brother and sister?"

"I'll check their pedigree tomorrow," said Steve as he stumbled along the dock. He pulled the dive gear across the rough boards and left tracks on the damp wood. "We might as well go to Seattle tomorrow while the captain is on the links. We can pick up some more high-speed film, get my adapter and check into that lab at the University of Washington. I have to contact a researcher out there anyway, so we can do the whole trip tomorrow." He sat on his gear and looked beat, reached into his pocket and handed me the necklace. "Here, stick this thing in your pocket. We'll take it to town tomorrow."

"Leave your gear right here and I'll wash it down." I pocketed the necklace, pulled him to his feet and guided him toward the front door of the houseboat. I knew he was tired when he did not complain, instead unlocked the door and went in without a word. I pulled the necklace back out, held it up and watched the late afternoon rays dance off the amber pendant. I held it close to my eyes and whispered, "Who do you belong to." A small brown head popped from the water and stared at me. "Is that thing yours?" I called to the disembodied head and then swung the pendant a circle above my head. "Would you like to have it back?" I made as if to throw the necklace at the animal when it barked and dove silently under the water. "Ha," I yelled at the vanished harbor seal and returned the necklace to my pocket. "Damn, I better get this gear cleaned before I go all the way around the bend," and I reached for the garden hose.

Chapter 5

"Good morning, Children." Lois smiled at her five little apostles and glanced out the window. Heavy fog blanketed the saltwater, spilled onto the beach before crawling up into the tree line. The pathway to the main house disappeared in the mist. A foghorn sounded lonely as it called out warning to other vessels of its blindness. The seagulls perched on tumbled, beached driftwood and waited for the fog to dissipate.

The girls sat on chairs they would someday grow into. They were dressed in white cotton robes, like their teacher, who stood at the head of the table and began the lesson.

"Today, you will learn more about yourselves. Our bodies are different. We are special. We are protectors of the sea, and as such our bodies have adapted over the years to be at one with the sea." She walked around the table and patted each child on the top of the head. "Quit fidgeting girls and listen."

"We see underwater without goggles. We swim underwater as fast as a dolphin, without fins. We breathe underwater without air tanks. We are fish that can live on land." Lois looked around the table at her charges; she had gained their attention. "Gather close and look at my eyes,"

Lois opened her eyes wide and a third, clear, membranous

53

lens slid down to cover her naked eye. The eye appeared to be much larger and bulged slightly. The eyelids locked into place so that it created the illusion she was staring at the children. Under the membranous lid, the color of the iris faded to light gray. The girls "Ooohed" and "Aahhed."

"Now you do it," Lois intoned quietly. "Open your eyes very wide, as wide as you can and the new lens will cover your eyes and protect it from the sea."

The five little girls tried, and found it came easily, naturally.

"But when it's down, everything's all blurry," complained Celia, the smallest of the five.

"That's all right, Sweetie. That's how it's supposed to look when you're not underwater." She explained that the lens made up for the distortion and the color changes underwater so that when they were submerged, everything they saw would be crystal clear. "That's why we don't wear the lens on land. Do you all understand?"

The girls looked confused. Lois knew that it would take time underwater for the acolytes to fully grasp the use of their new toys.

"To slide the lens back up over your eye, just close your eyes for a minute, until you feel it unlock."

Soon the girls mastered the art and turned it into a game. They blinked, giggled, and called one another names. Lois knew too, that this was part of the process, and it made these new transformations comfortable.

After a little while, Lois waved her arms for them to be seated, "Okay, Girls, settle down. Another thing you can do is breathe underwater just like a fish. Only other members of the Sisterhood can do this."

The girls held their breath and waited.

"Gather around me again, and watch closely." Lois collected her long hair and exposed her neck. She grasped her earlobe between her index finger and thumb and pulled her earlobe up out of the way. Beneath her earlobe, was a small split in the skin no more than three-quarters of an inch long. Lois held her breath a moment and the organ began to open and then close. A puff of air could be heard.

Again, the "Ooohs" and "Aaahs" filled the room as the children inspected this new mystery.

"Now you try it. Hold your breath and concentrate on breathing through your gill slits. Yours, like mine are right behind each ear." She demonstrated again, and before long the girls mastered the new skill.

"Now we will all lie on our tummies, put our heads into the pool and breathe. Just like the fishes." Lois lay face down and submerged her head underwater to demonstrate. For a few minutes, Lois held her head underwater, and then with a vigorous shake, she removed her face from the water and drenched her pupils. "Okay, your turn."

"I can't do this, Sister Lois." The tiny redhead turned toward her instructor.

"Yes, you can. You all can do this." Lois knelt down next to the tiny voice. "Watch again." She lay down so that her face was next to the girls and said, "You do it with me. We will do it together."

Five little girls acted as one, dunking their heads into the pool. They gagged and spit out misplaced water to begin with, then coughed and choked, but soon they all were breathing comfortably underwater.

"Watch this, guys." Sarah, the slimmest of the five,

plunged her head too enthusiastically into the pool and toppled in. She was then dragged out feet first by her unimpressed teacher.

As the girls dried their hair, Lois announced, "Wash your skin carefully, Girls." She ran a finger along Sarah's arm. "You see this substance?" She held her finger for all the girls to study. "This forms on our skin to protect us, and when we play in the saltwater, it will begin to ooze all over our skin. So, just wash it off."

"Yucky!" Five little girls toweled their skin vigorously.

Lois laughed and turned toward the door. "After lunch, I'll teach you how to
 <u>really</u> swim."

Chapter 6

The eight-ten ferry blew its departure whistle as we drove aboard and parked on the upper car deck. Three cars pulled on behind us, before the gates closed. The ferry rumbled out of the dock and hurried toward Seattle.

"Good timing, Partner. You buying the coffee?"

Steve pushed the car door against the side of the ferry and tried to squeeze out. "I'll have to slide out your door. Coffee, maybe, but no doughnuts."

I reached in and hauled him toward me. "We are going to have to stick you on a diet. Pull your door shut."

We climbed the two flights of stairs to the passenger cabin, shouldered our way through the ferry and found the back of the coffee line. I shook my head. "This place is crowded."

"Commuters. Do you have any money?" Steve patted himself down. "I think I left my wallet in the car."

"You wouldn't think that this little island would have this many commuters." We reached the coffee counter. "Two large black coffees, please."

Steve jabbed me, "I don't have any money, Gil."

"What a surprise." I paid and handed a cardboard cup to Steve. "Let's try and find a place to sit."

We actually found a window seat on the south side of the boat as the ferry made a turn out of the harbor. Black clouds soon displaced the rain and fog. I sipped my coffee and looked down the shoreline in the direction the <u>Spirit</u> had taken us the day before.

"Isn't that our dive boat?" I pointed my coffee cup in the direction of the harbor.

Steve removed his glasses and cleaned the lens with a paper napkin and then replaced them. He stood there, pressed his face against the window and squinted.

"Just turning the corner, see it?" I sat my coffee on the window's ledge.

"No, I don't think so. Unless the captain has to drive the boat to the golf course." He sat back down, leaned against the seat back and said. "You're seeing things again."

White caps began to develop and raindrops sprinkled the window. The massive boat glided effortlessly through the choppy water and pointed her bow toward the Space Needle on the Seattle skyline. The ferry docked thirty minutes later with a gentle nudge at the pier.

We drove north through the metropolitan area of Seattle to the campus of the University of Washington. The campus resembled a park with buildings and pathways concealed by an endless variety of hardwood and evergreen trees. We parked and proceeded on foot to the Science Building. The campus bustled with life, as students jostled one another to trek across campus. Autumn leaves gathered around massive tree trunks as their bare limbs shivered. More raindrops splattered against the cobblestone path as we entered the building and moved down the main hallway.

I stopped Steve before we went in the door marked, Marine Science Center, "What's this guy's name, Steve?"

"Dr. Francis Mark. He heads up the Department and he's an old friend."

I opened the door to the lab, stood aside and held the door for Steve. I expected to see a small man, frail with coke-bottle glasses and a Friar tuck haircut.

"Stevie," a voice boomed and nearly knocked me down. "Give me a hug, Big Guy." The man behind the voice ducked his head through the opening and engulfed Steve with gorilla arms.

I jumped out of the way as Doctor Francis Mark swung Steve around and then deposited him gently in the foyer.

Steve stumbled to gain his balance and then turned and jabbed his hand into the catcher's mitt that hung from the giant's sleeve. Steve's hand disappeared. "How are you, Fran?" Steve winced and tried to pull away.

"I'm a hundred percent, My Friend." He released Steve, stepped back and folded his arms across his chest. "It's damn good to see you, Stevie. How long has it been?"

Steve massaged his hand and smiled. "It's great to see you too. I think we met up at the Bahamas conference." He scratched his head. "Two years ago."

I could hear Steve speak but was unable to see around the professor's back. The white lab coats seams began to part, and threads dangled like shredded skin from an open wound.

"Yeah, that's right, Walker's Cay. We did the shark thing there. That was a good time." He laughed and the wounds on his jacket grew.

Steve peeked around the man who blocked his view of me and wiggled his fingers. "Fran, this is my friend, Gil. I don't think you've met him yet. He's a photo expert."

Doctor Mark spun toward me, grasped the top of the entry door and slammed it closed in one motion. "Gil." The voice roared. The black mop on his head whirled about his face and then settled on his shoulders.

He surrounded me in an instant I backed into a counter and raised my hands. "No hugs, please." I held out my hand, tentatively. "It's a pleasure.

He ignored it and bear-hugged me anyway. He slapped my shoulders, but held me tight. "Any friend of Stevie's is an automatic friend of mine."

"Thanks, ditto," I gasped.

He released me as quickly as he had snatched me up. I held onto the wall for support. Doctor Mark turned sideways and I was able to see Steve once more.

"What can I do for you two? Come, let's go into my office."

My ears began to ache from the sound waves he generated. He turned and bullied between us and pushed through the door that led into his laboratory. I winked at Steve and poked my fingers in my ears. Steve smiled and followed his friend through the door.

The lab looked as though a tornado touched down, spilling papers and paper cups. Reams of computer paper overflowed from the file cabinet onto the floor.

"Jesus Christ, Fran, don't you have a housekeeper or lab assistant?" Steve sat down in a steel backed chair and grinned. "Same old Fran."

Fran perched on a paper-strewn corner of his desk. The desktop groaned. "That's my wife's job," he complained.

"You don't have a wife, Fran."

"Well, there you go then." He stood, turned and began to

shuffle papers.

"I'm kidding. The place looks great." Steve removed his glasses and blew onto the lenses. Fran, Gil and I have some material…uh, maybe marine origin, and we thought maybe you could--"

"Identify it? You bet." He turned his palm up and we could have parked a Volkswagen in it. "Where is it?"

"Right here." I pulled the zip-lock bag from my coat pocket and handed it to him.

"Where did you get this?" He held the plastic bag to the light and squinted.

Steve crossed his legs and told Dr. Fran about the negatives and the possibility that someone had contaminated the films. He finished and asked, "If you have the capabilities and the time for a quick analysis, Fran, I'd be grateful." He took off his glasses again, but they slipped through his fingers and clattered to the floor.

Fran scratched his head with both hands and looked first at Steve and then me. "What have you boys gotten yourselves involved with?" He shook his black mane.

Steve and I exchanged a look.

"Okay, okay, maybe it's better I don't know. So, you think this material may be of a marine origin. I can work it up for you right now." He took the bag and bounded through the door into the lab, threw off his jacket and rolled up his sleeves.

We followed him, and found ourselves in a larger room filled with humming computers and desktop workstations. This room looked as sterile as a hospital operating theater, stark white with white tile floors and red, grilled, rubber mats.

Fran stopped midway and bent over an electronic centrifuge. He opened the plastic hatch on the top and placed some of the material from the index card into a small, white ceramic bowl. He then closed the hatch and activated the device. A computer keyboard slid out from beneath the centrifuge, and Fran's fingers raced across the tiny keyboard and gave the machine its instructions.

"No more dipping and comparing. These new computer programs I've developed can decipher in a millisecond what used to take a week," he bragged. "The computer is programmed to break down the component elements of any material that is marine-related, then reassemble that same material and match it with the listed categories or sub-categories that we have programmed. If it's from outer space, we probably won't be able to recognize it. Otherwise it's a piece of cake." He typed on the keyboard and said, "Aha, this one's easy." He pulled out a sheet of paper from the printer, scanned it quickly, and handed it to Steve.

"Cytoplasmic mucosa?" Steve read aloud. "On the slides?" He read it again. "Now that is interesting"

"A very high concentration, according to the numbers," Fran noted. "You would normally see those numbers if you came in direct contact with the animal, but not so if you simply rubbed against it."

I scratched my head. "Just a minute. What are we talking about here?"

"This material on your negatives is the same material that coats the outer layer of skin on many marine animals. It's a protective coating that sloughs off when the animal comes into contact with anything," Steve explained.

"What…"

"Remember at Devil's Boulder, when you swam into those large white anemones? You come out of the water with a slime that coated your gloves and legs."

"I remember."

That's what we're talking about." His hands fidgeted. "The problem is the high concentration could occur only if there were direct contact. In other words, the marine animal would have had to be present to leave the slime on those slides. You couldn't have contaminated them."

"Or maybe," I countered, "someone is playing a little game with us."

***

It was eleven-thirty, and traffic on the freeway was light. The rain sheeted our windshield and continued to build, being driven by the southerly wind.

"Where's the jeweler located, Steve?" I drove while Steve laid his head back and closed his eyes.

"Take the Pine street exit. It's right in the center of the city." He opened his eyes and sat up. "Let me see that bauble again."

"It's in the glove box. Does it ever stop raining here?" The windshield wipers scraped across the glass, too slow to keep up with the job.

He removed the necklace and re-closed the glove box, "This thing feels warm. I wonder what that amber liquid is, inside the glass." Steve held the pendant in his hand, and let the gold chain flow between his fingers. He opened his hand and examined it closely. "I can't quite-- Well, let me see." He fumbled his glasses off his nose as I swerved to avoid a hubcap in the road. "Watch out there."

"Sorry." A tractor-trailer passed and flooded our

63

windshield. "Shit."

Steve held the glass pendant in one hand and with the other held his glasses as if they were a magnifying glass. "There's writing on the back of this thing. I can't quite make it. Hmmm, Gaelic, I think. Not certain, though." He coiled the chain on top of the glass, and then pocketed the pendant. He looked out the windshield. "About a mile and we turn off to the right."

We parked next to an older brick building. People strolled down the sidewalks without umbrellas or hats, oblivious to the hammering rain. I suspected that North westerners accepted the rain like Californians accepted sunshine.

The lunchtime crowd on the sidewalk was heavy as we pushed our way through and entered the red brick building through double glass doors into a small foyer. An umbrella stand was conspicuously empty, and above to the left, a window etched with, "Jonas Goldstein, Antique Jewelry."

"How do you find these places Steve? We've been here three days or so and yet you can still find an antique jeweler?"

"My ex and I honeymooned here back in eighty-five. I bought her a nice little bauble here after a particularly great night. We stayed just around the corner, and would walk past this place on the way to the theater," he reminisced.

He looked sad for a moment and glanced out the window.

"As a matter of fact, it was raining then, too, and that was in August."

An old-world smell of polished leather and dust hovered in the air as we entered. Two leather chairs were positioned around a small, wood table at one end of the room.

I whispered, "No one's home. Maybe its lunchtime and he forgot to lock up. Let's steal something and get the hell out of here," I joked.

"Go ahead, take your best shot," came a Brooklyn accent from behind the counter. "But unless you're wearing body armor, I wouldn't try nothing"

I looked over the counter into the barrel of a twelve-gauge shotgun. A black man, no bigger around than a garden hose sat in an overstuffed chair, a shotgun in one hand, a half-eaten sandwich in the other, and a smile on his face. I raised my hands and said, "I was just kidding, Sir. We have business with you and when I didn't see anyone-- I was just joking around a little. Sorry."

"Yeah, sure. What in the Hell do you want, Boy?" He stood up and placed the sandwich down in one fluid movement. The shotgun didn't waver. He looked up at me and pumped a round in the chamber. "You think I'm bluffing?"

I backed up, trapped by the wall behind me. "No sir."

The wind had joined the rain outside and puffs of wind rattled the door to the jewelry store. The door latch slipped and the door began to swing open. Steve pushed it and the door closed with a solid click. Mr. Goldstein seemed unaffected. The temperature was as cool in the store as it was outside, yet he wore a short-sleeved T-shirt with Harley-Davidson printed across the front. The shirt fit him like a hand me down from a big brother.

"Look," Steve intervened. "We wanted to show you a necklace, get an opinion from an expert, and then be on our way. That's all. We don't want any trouble. Sorry for the bother. We'll be leaving now."

The gun didn't move but a smile began to break across the jeweler's face.

"Oh, sit down and show me what you've got." He pointed the shotgun at the ceiling pumped the fore stock and ejected two shells into the air, neatly caught the shells before they landed then placed the shotgun on the counter. He sauntered around the end of the counter and plopped himself down in one of the chairs. "Don't get all huffy on me. I could tell you two were lightweights the minute you walked into my store." He brushed crumbs off the front of his shirt and motioned for us to sit down.

Steve sat down across from the dealer, pulled the necklace from his coat pocket, and placed it on the jewelers display pad in the center of the table. There were only two chairs available, so I stood behind Steve and looked over his shoulder.

Mr. Goldstein carefully picked up the necklace and spread it across the felt surface. After he looked it over he picked it up, palming the necklace, and wrapped his fingers around it. The jeweler reached around behind him, and retrieved a lighted magnifying glass. Without a word to either of us, he continued his examination for several minutes.

Goldstein muttered. "Gaelic for sure, probably Goidelic, and either ancient Manx or possibly Scottish. See those symbols here?" He pointed and moved the magnifier closer to Steve. "They look like ancient Druid writings. You know about Druids?"

I shrugged.

"They were teachers and priests--learned ones. I'm no expert, but this is very old. The gold and the workmanship are incredible. As far as the gemstone inset, I haven't a clue. I've never seen anything like it. The stone almost looks alive. I feel like it wants me to warm it up. It's very unusual."

"Mr. Goldstein? Is this thing worth something?" I was always the bean counter. I noticed Goldstein's hands begin to rub together.

"To be honest with you, I got no idea about its true value. I can give you what the gold is worth if you want to sell it, and you could keep the gemstone." He sounded like a used car dealer. "I'll tell you what! The best I can do is a thousand bucks for the entire necklace."

"Mr. Goldstein," said Steve, "We don't actually want to sell this necklace; it is part of an on-going investigation. What we need to do is find out everything we can about the necklace, and its history. I don't want to appear to be disrespectful, Mr. Goldstein, but do you know anyone who can give us some more detailed information?"

"Dr. John Griffin," Goldstein spat out. "Evergreen State College in Olympia. You don't come in here to sell, then I got no time for socializing. He stood and turned toward the counter, snapped a rag from his back pocket and wiped at an unseen smudge on the glass. He half turned and said, "Be careful boys, who you show that necklace to; it's worth more than I'm willing to give for it. Maybe, a lot more."

Chapter 7

Catherine joined Lois and the girls for lunch.

"Okay, gather around." Catherine herded the girls so that they formed a semi-circle around herself and Lois. The fog lifted, but the rain began in earnest. Catherine sighed and turned to her pupils. "Come on, Ladies, stop lollygagging, gather around." She tapped her foot.

Lois stood within the semi-circle, loosened the ties on her white terry robe, stepped out of it and handed it to Catherine. Lois's body was long, hard muscled, with small breasts and muscular calves. Her skin was blue-white and fine textured as if it were painted on, so silky; it shimmered like a runner after a mile of hard work.

While the girls looked on, a magnificent metamorphosis began to occur. A liquid effluent emanated from Lois's skin and oozed from her pores. The substance coalesced, obscuring her skin and replaced it with a mucous sealant that began to dry. The skin lost its luster. Lois pirouetted like a model and the light glittered off her skin, iridescent.

"Touch Sister Lois's skin, Children." Catherine invited. "It's very smooth and soft, but in fact her skin is strong, and durable. This covering protects Lois from sharp rocks and barnacles, which would tear her skin."

The children gathered closer and ran their hands over Lois. "Can we make our skin do this, Sister Catherine?" Sarah asked.

"Not yet, Sarah. When you turn thirteen or fourteen you will be able to do everything Sister Lois will show you today."

Catherine brought the children's attention back to Lois's body. "Watch Sister Lois's legs now, Children."

Lois lay down on the tile next to the pool, her legs tight together. The seam between her legs began to fill with the mucous material that was liquid with the consistency of glue. The grayish substance flowed quickly and then hardened. A new appendage was created, two legs into one powerful, extremity. The muscles in her upper thighs fused with her calf muscles and formed a longitudinal muscle that rippled under her new skin. Her feet splayed at a forty-five-degree angle and a web-like structure molded itself in the intervening space and formed a single lateral fin.

"Sister Lois can now swim like a dolphin, Children," Catherine said.

The girls whispered and pointed.

Lois rolled off the edge into the water and demonstrated her powerful new body to the girls. She dove to the bottom of the pool, and leaped out of the water to touch the ceiling. She splashed back into the pool and soaked the children with the cold water. Lois enthralled them with more tricks and splashes.

"Weee! Sister Lois, more, more." The girls ran the length of the pool and squealed. They jumped and raised their arms, and Lois would leap again.

Before long, Lois swam to the shallow end of the pool and rolled up onto the side. The children gathered around to touch, prod and compare this new body to their own. They took no notice of the needle sharp teeth or of the fingernails that had transformed into razor sharp claws.

"Okay, Children, it's time to get wet, everybody in the pool." Catherine clapped her hands, and five little girls threw off their robes and leaped into the pool. They squealed and splashed, dove to the bottom and back up again.

Lois joined in the fun and games in the water and encouraged the children to ride on her back as she dove to the bottom and then soared into the air with them.

Catherine clapped her hands, "All right, Ladies, out of the pool and dry off; it's time to take you home."

As the little girls dried off in the classroom, Lois lay on the side of the pool and began the slower process of reconstructing herself into a human woman again.

"He's got my necklace, Catherine, and I want it back." Lois whispered bitterly, "I should have let the dumb bastard drown."

"Why were you there? I thought I told you we had to be careful." Catherine kneeled and scrubbed at the skin as it emulsified and trickled into the pool. "Besides, what makes you think he has it?"

Lois spread her legs apart and the skin cracked and then separated longitudinally. "I'm sorry, Sister; I just wanted to see him." She kicked free of the shredded skin and sat up. "I know he has it because I felt his hand on my neck, and when he was gone, so was the necklace." She scrubbed herself to divest herself of the remainder of the skin.

"Don't worry, I'll find it and get it back for you. You did the right thing; I should have watched him more closely." Catherine encircled Lois's upper arm with her hands and squeezed.

Lois melted into Catherine's arms and whispered. "Come swim with me tonight, it's been so long."

"We'll see, Sister." Catherine kissed her on the side of her nose. "We'll see."

Chapter 8

We stopped at the ticket booth for the Bainbridge ferry and I rolled the window down. "Two and a car," I yelled through the blast of wind.

"Nine-seventy-five." A hand snaked out from the tiny window. "The three o-clock is about ten minutes late. Pretty windy out there, but you'll make the boat."

The boat was full and the cabin crowded. A thirty-knot southerly wind drove the rain sideways and rocked the boat brutally as it fought its way out of the ferry slip.

"Does it ever stop raining here," Steve whined.

"It's your turn to buy coffee, Partner. I'll take a latte." I pushed him in the direction of the galley. "I'll find us a window seat."

"What's a latte? Where are you going to sit?" He fumbled with his glasses and I strode over to the south side of the boat.

We drank our lattes and watched the storm through unfocused eyes and thought about the last few days.

"What the hell is going on around here, Gil?" He balanced his cup as the boat dipped and rolled. "I mean, well, a dead woman, allegedly. The cytoplasm on the negatives: The necklace? What do you think?"

I placed my coffee on the windowsill, stood and leaned against the glass. Two seagulls played crazily in the wind. "I don't know, probably coincidence." I sat down and picked up my coffee. "Our imagination is playing tricks on us. That's what I think."

Latte foam formed a white moustache on Steve's upper lip. "It seems that we are being given puzzle pieces, and when it's complete, we may not like what we see."

"I'm as much in the dark as you are, Steve. Hey, that reminds me I haven't told you about the octopus-wrestling match. You know, how I got the necklace in the first place. I'm guessing that once we find out about the necklace, we'll find out if there is any connection."

"What wrestling match. Keeping secrets from me, eh?" The foam slid down the corners of his mouth. "I think I need a napkin." He looked around a bit, finding none he cleaned off his mouth with the back of his hand and then wiped it on his trouser leg.

I held my cup in both hands and tried to warm up. Then relayed the story about the octopus, and the reason I was reluctant to tell him about it on the boat. "I think the necklace was worn by whoever helped me get away from the octopus?" I sipped my coffee. "It couldn't have been Catherine, so--"

Steve smiled. "Maybe it was your naked lady,"

"I'm serious, Partner. I think, whoever owns the necklace will put two and two together and come up with your favorite dive buddy." The coffee suddenly tasted bitter.

Steve downed the remains of his drink. "Thanks for telling me. Christ!"
He stood and dropped his cup in a nearby trash container and mumbled,

73

"Looking over my shoulder, underwater, it's..."

A middle-aged, rather plump woman walked briskly through the crowd. She elbowed passengers who blocked her way in her rush to line up to exit the ferry. She slipped on the wet tile deck and fell with a loud thud scattering papers in her wake. She landed on her rear end, which was padded enough to afford her a soft landing. Her purse shot out like a hockey puck. I helped her to her feet, while other passengers gathered her papers. A little boy ran back to her with her purse.

"Oh, I'm so embarrassed," she cried, and brushed at her dress.

"Are you all right?" I held her arm until she regained her balance.

"Oh, yes, I'm fine, always in a hurry, you know." She smoothed her coat down and organized her parcels. "Thank you, young man, for your help."

I let her go and noticed the ring on her middle finger. The gem looked identical to the one in our necklace. "That's a beautiful ring." I said with a smile. "What an unusual stone."

She snapped her head in my direction, paused a moment then said, "You're one of the divers photographing our wolf eels." She adjusted her packages so that the ring was concealed.

"Yes, that's right. How did you know that?"

"We all know about you," she murmured, before disappearing into the crowd.

Steve shook his head and grinned.

"A bit rude, wouldn't you say?"

"Hmm, small town. Stuff gets around," he replied.

I shrugged my shoulders.

The ferry hit the dock hard to the tune of groaning timbers. Passengers swayed as the boat rocked from side to side, and elicited comments of, "Captain Johnson must be driving today" and "Should have waited and ridden the <u>Spokane</u> today." We jostled our way to the auto deck, found our car and drove off.

* * *

The rain settled into a steady, light drizzle. The street was lined with little beach cottages. Lofty evergreen trees stood like giant fence posts, limbs trimmed twenty feet above the roadbed, their tops entwined to block out the sky. Streams danced merrily down either side of the blacktop. A shaggy black dog chained to a porch, stood up and dared us to tread on his territory. Near the end of the road where blacktop met boardwalk, the trees trunks grew thicker and closer together. We tiptoed along the boardwalk like ice skaters and hung on to each other's sleeves.

The wind still blew, but quieted since our trip on the ferry. Wavelets bounced off the south side of the dock and sent spray into the air. The sky grew dark as we approached our houseboat. Lights shimmered, reflected off the windows from houseboats, that pushed against taut mooring lines as the wind increased. Smoke billowed from stainless smokestacks and, mixed with the wind and carried the smell of burning firewood.

"Honey, we're home," I called out. "I hope you are contemplating building up a nice hot fire, Steve, so I can warm my wet feet."

"Deal, and you can start on dinner." Steve shivered, and shook himself like a wet dog.

The house was cold and damp. I walked through and turned on lights on my way to the kitchen. On the counter piled pyramid style, sat half a dozen little white boxes. They were still warm and filled the kitchen with smells of the far east. A note affixed to the top read, "Bon, appetite, be ready by 0700 Saturday, Catherine."

I was becoming accustomed to people breaking into my house, after several days of uninvited guests, so I decided to keep my cool and enjoy dinner. Once the food was sorted into small dishes and arranged onto a tray, I walked into the living room with a white towel draped over one arm, and the food held high. "Dinner is served." I bowed.

"I'm not surprised at anything anymore." Steve sat down and began to help himself to the feast.

After we both wolfed down dinner we moved over to the couches facing the fireplace.

"You know, Steve, the boat will pick us up O-dark hundred tomorrow morning. The water will be freezing and the wind will probably be blowing." I shivered. "In other words, tomorrow looks like a shitty day to go diving." I sipped at my scotch and watched the fire dance in the stove. "Maybe we can finish this thing up earlier than we thought, catch a plane to Belize and finish the rest of it there. What do you think?"

Steve stretched out on the opposite love seat nearly asleep. He twisted his arms over his head, yawned, and sat up. "We have at least two weeks before that one batch of eels hatch, and we need shots of them. So, as nice as Belize sounds, we have to hang in here until the hatching." He picked up his half finished-drink and rattled the ice cubes. "Do you remember the look Catherine gave you at the pub? You know, I think she wants your body. But sex aside, there's a lot more to that woman than meets the eye. I think you should do a little investigation and if anything happens, give me all the dirty details." He put the drink back on the side table and winked.

"I think you should lay off the booze tonight."

Steve yawned and closed his eyes.

I sipped my scotch. "Remember San Pedro?"

"Yeah, the small town on Ambergris Cay. So?" He took off his glasses and laid them on his chest, hoisted his feet up onto the couch and laid his head on the armrest.

"I was dreaming, you know, the little dirt road, and the warm Caribbean water. I guess the rain, makes me think of the hot sand and cold gin." I said.

"Yes, cold gin--hot-- sand." He drifted into sleep.

I picked up my drink and walked into the kitchen. Through the window I watched a small tugboat navigate through the anchored boats. Eventually the tugboat tied to a mooring ball and settled into the wind, extinguished her lights, and became still. I shivered again as the rain beat steadily on the steel rooftop. The scotch warmed my insides, as the fire had warmed my hands. A thought flashed through my mind as I watched a lightening bolt explode over the black sky. I remembered how warm Catherine's hands were after our last dive in that frigid water. How could that be?

I turned to watch Steve sleep and listened to him snore contentedly. I wondered if he dreamed of the clear, warm Caribbean waters. I was afraid that if I were able to sleep at all, my dreams would turn to nightmares before morning.

Chapter 9

On Monday morning, Steve and I were up early, ready to dive, only to find a note pinned to our front door advising us the Spirit would be out of service that day.

Steve slammed the door. "We could have slept in for Christ sake."

"Quit whining. You're starting to sound like me. Let's go up to that diner in town and grab some breakfast. I'm still hungry from yesterday." I slapped him on the shoulder.

"Okay," he relented, "I want to pick up a newspaper and see if there's any more on the missing diver from Saturday."

"There's been a rash of missing or drowned divers around the island, hasn't there?" I slid into my rain parka.

"Sometimes they run in batches. I guess…the current, storms and such."

Steve pulled the hood of his rain jacket up and opened the door. "I heard talk on the ferry that the divers were mostly spear-fishermen. Sounded like these guys weren't too popular with a lot of the tree huggers on the island."

"Well, come on, I'll get you a paper."

The diner was a local hangout and featured old-style cooking. The breakfast consisted of cholesterol over easy and heavy, black coffee. Steve picked up a newspaper and sat next to me on a stool facing the cook.

He spread the paper out over the counter, "It says here that none of the divers were from the island, and all were spear fishing. In six months, only one diver among those killed was an inexperienced diver." He sipped his coffee gingerly.

"Four divers in six months, seems a bit much wouldn't you say?" I said, stirring my coffee.

"Yes. Is your coffee as hot as mine?"

"Hotter." I slapped my hand on top of the newspaper. "That reminds me. Do you remember how hot Catherine's hands were after the dive?"

"No, but then again I wasn't holding hands with her. So what?"

"So, probably nothing. Just thinking out loud."

"You looking for an excuse to hold her hand?" Steve folded up the newspaper and slapped me on the shoulder.

I sipped my coffee. "Maybe."

Our orders arrived and Steve stuffed the newspaper between his knees.

"What do you say we drive down to Olympia and try and find that professor of antiquities, or whatever he is? We have the day off," I said.

We drove the back way through tall evergreen forests that seemed to go on forever. Clouds with ghosts for tails slipped across patches of blue sky.

"This looks like Vermont, don't you think?" We crossed the bridge from Bainbridge Island and drove up a ribbon of highway that snaked through the woodland. "I'll bet your girls would love it here."

Steve wrestled with his raincoat and tried to remove it without disconnecting his seatbelt. I reached over and unhooked it.

"I told the girls that I would send them the tickets for Belize." Steve tossed the coat in the back seat. "Melissa loves the regulator you sent her."

"Great. She's a good diver, for a teenager. So is Marnie. I can't wait to see them again." I pulled the map off of the dashboard and tossed it to Steve. "Navigate for me, Partner."

He opened up the map and squinted. "I hope the ex doesn't get pissy with the trip." He drew his finger along the blue line. "Look for highway sixteen."

"Oh, come on, Kim's a sweetheart. She won't screw up the kid's vacation." I turned onto sixteen. "You're lucky you don't have to deal with my ex."

"That goofy insurance salesman seems to be handling her. Maybe if you stayed home more, she wouldn't have dumped you." He wriggled in his seat. "But then, what am I talking about?"

He sighed, took his shoes and socks off, and planted his feet on the dash. Maybe you should settle down and try it again, Gil. You could start a family. You're good with kids, and I know you'd like to have them some day."

"What would I do for a living: sell insurance?" I said.

"Find yourself a little Bainbridge Island woman. God knows there's a bunch of beautiful women on that island. Get yourself a rich one; you won't have to work again." He grinned.

"They are a fine looking bunch," I admitted. "But they're a cold bunch, too." A cold bunch with hot hands; I thought to myself.

"Evergreen State College. That's the exit up ahead, Gil."
Steve waved his arm to the right like a cop in an intersection.
    We turned off the main highway and followed the signs
that directed us onto a winding two-lane road bordered by tall,
thin, fir trees. The college hid inside a thousand acre forest. A
three-story clock tower watched over the comings and goings of
the students. We parked under a dripping oak tree.
    "This is some kind of hippie-college isn't it?" Steve
asked. "The kids dress like they're still in the sixties."
    "It's an ultra-liberal-arts college. Kids here can major in
organic farming, things like that. The medieval history professor
teaches here because the college is a hub for teaching ancient
mythological lore."
    "There's the Administration office." Steve and pointed to
the building, beneath the clock tower.

    "Can I help you, Sir?" A soft Georgia voice spilled over
the counter from the mouth of a black woman seated behind a
computer.
    "We're looking for Doctor John Griffin," Steve said. He
took off his glasses and folded them into his hand.
    "Yes, let me see." She thumbed through a directory
connected to the counter by a chain. "Yes, he's in class right
now, but his office is in the library building on the bottom floor.
His secretary's name is Flora, and her office is at the bottom of
the staircase just before you get to his office." We followed her
directions and passed no one. The hallway smelled of dusty
books and marijuana. We talked in whispers, although there was

81

no one to disturb. Steve and I sat down on the wooden bench at the end of the hallway to wait. Footsteps tapped against the concrete floor from around the corner.

"Good morning, Gentlemen. Do we have an appointment?" The shock of unmanaged white hair danced to the rhythm of his hurried step. He stopped and snapped his heels together.

We both stood.

"Doctor Griffin?" Steve began.

"Yes Sir! You have business with me?" He buttoned his tweed jacket and stood at attention. He looked up at us. The Scotch accent was easy to listen to.

"Yes, well, no." Steve sputtered.

"Is that a yea, or a nay, then? My secretary seems to have gone on vacation, or died, or is smoking dope in the latrine." His R's rolled like a steel ball in a pinball machine and there was no hint of a smile on his whiskered face. His taciturn manner made me ill at ease.

"No, Doctor, we don't have an appointment. I'm sorry, but--"

"Well, never mind," he interrupted, "What can I do for you?" He opened his office door, turned and walked in briskly. "Please, take a seat."

"I'm Doctor Hopkins from the Vermont Marine Studies Endowment Center and this is Gil McCrae, a photographer for National Geographic."

"McCrae, you say?" Dr. Griffin smiled and directed his attention toward me. "Your people have quite an historic reputation, Young Man. Have you been to the Isle of Skye?"

"Is that near Barbados?" I smiled.

"Scotland! My boy. Surely, you've heard of the Isle of Skye. Oh, never you mind. How can I be of help to you

Gentlemen? I am done for the day, but promised Mother I'd be home a wee bit early."

"We won't take up much of your time Doctor Griffin." Steve took out the necklace and placed it carefully on the desktop. "We were told you might be able to decipher the characters on this pendant. Possibly give us some of the history? It has some bearing on our work in the waters around Bainbridge Island."

Dr. Griffin took the necklace and arranged it carefully in a circle in his palm, then placed reading glasses on the end of his nose. He studied the necklace intensely for a moment and then sat down heavily in the wooden chair but kept his gaze riveted to the necklace.

As the professor studied the necklace, I looked around at his windowless office. The red brick walls were barren, save a calendar. The desk wiped clean and buffed to a high sheen.

"Where did you get this necklace?" He demanded. His ruddy face turned ashen; his hands shook. He turned and looked at me. "Do you know what this is?" He whispered, as if he suddenly lost his voice.

"An old necklace?" I shrugged my shoulders.

"Aye, 'tis that." He shook his head and turned to Steve. "Where did you get this?"

Steve cleaned his glasses with his handkerchief. He turned his head and said, "We found it diving." He dropped his glasses on the desktop and they skittered across, landing neatly in my lap. "Can you decipher the writing?"

Dr. Griffin took a deep breath. He stood up and removed his jacket and hung it carefully on the back of the chair, then sat down again. He palmed the necklace once more. "If the legend were true," he began, "this necklace, or at least the charm, was worn by the Sisterhood, a migrating Celtic tribe known as the Bructeri. In as early as one hundred B.C., they traveled through Scotland and Ireland, led by the prophetess <u>Veleda</u>." The professor's eyes were shut, his hands closed tightly around the necklace as he recounted the story to us.

The basement office space was quiet. Steve whispered, "What are you talking about?"

Dr. Griffin lectured us in a hushed lilting voice. "<u>Veleda</u> means inspired sight, and is spelled out clearly in Gaelic at the base of the gemstone. The Sisterhood was an offshoot of the Druids, an order of men who were trained as priests and teachers. The recruits were drawn from the children of the aristocratic warrior class. They were judges and executioners as well, and their word was law. The Druids were highly respected, even by the Romans. The ancient legends had the Druids assembling once a year at a place called Carnutes, which was believed to be the center of Gaul.

At one such meeting, the Sisterhood was born to bolster the stature of women--a kind of women's liberation movement. Not too much was heard of them after that, but the legend persisted. Some historians uncovered evidence that these women possessed magical powers and great strength. There are indications that they were tied to the sea and lived in underwater caverns and that they would pull fishermen from their boats and kill them, feasting on their flesh. Their last known address, if you will, puts them in Northern Scotland." He finished, and the necklace slid out of his hand onto the desktop. "If this necklace is genuine, it would be an amazing find." He slumped in his chair.

Steve picked up the necklace and wound the chain around his middle finger. "What about the gem, Doctor. What is it? Is it significant?"

"I have no idea. The readings that were interpreted from ancient lore indicate that anyone in possession of the gemstone, and not a member of the Sisterhood, carried a death-sentence. However, I've never seen a pendant like this. Even drawings gleaned from Roman historians showed only vague impressions of the jewelry, nothing to assist us in authenticating what you have there. Although the Gaelic verse and the sacred mistletoe above the verse, suggest that this may be an original." He held out his hand, palm up and ordered, "Give me the pendant and I'll have it dated, then we can go from there."

"I'll need a receipt," Steve said and unwound the necklace. "How long do you think you will need it, Doctor Griffin?"

"Not long. We have the facilities for carbon dating on campus, and I can verify the Gaelic translation myself. A few days, up to a week at most, I suppose." He took an envelope out of a desk drawer, placed the necklace inside it, and then slid the envelope into his breast pocket.

"Just a moment, doctor." I looked at Steve and then back to Dr. Griffin. "I need to see the necklace again for a minute."

"Absolutely." He reached into his breast pocket once again and retrieved the envelope, opened it and poured the necklace, somewhat reluctantly into my hand.

I laid the necklace on the desktop so that the gemstone faced down, exposing the gold back of the pendant. "Do you have a magnifying glass doctor?"

"Yes, I do." He rummaged through a lower desk drawer and fetched a large oval glass.

The light from the ceiling fixture was magnified and as it touched the back of the gold pendant an array of vivid colors exploded before my eyes as if I had magnified a rainbow.

"It's beautiful," Steve gasped. "What are you looking for Gil?"

"See these markings; probably scratches on the top left? They look as if they have been there a long time." I looked closely and the scratches appeared as a tiny cross with a loop in the center. I removed the glass and could still make out the markings if I squinted. "Good enough," I concluded and handed the necklace back to the doctor.

"Worried that you won't get the same necklace back from me?" Dr. Griffin shook his head and continued, "Where's the trust?" He replaced the necklace delicately into the enveloped and back into his pocket.

We all stood together; Dr. Griffin at attention. He made out a receipt, sealed it into another envelope and handed it to Steve. "Keep this under your hat boys. If there is any remnant left today, well, the Druids could be a nasty bunch. Who knows how they'll react when they find one of their religious relics in the hands of Christians."

I looked at Steve and smiled. "I guess that leaves us out."

Steve slid the envelope into his jacket pocket.

Rain drizzled from the dark sky when we opened the doors and stepped into the square.

"You don't trust the good ol' professor, Gil? Steve pulled the raincoat around him and folded his arms across his chest.

"Actually, I kind of liked him. I just don't want to lose control of the necklace, you know?" I unlocked the car door and slid in. "I feel like I stole something from someone who probably saved my life. It doesn't feel too good." The car started with a roar. "So what kind of a jerk does that make me?"

"Number one," Steve reasoned, "You didn't steal her necklace, you thought it was…what, a flashlight lanyard? It was an accident when it pulled free. It was a treasure that jumped into your hands." He turned and looked at me, "and to answer the second part of your question, if you have to ask, then it doesn't matter what kind of jerk you are."

"Thanks a lot! Here." I tossed the keys, he missed and they jingled when they hit the pavement between his feet. "You can drive home."

***

The drive back got us to the island by four o'clock. We hadn't stopped for lunch, so decided on an early dinner. Steve parked the car in a nearly empty parking lot adjacent to the pub. The dinner crowd would not show up for at least two hours, so we had the place to ourselves. We sat in a booth that overlooked the water; rain beat a tattoo on the deck railing outside.

In the center of the harbor, I could make out the <u>Spirit</u> as she maneuvered around the anchored boats that called Eagle Harbor home.

I pointed her out to Steve. "You suppose the captain is doing some sea trials today?" The tide was high and water swept across the boardwalk. Walkers were forced to crowd to one side to keep their feet dry.

"Yeah, I suppose." He toyed with his napkin.

"You getting grumpy, Partner?"

He raised his hand in the air and waved at the waitress. "You know, Gil, I really don't care what the captain is doing. I'm hungry and I can't seem to get the waitress' attention."

"Catherine said that this week was a full moon week."

"So what?"

87

"The full moon affects people's moods." I spread my napkin on my lap.

"As the captain would say, fuck you." He raised his hand again.

The waitress glared at us from behind purple eyeglasses. "What the hell do you want? You're too late for lunch and too early for dinner."

"Hi! We need a menu." I smiled.

"You don't need a menu," she growled, "because the only thing we have to eat this time of day is beef stew, and that's because it's been cooking all day." She placed her hands on her hips.

"Then stew it shall be, and a light beer for each of us, please."

She turned and marched back to the kitchen.

"No tip for the waitress today," I whispered.

Steve stared through the rain-streaked glass out into the harbor. His brow was furrowed; eyes focused a million miles away.

"Hello?" I snapped my fingers in front of his eyes. "Earth to Steve, are you prepared to copy? Over."

He slowly regained focus, took his glasses off, and cleaned them with the napkin.

"Aren't you at all worried about what's happening around here, Gil? You mentioned something the other day about finishing up here quickly and then getting the hell out of here. What about now? What do you want to do?"

"I think that we've run into a little mystery here and we're letting it get the best of us. You were right, we should go about our job, get it done, and then get the hell out of here." I held up my hand to quiet him. "We found a little slime, a pretty little necklace, and I had a couple of bad dives. That's the extent of it. Right?"

Steve replaced his glasses when the beef stew arrived. It smelled good enough to eat. I could see that Steve was not completely satisfied.

"Ah, come on Steve, the only stewing you should be doing right now is in that bowl in front of you."

"Hmm, I suppose you're right."

The stew was as good as it smelled.

"Come on; let's get back to the houseboat. I've got some processing I have to finish, and I need to replace those o-rings in the camera."

When I threw Steve his Jacket, I didn't see the white rectangle drop out of his jacket pocket and land beneath the table.

Chapter 10

Twelve figures cloaked in black stood around a stone altar, arms outstretched, their fingers touched lightly. They stood barefoot, cloaks brushing the granite floor. Hoods sheltered their faces as lanterns burned high on the rock wall and cast flickering light on the figures below. Wisps of red hair spilled from beneath the hoods and caught fire as the locks reflected the yellow light from the lamps. The room in which they stood was circular and measured twenty feet high and at least thirty feet in diameter. An arched doorway that was cut into the stone at one end of the enclosure led to a staircase and was the only visible exit from this dungeon. Steam vented up into the enclosure from various junctures where walls met the floor. Opposite the entryway on the far side of the chamber, a black pool of water undulated and splashed gently onto the stones. The humid room smelled of dead kelp, kerosene and ancient taboos.

Barely audible above the splash of the water and the sizzle of the lanterns, a low hum emanated from the enclosure. The hum grew into a chant and increased in volume. The twelve bodies vibrated to the timbre of their voices. They clung to one another, lest one fall. The sonorous tones of the chant were ancient Gaelic; uplifting one moment, low and melodious the next. The figures summoned their prophetess <u>Veleda</u>.

As the hymn reached its climax, sound waves reverberated off the stone walls, kerosene lanterns shuddered and threatened to fall from their perches. The twelve doffed their robes and fell unclothed upon the altar, breath grated from their lungs. The women lay naked; light reflected from their bodies and glistened in the shadows. Their hair was thrown forward and fashioned an auburn carpet upon the stone.

Catherine lifted her head, rose and stepped into the center. She gazed at the women lying prostrate at her feet. Her eyes glazed over, and a hint of a smile parted her lips

Above the underground chamber a quiet brick and stone house on a bluff overlooked the little harbor. The building was dark. This home protected the entrance to the hallowed chambers where the sisterhood practiced their ancient ceremonies. Here, they asked their beloved prophetess for help to prepare for the future.

Chapter 11

I stood with Steve at the end of the dock and waited for the Spirit. She was late. It was 7:30 in the morning and drizzle enveloped us. A pair of mallards swam by and looked at us before they turned and swam out into the harbor.

Steve stamped his feet and flapped his arms. "Damn, it's cold. Where's our ride?" He leaned against a black piling that rose out of the depths and held up the corner of the dock. "I need windshield wipers, for Christ sake." He shivered, removed his glasses and shoved them into his jacket pocket.

"There she is." I pointed across the harbor. "You ready?" The blue and white boat churned our way through the calm water.

"Ahoy there!" I called out too loud on this quiet morning. I teetered on the end of the dock prepared to grab a line. The Spirit swung alongside the dock with a thud. I reached down to the gunwale, plucked the tie-up line off the deck, and secured it to the cleat on the dock.

The captain came out on deck and spat over the side. "Grab that bow line and tie 'er up, Sonny."

"Where's the boss?"

"Catherine's in the galley fixin' up some coffee and doughnuts or something." He replied. "Toss me the gear bags."

92

He shouldered our bags over the transom, and then spat more brown juice over the side. The dock received the majority of what didn't hit the water. He called over his shoulder, "Grab that line and bring it aboard so's we can get this show on the road!" He eased himself through the doorway and into the pilothouse.

The Spirit heeled over to port as the captain turned his rudder hard and applied power. Steve and I fell to the benches on the port side and grabbed on to each other for support.

"Captain's in a big hurry today," Steve grumbled as he let go of me and grabbed for a handrail.

Ten minutes passed before Catherine came aft with coffee cups balanced on a tray with of pastries and donuts piled to one side. "Good morning, Gentlemen. Coffee and carbohydrates for the divers today." She moved slowly and glanced at us through bloodshot eyes.

"Hard night last night, Catherine?" I picked up two coffees and handed one to Steve.

"Something like that," She chewed on a doughnut and gulped her coffee. "We have a dive plan, Gentlemen. Today we dive Blake Island, an artificial reef. A gift from the Navy. The government calls it an artificial reef when they dump their garbage and rusted leftovers into the bay. After a good amount of time, marine life covers it over. As more marine life is attracted, it looks less like military trash and more like a living reef." She shook her head, filled her cup again and sat the pot on the deck next to her feet. "With the full moon this week we will encounter excessive currents. To use these currents to your best advantage, move with them. Steve, you will be able to see how the wolf eel interacts with his mate during times of heavy current. Gil, you will need to be ready to shoot downstream with the current. Line em' up and shoot fast."

Steve looked up quickly. "What about the boat, Catherine? Won't the captain have trouble finding us once we ascend?" He patted his shirt pockets and then found his glasses on the bench next to him.

The pilothouse door slammed and the captain emerged in front of us, "Never fear, your captain is near." He gulped his coffee and then sat on the gunwale so he could spit over the side. "If you make it to the top, I'll fuckin' pick you up." He leaned sideways and spat over the side of the boat.

"That's encouraging," Steve said.

The Spirit departed Eagle Harbor, turned right, and as Seattle loomed through the drizzle, we headed south. I could almost make out the forested bluff of Blake Island in the distance.

We dove twice at the site with the ebb tide that propelled us through the water at three to four knots. Old concrete slabs and sunken boats rushed at us, giving us only seconds to turn and avoid collision. Fish, especially wolf eels, utilized the lee side of structures to avoid the current, but when startled by our mad dash through their territory, jumped into the current and disappeared. We flew through the underwater world like an eagle soaring effortlessly through the thermal climes.

As the day closed the Spirit deposited Steve and I on our houseboat dock once again. Catherine slumped against the doorway and asked if I would join her for dinner that evening.

"Yes, I would enjoy that," I stood for a moment with my dive bag over my shoulder and looked at her. "Are you okay?"

She looked at the deck, shrugged her shoulders and turned. I dropped my gear and stepped onto the boat and touched her elbow as she stepped into the pilothouse. She turned into my open arms and laid her head against my neck. She smelled of the sea. "Catherine, I--"

"Don't say anything," she whispered.

"Anybody gonna drop my fuckin' lines?" The captain started aft, looked at Catherine in my arms and spat. "Jesus Christ all Friday." He turned back to his logbook and mumbled.

Catherine disentangled herself and looked up at me. Tears stained her cheeks. I brushed them aside with my thumb. She smiled, "Don't come early tonight, Soldier, just on time."

I jumped back on the dock and tossed the lines to her and watched the captain shake his head and then increase throttle and turn the little boat hard over and disappear into the south end of the harbor.

Chapter 12

"Can I borrow your raincoat, Steve. The good one?"

"It's not even raining." He laid the trench coat on the kitchen counter, and then picked it up and brushed at the wrinkles. "Where are you meeting her?"

"Main Street café. I think its a couple blocks up the street. What time is it?"

"It's almost seven. You're going to be late." He pulled at my sleeve. "Come on, go. I remember the captain said that Catherine does not like to be kept waiting."

"I'm hurrying, Mother." I pushed his hand away. "Don't wait up for me. I might be late." I gave him a wicked smile and then winked. "Wish me luck, Partner."

"Luck, and I want to hear all the details." He slammed the door and I jogged up the dock.

I stood for a moment in the dark foyer and let my eyes adjust. The restaurant had the texture of old money; dark wood, leather and brass wall sconces that poured candlelight in minimal pools onto the rich carpet. It smelled of cooking spices, old wine and floor wax.

"Excuse me, Sir. May I help you?" A tuxedoed black man

blocked my way.

I looked around him and saw a tiny hand wave from a dark booth in the corner. "Thanks, I can find my way." I stepped around the maitre d' and waved.

Catherine raised her glass. "Hi there, Soldier. Care to buy a lady a drink?"

My mouth dropped open and then I smiled. Catherine's auburn hair flowed down her shoulders and lay against her breasts, wild and unaffected. Her gray-blue eyes twinkled as they reflected the light from the single candle on the table. She looked rested; she smiled and stood as I approached. Her simple white shift fell to just below her knees. The dress was provocative, but not carnal, a sensual yet graceful embellishment that floated on her body as she moved, as if the garment were unattached.

She placed her right hand on my chest, drew close and kissed me under my left ear. Her soft hair floated into my face and blinded me for a moment, then drew back and left behind a scent of seawater and honeysuckle. I was enthralled and remained standing. I stared at her, mesmerized.

"Sit down, Soldier, I've ordered you a drink," She said. "Scotch, single malt, with a little spring water."

"Yes, thank you." I saluted her and then removed my coat and tossed it on the bench seat and then slid in. "Do I look like a soldier to you?" I pointed to her drink, "How about you?"

"I'm good, maybe later." She smiled raising her glass again.

"I'll bet you are." I pushed the water glass to one side.

"You're a McCrae aren't you? We're probably related somewhere back in history. My family seems to be rooted on the Isle of Skye, just like the McCrae clan." She winked. "All the McCrae men were soldiers."

For the second time this week, someone knew more about my ancestry than I did.

"I hope we're not brother and sister."

She laughed and signaled to the bartender to bring my drink.

The scotch was smooth and slowed down my heart. I looked at Catherine and wondered what the draw was. Was it her beauty or her manner or the way she looked at me? What was this feeling she provoked in me? It was not raw lust, which was a part of it, though I couldn't imagine myself in bed with this woman. Was she more woman than I could hope for? Would she be disappointed in me? So many thoughts ran through my mind as I lifted my glass and drank.

We sat across from each other. I noticed her necklace and reached across and placed two fingers beneath the charm and examined it.

She gasped and her breasts swelled as my fingers brushed against the silk. "Careful there, Soldier," she breathed.

The pendant was warm. It looked like an old coin cut in half with a gold scuba diver, inverted as if swimming downward, attached to the half coin. The gold chain was heavy and fashioned like three-strand rope. "Beautiful," I said, "and I like the necklace, too."

She gazed at me steadfastly for a moment. "Are you color-blind?"

"Am I color-blind?"

"Yes, color-blind. Are you color-blind?" She persisted.

I thought for a moment that I was on the wrong page or that she was being whimsical and wanted to change the subject. She looked at me serious and unblinking.

"Yes, as a matter of fact I am, and have been since I can

remember. I can't see those little shapes in that idiotic DMV test."

"Whoa, Soldier," she said. "Color-blindness in Scots, and especially McCrae's, is a sign of nobility. You can be proud of it. The Scots lost their sense of color many centuries ago because colors in Scotland and Ireland are at best non-existent much of the time. At higher latitudes the sun slants its rays to a degree that the colors we do perceive are muted. That, and the fact that overcast and rainy skies much of the year further dilute color, made it unnecessary for our people to perceive color to survive. So, many of us lost it." She exhaled and I could smell the scotch sweet on her breath.

When she talked of Scotland, her eyes reflected a thousand pinpoints of light from the flickering candle. Her gaze held mine unblinking until I had to break away. I asked her, "What do know of the Sisterhood?"

Her face turned to stone; her eyes lost their color for an instant. She blinked, and smiled. "What would you like to know?" She cooed.

"Is the Sisterhood just a myth, an old wives' tale or is there some truth to it?"

She took a long drink and then began. "Many of the women in ancient Scotland were persecuted like the witches of England and early America. They were midwives for the most part and delved into magic potions or herbs to try to cure the sick."

She looked at me over the top of glass.

"For hundreds of years they were highly regarded by both men and women alike, but when the Druids became powerful they demanded the knowledge midwives had garnered for years. A struggle ensued and in the end the midwives went underground to save their knowledge and to save their lives."

Her voice was so soft, and I leaned closer. She took hold of my wrist in her tiny, powerful hand and leaned across the table.

"The Druids placed the midwives in large, woven baskets and set them on fire. So, the midwife disappeared one day from the face of Scotland and then appeared later as the Sisterhood with much greater powers--so powerful, it is said the Druids were fearful of them. The greatest enclave of the Sisterhood practiced their magic on the Isle of Skye and was protected by the local clansmen." Catherine took a sip of her scotch and asked, "Where did you hear of the Sisterhood?"

"I don't remember," I lied. "I wake up in the mornings with trivia swimming through my head."

The meal was sumptuous. I had forgotten how hungry I was until a sixteen-ounce rib steak was set before me still sizzling, pink on the inside, seared on the outside, nestled next to new potatoes and brussel sprouts. Catherine ordered blackened cod on a bed of long-grain rice. She ate quietly and did not speak through the meal. She concentrated fully on the meal as if the task at hand was one to be completed before another could be contemplated. Even her wine was consumed after everything on her plate had disappeared, and then was downed at once like a glass of water to a parched man.

When we had both finished, I ordered more scotch. I sat back in my chair, sipped my drink, and contemplated this woman across from me. Her skin was white-on-white and so smooth. A fine sheen reflected the ambient candlelight as if she had just applied a coating of oil to her skin.

"Walk me home, Soldier; I'll buy you a nightcap." She smiled at me.

"I can't wait." I tossed my coat over my shoulder. "Let's go."

Not a word passed between us as we walked. The night was dark and still, with a hint of rain. The bare tree branches left their dead leaves to spread with the wind. Streetlights glowed dimly. After three blocks the main street turned into unlighted side streets. We passed the pub then turned left down a lighted, paved drive and the three-story condominiums loomed ahead.

"Down these stairs, here." Catherine led the way as we descended stairs to the bottom of the building that fronted the harbor. Her apartment was on the far corner where concrete steps led down a short bank to a lighted concrete dock. Black, oily water oozed around the pilings.

She opened a sliding glass door and walked into the apartment ahead of me. I closed the door while she lit a bank of candles above the fireplace. The darkened room was warm and the carpet soft under my feet. I tossed my coat onto an overstuffed couch that faced the fireplace.

Catherine called out from the kitchen, "Brandy all right?"

"Sounds perfect."

She entered the living room with two brandy snifters half full of dark amber liquid and motioned for me to sit. I sat opposite the unlit fireplace and took the drink. She sat next to me. Her thigh touched mine. The brandy was warm and I surrounded the glass with both hands.

"This is an old Scottish brandy to savor after a particularly delicious dinner." She held the drink up in a toast, took a small swallow then set her glass on the side table. The candles flickered as if a door had been left open somewhere creating shadows that danced across the ceiling.

The rich, smooth brandy had a heady aroma of honey and

tangerine and maybe a hint of mint. It was strong. It fired my body with a flush that spread to my arms and legs and radiated outward to my skin surfaces.

Catherine stroked my arm and set my skin on fire. Her lips touched my ear, "What do you want to do now, Soldier?" Her voice was soft, barely audible, her breath sweet.

She kissed the corner of my mouth, licking my upper lip with the tip of her tongue. Helpless, I yielded to my desire for her. Her tiny hand slid inside my sweater, her fingers caressed my nipples, while her tongue traced circles inside my ear. My heart beat wildly. I put my brandy down on the side table next to her glass before I spilled it. She stood up, unhooked her shift, and let it fall to the floor. She did a slow pirouette in front of me to let me see what she knew I wanted. Her body was perfect, a marble statue in living flesh. I reached up to touch her but she sidestepped, turned and knelt in front of me spreading my knees apart and then laid her head against my chest. I held her in my arms, encircled her small back.

Her skin was silky; an almost invisible red down covered her entire body. The tiny hairs created a current and sent tingling electric shocks that traveled from my fingers to my shoulders. My hands shook. I could feel her body throb as the tension accelerated. I stood, lifted her up and massaged my hands down her buttocks. She clung to me as I caressed her inner thighs.

She reached around my back and pulled my sweater up and then drew it up over my shoulders, and then tossed it to the floor. She unbuckled my belt and pushed my slacks down over my hips. As I bent to remove them, she pulled my face into her breasts and pressed a nipple into my mouth. She threw back her head as I suckled, a high keening sound emanated from her throat. I dropped further to my knees and licked her skin. I pressed my face into her pubic hair, my hands mauling the muscles on the back of her legs. My heat was so intense, the more I tasted of her the more I demanded from her. She tasted like she smelled--of seawater and honeysuckle. I felt her body heat reach an unbelievable fever pitch; my penis became erect and throbbed. She took hold of my erection and stroked it, and then placed her mouth around it as we lay head to toe, my tongue buried deep inside her licking the sweet nectar that dripped from her moist slit.

She stiffened and screamed as she thrust her hips down hard onto my willing tongue. At the same instant she released my throbbing member and moaned her release again. Then like a gymnast, she broke contact, swung her legs over me, and buried my erection deep into her hot recess. She screamed again as if I had plunged a sword into her belly. Her full, womanly lips closed warmly around my penis and burned into my being. My mind lost touch with reality. Her hands pinned my shoulders as she thrust herself repeatedly down onto my erection until I exploded into her again and again. I shuddered; my semen flooded into her and quenched the fire.

Catherine rolled us over once again. She lay on her back and locked her legs around my buttocks and her arms around my back. As she nibbled on my ear, her inner muscles milked my erection, clamping down so tightly I stayed hard inside her. She whispered into my ear, but I couldn't understand her. The blood screamed through my eardrums; my breath abraded my vocal chords and made speech impossible.

We lay joined for a while, as my breath finally came easier and my erection melted like summer snow. As she slept beneath me, I held her and stroked her skin. Her skin was more than wet; it felt slippery and oily and it coated us, creating a sucking sound when we moved. Her body was still hot to the touch, while the air that surrounded us felt cold. With her head tucked under my chin I drifted off to sleep.

Chapter 13

Catherine lay supine, naked on the stone altar surrounded by vaporous steam that heated the large stone enclosure and masked the participants. Eleven women darkened by subterranean shadows bent in prayer and supplication, their naked bodies shimmered as their skin reflected light from the kerosene lamps hung high on the walls. Their heads touched stone, their bodies bent double, arms stretched forward. Twenty-two palms rested on the smooth floor.

They rose as one, approached the altar and bent to their knees. They placed their palms downward on her and chanted in Gaelic. "Let the egg be fertile. We implore you, sacred Veleda, let the egg be fertile."

This chant ascended in volume until the cacophony of voices filled the chamber. The lone woman upon the altar began to vibrate. As the chant reached a fever pitch she began to convulse, a moan escaped her lips. The other women held her down as her legs pummeled the end of the altar. Her face contorted, the moan became a scream.

Abruptly, the massive chamber was still, except for the ragged breathing emanating from the center of the altar. The participants watched her chest rise and fall.

After some time, Catherine sat up, swung her legs over the edge of the altar until her feet touched the stone. She stood, walked to the black pool of water at the edge of the chamber and dove in.

When the ripples subsided, the women donned heavy black cloaks, fell to their knees and gazed upward into the darkness. The whispered prayer echoed in the hollow chamber like wind rustling across the heather on a forgotten island. "Omo chreach, Veleda, tha mi an dochas gum bi e math."

Chapter 14

As the morning daylight flooded the apartment, I awoke alone, covered with a red flannel blanket. I was on the floor and a pillow had been placed under my head, my clothes neatly draped over the back of the couch. I smelled coffee brewing and saw a light on in the kitchen. I stretched and called out, "Good morning, Catherine."

Silence.

"Hello. Coffee in bed sure sounds good." I propped myself up on my elbows. "A little morning roll in the hay wouldn't be so bad."

More silence.

I peeked beneath the covers. "You might as well relax, Buddy. I think she's gone."

I rolled over, stood up and grabbed my clothes. Standing naked in the apartment I surveyed my body. A shower was necessary, not only to wash off last night's delicious smells, but also to wash off the strange material that coated my skin. Crust that could be peeled off like a bad sunburn, covered me everywhere. I wiped my hand from my chest to my stomach and watched the material flake and fall to the floor. "Wow!" I said out loud, and smiled at the recollections of our lovemaking.

I located the bathroom down the hallway past her bedroom. It was spacious and the shower afforded me plenty of room to move around. The crusty mucous was water-soluble and came off under the hot spray. After I dried off, wrapped myself in a towel and made for the kitchen for some much needed coffee. I was surprised that Catherine hadn't awakened me; we were supposed to dive today.

The spacious kitchen was decorated with pastel watercolors on the walls with an atrium that afforded a nice view of the harbor.

A pot of strong, black coffee steamed on the counter. Under the coffee mug was a note. "When you're done sleeping in, get your ass down to the public dock. We dive at noon today. P.S. Thanks for last night. Catherine."

I walked along the waterfront on the boardwalk toward the houseboat. The day was overcast, although the promised rain had not yet materialized. The harbor churned under the onslaught of the wind, boats lay hard on their anchors. The high tide left the boardwalk awash on the harbor side so people who walked by sidestepped each other as they passed. The last of the leaves fell from the trees and painted the sidewalks with their dead bodies. I buttoned Steve's raincoat to the neck and hid my hands in the pockets.

As I approached the houseboat, the door swung open, Steve lurched out and slammed the front door. He saw me and called out, his voice was lost in the wind. He held a newspaper in his hand and waved it in my direction. We met mid-dock and he thrust it into my hands.

"Read the headline," he ordered. "Come on; let's get out of the wind. You can read the article in the diner."

We hurried, as I read the headline: "Evergreen Professor Missing After Car Crash Into Puget Sound."

The diner was quiet; a couple in the corner lingered over coffee. We sat at a side table, ordered coffee and menus; I spread the newspaper on the table in front of me. Steve looked nervous and glanced around the diner.

I nudged Steve. "Listen to this."

"I already read it." The coffee arrived and he sipped it tentatively.

"The car driven by Dr. John Griffin plunged over an embankment and plummeted into Puget Sound, south of the Narrows bridge near Steilacoom. There were no skid marks or other indications as to why the car left the road." I fumbled for my coffee and looked at Steve. "Did you read this?"

"I told you, I read it," he whispered.

"Dr. Griffin's body has not been located in or near the car, and divers are searching the water near the accident for the professor. The fire rescue team indicated that most of the search would be concentrated south of the accident where the current would most probably carry the body."

Steve swiveled his stool around to face the windows and whispered, "Don't read so loud."

"That's strange, I wouldn't have believed that the professor would be a reckless driver. In fact I would have pegged him for one of those drivers that would travel at fifty-four in a fifty-five zone."

Steve turned his stool around and leaned his elbows on top of the newspaper. He pushed my coffee cup to one side, took off his glasses and tapped them on the article. I bent my head toward him, he whispered. "So, what do you think happened, Einstein?"

"What? Wait a minute. You don't think--" I lowered my

voice. "You don't believe someone killed him, do you?" I straightened up.

Steve sat up straight and shrugged. He reached to his left pocket and closed the other hand around his coffee cup. "He's dead. We just visited him, and he has in his possession our valuable necklace." Steve replaced his glasses, pointed to the article and said, "We're connected to him."

"So what?" I sipped at my lukewarm coffee.

"There's more." Steve gathered the newspaper together, folding it.

"More what?"

"The receipt he wrote to us for the necklace is missing. Either I misplaced it, or it was taken from our houseboat while we were diving. And who do you suppose knows when we're not home?"

My mouth fell open. "No, You don't--"

"That's right, your little sex kitten."

I gestured to the cook to refill my coffee and shook my head at Steve. "No, no, no. You should have seen her last night, Steve. She was fantastic. She--"

Steve grasped my arm and squeezed. "You tell me what the hell is going on here then."

My coffee arrived with a thump, splashing over the side, onto the counter. I nodded my thanks as he swiped at the spill.

I took a deep breath. "All right, let's not go paranoid." I said. "Do you want to cut our losses, pack up today, and get the hell out of Dodge?"

"Shit Gil, you know I'm no hero, I know I must sound paranoid, but too many strange circumstances are adding up to something. I don't know what, but something that we don't understand." He wrung his hands together

I pulled a napkin from the holder on the counter and handed it to him. "Here, clean your glasses."

"Thanks." He blew on the lenses and wiped them clean. "Let's finish this week, so we can get those hatchling shots then process everything in Belize."

"Okay, good. You want some more coffee?"

"No thanks." He sighed.

"Now why don't you ask me how it went last night?" I said grinning.

"I didn't have to; it's written all over your face." He swung his stool back and clapped his hands. "I know you're going to tell me all about it. Right?"

I felt someone's presence. I turned my head to look. At a table in the corner, half turned toward us sat a woman who stared at us with obvious interest. Her age was hard to estimate. She combed her hair with her fingers showing off streaks of gray in the brown curls. She tapped her toes on the air and flexed the muscles on legs too short to touch the floor. She looked at me with disdain and seemed unabashed that I watched her stare at me. A life of adventure was evident by the lines on her face, but her eyes were soft and sensual. I was immediately drawn to the woman in ways that were hard for me to understand.

She continued to stare and tap her foot, so I acknowledged her with a nod. Her foot stopped, but the cold stare persisted. I turned to Steve. "You see that woman?" I whispered.

He lifted his cup to his lips and whispered over the brim, "I don't like her."

"I think she's a fox, in an earthy sort of way." I turned back. She was gone. "Where the heck did she go?"

Steve slid off the stool and pulled his coat on. "Jesus Christ, Gil, you got laid last night." He pulled on my arm.

111

"Leave that one alone. Come on, let's go."

The back door to the restaurant closed quietly and a shadow disappeared behind the opaque glass.

Steve shook his head and signaled to the waiter for the check.

***

We met the <u>Spirit</u> at the public dock at noon. She was tucked beneath the bowsprit of a four-masted schooner. The captain was on the cabin roof. He tightened a nut that held the radio antennae mount in place. "Come on you cocksucker, hold still or I'll cut your balls off." Although he talked to himself, he could be heard the length of the dock. With a last turn of his wrench, he jumped off the cabin deck onto the dock and waved us aboard. "We're ready boys, let's go divin'."

I was looking forward to seeing Catherine again and called out, "Where's the boss?"

"Who the hell knows," he waved his hands. "You ever figure women out, and I'll give you a fuckin' medal. We don't need her today anyway."

Dark clouds scudded across the skies and brought with them promised rain. As the <u>Spirit</u> pulled away from the dock and headed into the wind, spray cascaded from her bow shooting up over the sides. The spray collected on the cabin roof, pooled, and then ran down into the wet deck where Steve and I readied our gear. The little boat rolled up into the swell, before it dropped with a loud thud into the trench. Then she shook herself off like a wet puppy and rose to begin the cycle anew.

We clung to handholds and attached our gear fittings. When we finished preparing our gear I opened the hatchway to the pilothouse and crowded in with the captain.

He sat in his captain's chair and alternately drank coffee and spat tobacco juice into a cup. He placed it down next to the throttle control. "Grab yourself a cuppa Joe. It's hot on the stove behind you," he said. He horsed the steering wheel right, then left to compensate for the rough water. "God dammed dive master's playing golf or somethin' and can't make it. We're gonna anchor up on the lee side of the island today, out of this fuckin' wind. The eels should be feedin' in the eel grass today, what with the hatchin' coming on. Should be able to get some good shots out there today."

"You diving with us today, Cap?"

"Goddamn right I'm divin' today!" He spat into the cup and wiped his chin with the back of his hand. "I've been divin' these waters for thirty seven-years now. Think you can keep up with me?"

"I kind of doubt it," I winced. "What's the big hurry?"

"Same old shit," he said. "Gotta dive the slack tide, then get back aboard before the flood begins. Only today, the <u>Spirit</u> will be hooked to the bottom, and won't come to get us if we lollygag. So we're goin' to do a circular pattern for twenty-five minutes, then jump back on the boat."

We turned around the headland and were immediately out of the weather; the seas calmed and the air was quiet.

"Okay, boys, go ahead, gear up while I set the anchor." He slowed the boat to a crawl then swung himself over the gunwale and up onto the bow. He released the anchor, and pulled out another twenty feet of line and attached it to the forward cleat. When he was satisfied that the anchor would hold, he shut the engine off and stepped onto the wet deck.

With the engine shut down, the only sound in addition to our gear clanking was the water that splashed against the side of the hull. The rain hadn't materialized, but the air temperature dropped a few degrees and made me wonder if they got snow this early. This side of the island was protected from the south wind but open to the fierce north winds of the winter, as evidenced by the windswept shoreline. Trees grew at odd angles; all of them bent in the same direction. A beach of steep, rock cliffs terminated at the shore where large boulders dotted the shallow water like so many marbles tossed aside.

The captain suited up as Steve and I hoisted our gear up on to each other's shoulders. The captain wore an old-fashioned wet suit without a hood or gloves; a set of twin-fifty tanks like Mike Nelson used to wear on "Sea Hunt." Steve and I climbed laboriously over the stern onto the dive step and watched the captain topple over the gunwale into the water. We stepped into the water only to realize that the captain had submerged without us.

The captain waited for us on the sandy bottom. We had thirty feet of visibility. The captain motioned for us to follow him, then turned and headed in an easterly direction. He set a fast pace.

Steve and I worked as a team to set up shots. The eels were plentiful and swam gracefully along the rocks and sandy bottom. We watched as they snatched up small crabs, and brown sea urchins, which they cracked with powerful jaws and inhaled the contents. The captain played with the eels and grabbed them by the tail and then released them before they could take off one of his fingers.

When we began to feel the early stages of the flood current the captain pointed his thumbs up to indicate it was time to surface. We had come around full circle and when we broke surface we were within five feet of the stern of the boat. The captain launched himself out of the water onto the dive step, shrugged his gear into the wet deck and then helped both of us into the boat.

I shivered as I extricated myself out of the suit. The captain fired up the diesel heater and put the soup on to heat. He thumped the outside thermometer with his middle finger. "Feels like snow. Sometimes we get a good blast right before Christmas."

"Where is Catherine really, Captain? I know she doesn't play golf."

He winked. "Who the fuck knows, Gil? She said somethin' about a woman's meetin' last night. I don't know, and frankly I could fuckin' care less."

With that, he ladled us each a bowl of bean soup, turned his back and walked into the pilothouse to start the engine. He obviously wasn't anxious to talk about Catherine, but I suspected that he might not really know too much about her private life.

Steve elbowed me, and between spoonfuls of soup, said, "You must have done a good job last night, Partner, if the dive master can't make it to work the next day." He smiled and winked.

"I wish that were the case," I said, "but the fact is, she was up and gone before I ever woke up."

The captain leaned through the doorway and called out, "Okay, boys, we're goin' back to the barn. Haul that anchor up for me, will you?" The captain shouted out orders from inside the pilothouse. "The wind's pickin' up from the north, and I'm thinkin' we should get the fuck out of here before we wished we already had."

I crawled out to the bow and engaged the electric windlass that pulled up the anchor line. With a final tug on the chain, I secured it to the cleat fixed on the bow, and we were off.

Back inside the warmth of the pilothouse, the captain filled his lip with tobacco and mumbled, "The south wind's blown her self out." He spit into his cup. "That icy breeze is out of the north." He cranked the wheel hard around the buoy. "That's a snow wind, and it's gonna get fuckin' cold soon."

I could feel the iciness sharpen the edge of the initial gusts. "Snow tonight, Cap?"

He pushed the throttle ahead. "Could be."

We were back in the harbor before the wind picked up any more, but daylight was almost spent. At four-thirty in the afternoon the houses were already lit up and sparkling in the semi-dark afternoon. The <u>Spirit</u> landed neatly alongside our dock. We waved and the <u>Spirit</u> lumbered off.

The houseboat was dark and cold. Steve knelt before the wood stove and built a fire before he shrugged off his jacket.

"I'm going to clean this camera and process the film, Steve. You need any help?"

"No thanks, I'm going to finish building up the fire, then jump into the shower. Hey, did you take a shower this morning? You don't smell too funky." He laughed and stirred at the hot ash beneath his kindling.

I ignored him and slammed the door to the darkroom, shivered and thought how nice the Belizean sun was going to feel. I re-opened the door and called out, "Hurry that fire along, Partner, it's freezing in here."

Chapter 15

I awoke in the middle of the night with a start. A woman was beside me. Her hand encircled my penis, which had risen to the occasion without permission. At first I thought it was Catherine but realized quickly it was not. This woman's body was longer and more compact than Catherine and her short hair tickled my ear. I began to speak, but she shushed me and whispered in my ear.

"I realize you think with your little head, so pay attention to me when I try to teach you to think with your big head."

I was not in any position to complain, nor did I have an inclination to, so I listened.

"The woman, you know as Catherine, is not like us. She's not entirely human and she's using you."

I started to speak and her hand contracted.

"Wait, wait, wait--" I grasped her wrist. "Easy," I managed through clenched teeth.

"Shut up and listen." She slackened her grip. "You will become her soldier, one of the protectors of the Sisterhood. You may not even have a choice. You must get away from here as soon as you can. Do not; under any circumstances have sex with that woman."

She stroked my erection pleasurably and I released my grip on her wrist.

"Look, Catherine is just the dive master on…"

She squeezed harder and whispered bitterly. "Or is it already too late? If she becomes pregnant, the hatchling will begin a new and stronger generation of monsters. Doctor Griffin realized the danger, but paid with his life." She released me.

I grabbed her wrist, rolled her over and pinned her hands next to her ears. Her curly hair tickled my nose as I bent closer.

"What in the hell are you talking about, and what do you know about Doctor. Griffin?" The zipper of her jumpsuit stuck into my chest. "Who the hell are you to come in here and," recognition dawned. "Wait a minute. You're that woman from the diner, aren't you?"

She nodded and continued in a whisper. "Doctor Griffin was killed for what he knew about the Sisterhood. You are a McCrae, and potentially you have the gene needed by the Sisterhood to strengthen their line. Listen," She lifted her head from the pillow, held her breath and looked from side to side. "I don't have time to explain everything right now. You are being watched and that puts me in mortal danger. If they knew I was here, I would be killed. Just keep two things in mind right now; keep your cock in your pants, and get away from the island as soon as possible."

I released her wrists and sat up astride her. My knees clutched her narrow hips. "I have no idea what you're…"

She moved like an eel and flipped me on my back, slipped out of the bed, and was gone.

I propped myself up on my elbow and faced Steve's bed. "Did you get all of that?" I heard his blanket rustle and the bedsprings squeak

"I knew that woman would be trouble," he groaned.

"Which one?"

"Which one isn't?" He rolled over. "Go back to sleep and tell me all about in the morning."

"What do you mean, tomorrow morning? Didn't you hear what that crack-pot said?" I swung my legs over the side of the bed and slipped on my jeans.

"I heard too much for one night, thank you. Tomorrow I'm moving my bed into the processing room. Either that or she can bring a friend for me next time. Good night, Romeo." His head disappeared under his blanket.

The clock on the bedside table read 2:40. Not a sound could be heard over the ticking of the clock and Steve's light snoring. The darkness was so total I was unable to see him three feet away. Then a faint echo struggled to make its self known. I felt more than heard an imperceptible splash and thump. Half crouched I tiptoed down the staircase into the living room and peered out the side window. A streetlight cast a faint light onto the docks surface.

I crept around the love seats and into the hall that led to the front door. I heard a noise like a shuffle close outside the door. I grasped the handle, took a deep breath, jerked it open and stepped out onto the dock.

A giant figure loomed outside my vision and closed in quickly. A sea lion, I thought as it rolled ungainly forward. I had no time to speculate or to adjust my balance before a blow to the side of my head sent me sprawling sideways onto the dock. I recovered and rolled to my knees. My head reeled from the punch, and then another blow to my ribcage sent me in a cart-wheel off the dock and into the water.

I sucked in seawater and started to sink into the blackness.

I grasped out for purchase and struck my hand against a piling support. I held onto its barnacle-encrusted surface. I climbed upwards; hand over hand, as if it were a tree. The cold water sucked my body heat from me. My arms and legs became leaden, filled with concrete. Finally, my head broke the water's surface. I heaved myself up onto the dock and laid out full length, face down as I gasped for breath.

I raised myself to my elbows and as strength returned, I got up on my knees. The dock was cool, but my bloodied hands burned like they had been seared on a hot stovetop.

My breathing came in ragged gasps. I spun on my knees and called out, "Steve, help." The houseboat remained dark. The dock was deserted. I began to shiver. Behind me I heard a splash. Crawling toward the houseboat, I stumbled and fell flat onto the dock, my foot clamped in a vice grip that dragged me backwards. I clawed frantically at the deck to no avail. My voice was hoarse and shallow as I screamed for help. Fierce cold enveloped me as I slid from the dock back into the frigid water. Blackness settled over my entire being as I lost consciousness and did not resist.

*****

I awoke sometime later amazed I was still alive. My ribcage ached and my head hammered in pain. Something was wrong. I was naked in a cavernous room with flickering wall-mounted lanterns that glowed in the otherwise dark enclosure. It was warm and steamy like a bathhouse. The smell of seaweed overwhelmed me.

My first thought was to cry for help, but decided my captors need not know I was awake, thereby giving myself time to assay my predicament. My head rested in a slight depression in the stone. My body ached and my hands and knees burned from the abrasions I suffered during the attack. I was able to turn my head from side to side, but could see no other person, and heard nothing but the lapping of water. My hands and feet were secured with what felt like heavy leather straps, my hands alongside my body and my legs spread about a foot apart.

The steam misted into tiny droplets of warm water and enveloped the full length of my body. Then, suddenly, the mist separated. A current of cooler air sucked it in a different direction toward an open door or window. I closed my eyes and feigned unconsciousness and heard a light shuffle. A presence began to fill the void around me. A silken cloth was hastily tied as a blindfold and knotted behind my head. My heart beat loudly in my ears, my hands and feet involuntarily twitched as I waited with dread. The aroma from the cloth reminded me of Catherine's fragrance-- honeysuckle and seawater.

I heard a throaty whisper, say, "Drink this."

I opened my mouth to speak. "What…" My vocal chords vibrated, but no other sound came forth.

A glass decanter clicked on my front teeth as it was pushed to my lips. Strong hands held my head while another pair of hands pried my mouth open and forced me to swallow a thick viscous liquid. It burned as it trickled down my throat. I gasped and sputtered and expelled some of the fluid while the remainder flowed down my throat. The flavor reminded me of honeyed scotch, and warmth spread throughout my body. I relaxed as my body fell away from me, an extraneous extension of myself. I felt disembodied and fully aware at the same time, a warm sensuality replaced my earlier fear. My eyes drifted closed under the blindfold, the silk caressing my eyelids. As much as I tried, I was unable to re-open them again.

A soft touch that progressed feather-soft up and down my body raised the hair on my skin like an electric current. The hands were fiery and scalded my skin where they made contact. My muscles contracted, and contorted my body in waves of pleasure. I yearned for the attention and shivered with desire. My erection became enormous, and the sensual massage became centered there, a pulsating focus of carnal desire. I could not help myself, nor did I desire to, aspiring only the abiding touch.

When the touch ceased I drew in my breath and strained against my bonds. My body arched involuntarily upward. Two hands pressed against my chest as my tormentor straddled my body and entombed my erection. She gyrated slowly up and down, increasing her tempo until I spent myself inside her. When she was finished with me, I was mounted again. Incredulously, I was raped again and again. My body seemed to have no limits as my semen was sucked from me. I felt the room spin faster and faster until at last I collapsed into unconsciousness.

Sometime later, I heard movement around me. Water was being wrung, twisted from a cloth and dribbled into a container. Warm breath against my skin made me shiver as my nurses moved in closer. A soft hand held mine and applied a silky, warm liquid to the torn flesh on my palms and then my knees. The delicate breath smelled of ripe peaches and I breathed deeply. Many hands washed me with soft cloths, teasing gently over my burning skin. I relaxed, content to let them minister to me. Gardenias and honeysuckle quietly replaced the earthy scent of sex. The stone altar beneath me became pliant and I melted into it.

I jolted awake safely tucked into bed in the houseboat. I

sat up, shook my head and looked around. Steve was still asleep and snored lightly; my pants were on the floor next to my bed. My headache was gone, replaced with a feeling of vacancy. My recent memory was becoming distant. From the window faint streaks of dawns arrival lightened the sky. How long had I been asleep? There were no abrasions to the skin on my hands and knees. Was what had taken place during the night only a dream? It must have been. I examined my body for telltale signs of last night's debauchery and found none. Something caught my eye and pulling the wrinkles taut around my belly button, there, hidden inside a fold of skin at the top of my navel, I discovered the same dried mucous material I had washed off the morning after sex with Catherine. Filled with a nameless apprehension, I wondered, was I dreaming, or was I simply losing my mind?

Chapter 16

I must have fallen asleep. Last night seemed an eternity. "Hey, Steve, look out the window." I did a tap dance on the cold floor as I peered out the bedroom window. I could hear him rustling in the kitchen. "The dock is covered in snow, at least nine inches deep and it still falling in soft, puffy flakes." I couldn't see the beach across the harbor through the heavy snowfall. I threw on a sweatshirt and jeans and tiptoed to the kitchen. "Hey, Steve, what did you do with my clean socks?"

"Cheeseburger in paradise." Steve sang an old Jimmy Buffet song as he built up a fire in the wood stove. "Ninety-five degrees in the shade, eighty-five degrees in the water, I'm ready. Are you going over and square with the dive boat before we catch our ferry?" He pointed to the coffee table.

I spied my socks beneath, "Yeah, did you get our flight arrangements confirmed? We're catching the two-ten boat this afternoon, right?" I asked, donning my socks.

"That's right; we're booked on the four-thirty to DFW." He hummed 'latitudes and attitudes'

I started to pack up my camera equipment, "Yeah, I have lots of time to pay off the boat captain unless I have to chain up to get over there." I took another sip of coffee

124

I hadn't mentioned to Steve anything about my dream, if that is what it was. I thought it might be a good story told from a hammock in the Caribbean.

"We are staying at Winfred resort, right?"

Steve heaved himself off the floor, poured a cup of coffee, sat opposite me on the couch and stared at the fire. "Of course we're staying at Winfred. Where else would we stay in Belize?" He put his cup down and removed his glasses, massaged his eyes with his thumbs and then placed the glasses next to his coffee cup.

"It is tourist season, you know. They could be full up." I knelt on my plastic camera case and closed the latches. "Did you check?"

"Dave will find us a room. He always does. Quit worrying." He put his glasses back on. "We have a simple plan for Belize. We'll compose our notes and photos in the morning when it's cool and drink all afternoon."

"Okay, my kind of plan. I better get moving." I grabbed a last sip of coffee and threw on my windbreaker. "See you in a couple."

"Don't forget to tell the captain to let us know when the hatching is imminent so we can fly up for a quick shoot." Steve shouted out the door as I skidded up the dock.

"Okay, no problem." I bent my head into the heavy snowfall and wished that I had chosen something warmer than the windbreaker.

The fresh snow crunched under my feet as I made my way up the dock and the north wind blew snow into my face and forced me to stare at my feet as I walked. Belize seemed too far away.

I walked about fifty yards when a woman in my path

blocked my way and almost knocked me down.

"I watched you last night writhing on their altar, and it was disgusting." She spat in my face. She was bundled up in a long, quilted parka with a stocking cap pulled down over her ears.

I stumbled back a step and stared. "Who the hell are--Oof!"

She stepped up to me and struck me in the chest with both hands balled into fists. "I thought I told you to get out of town. Do you know what you've done, you idiot?" Her face was red and contorted; her voice a hoarse whisper through the blowing snow.

I squinted through the snow. "The woman from the diner?" I wagged my finger. "The woman in my bed?"

She stood her ground and snarled. "The same."

I looked at her aghast, the rape had actually taken place and at the same time I was ashamed for what she must have seen. "I thought it was a dream," I said weakly.

"Bullshit! You know it was no dream. You enjoyed every second of it, and now you're looking for an excuse for your behavior." She switched to a whining voice. "I didn't know it was happening." She stood and shook her head at me.

"Look," I said angrily. "In the first place, I was kidnapped, drugged, and raped. I had no control over what happened last night."

"Right, any court in the country would believe that you were raped three times, and that you had no control over your hard dick. Give me a break, and start thinking with your big head for a change." She thrust her glove-less finger into my face. It shook, either in anger or because of the cold. "You've helped the Sisterhood create more monsters, and it has to got be stopped."

My anger subsided, "Hang on a minute, how did you see

126

what happened last night if you're not involved with these people? This whole thing is smelling fishier by the moment."

"I know a secret entrance to the broch," she whispered.

I shrugged my shoulders. "I don't have a clue as to what you're talking about."

"That cavern is called a broch. It's a giant oval with a single opening in one wall. It was originally designed in Scotland as a type of fortress to defend against the Druid attack. The broch on the island has a single opening, but in addition can be entered through the water. You must have seen the house on the beach in Blakely Harbor with the turrets. That's Catherine's house and the cavern is below the right turret. I was there, believe me." She took hold of my arm and said, "Let's get in your car, I'm freezing."

She held my arm as we walked up the drive toward the parking lot. The huge snowflakes fell like autumn leaves during a windstorm. The flakes collapsed vertically from a broken sky. I discovered my car after three misses and began to brush the snow off the windshield, but she restrained my arm. "Just get in and start the engine. The snow will hide us for awhile." She squeezed between me, and the car, to get in first.

Once the engine was started, I turned the heat up full. The inside of the darkened car could have doubled as a refrigerator. I watched her rub her hands together.

"I hate talking about my sex life to a stranger. Do you have a name?"

"Yes, it's Emma."

I took her hands in mine; they were cold and dry. "Look Emma, I can't explain last night, but if it means anything, I really don't know what happened, and by tomorrow I'll be lying in a hammock in the tropics."

She closed her eyes and shook her head vigorously and then looked up at me.

"Listen, Steve and I are booked on the four-thirty to Dallas-Fort Worth."

"There's a lot you still don't understand," she said, pulling her hands away. The snow on the windshield cracked as the warmth from the defroster began to melt the ice. She reached over and turned off the defroster. "Initially the Sisterhood began as a defense against the Druids, a sort of protection for women. After many years practicing the black arts the women became powerful and marshaled their powers of magic to destroy the Druid priests, becoming more powerful than the Druids."

I shifted in my seat. "What's this, a history lesson?"

"Be quiet and listen." She balled her hands into fists. "Next, the mighty forces of the Roman army invaded. The Druids enlisted their help and nearly eradicated the Sisterhood. As a result, the Sisterhood went underground, or better yet they went under the sea. They became adept at living underwater. When their broch was attacked, they simply slid into the water and vanished. They developed gills and learned to control their body temperature, all to adapt to their new environment. The largest and most powerful group lived on the Isle of Skye and was protected by the clansmen there, in particular the McCrae clan, who bred with the Sisterhood for many centuries. In turn, the Sisterhood protected the fish species the fishermen needed to survive. The McCrae clan became known as the Soldiers of the Sisterhood."

"Not more of this soldier shit!" I opened the door and started to slide out. She reached across me and pulled the door closed with more strength than I had imagined she possessed.

"Don't," she growled.

I settled against the seat with a sigh, and shrugged. "Please, continue.'

"The breeding took place inside a broch, and was witnessed by the entire coven of the Sisterhood. They became so adept at living in the water that when they gave birth, there was no longer live birth. They produced an egg, and then the egg was expelled and nurtured by the Sisterhood until it hatched. The reason for this is so the women wouldn't be burdened by pregnancy and the weakness' it incurred." She sat back and took a deep breath.

I was enthralled. "You want me to believe we have a coven of witch mermaids swimming around and laying eggs?" I struggled out of my jacket and laughed at the thought of Catherine laying an egg. Emma grabbed me by the ear and pulled my head down.

"Ouch! Let go--"

"Listen to the rest of the story before you laugh." Her eyes burned like fiery coals. She let go of my ear. "The eggs are laid two days after fertilization. They are placed into the salt water where they are constantly guarded and kept safe. After three weeks, a new member of the Sisterhood emerges.
"Sounds like a fairy tale." I rubbed the top of my ear.

"Be quiet," she snapped.

I nodded, still massaging my ear.

"Their metabolic rate is incredible; they can walk within a week, swim in cold saltwater in a month. I have personally witnessed, a hatching, it's a gruesome sight. The mission of the Sisterhood remains the same as it was in the past, to protect the natural environment of the sea."

"So what's the problem?" I interjected. "We have a bunch of mermaids that swim around, protect fish and lay eggs. So what? They might have raped me, but on the other hand, if they had asked me I might have agreed whole-heartedly to party with the lot. What's the rub?"

"The rub is that these women, these monsters, feed upon human flesh to retain their human disguise. They believe that without human flesh they change into a more adaptable form for living underwater and are less and less able to survive on land. Without human flesh, they will take on the appearance of the wolf eel. Those scuba divers that disappear underwater and are never found--they're part of the Sisterhood's diet! That's the rub!"

The thought sickened me, "You mean to tell me that Catherine is some kind of a monster living on human flesh, breathing underwater, and laying eggs? You're asking me to believe a story that Stephen King could have made up."

She nodded. "Not only is she a monster, she is the head monster. Catherine is the prophetess of the Sisterhood."

"Are all the mermaids we hear about in legend are actually flesh eating monsters?" I shook my head, grabbed my jacket and reached for the car door handle.

"No!" She put her hand on my arm. "Wait, please stay and listen to me." I watched the condensation building on the windows. She slid her hand up, lightly caressed my jaw and turned my head toward her. "Please."

I released the door handle and sighed. "Okay, I'm listening."

"There are thousands of mermaids in the world, even today. Most of them simply live off the bounty of the sea and can return to land when they please. The sisterhood that originated

from the Isle of Skye has always lived off the flesh of humans."
She wiped at the condensation on the side window. "That's the
other rub Gil; they don't need human flesh to survive, but they
still believe they do. Catherine makes them believe they need the
blood of humankind to survive." A single tear appeared and
trickled down her pale cheek.

The snow continued to fall outside while silence reigned
inside the car. I digested Emma's story. The windshield was
clear and snow began to slide off the side windows as well. A
patch of blue hood appeared where the engine's heat had melted
off the snow. The heavy flakes that plopped there melted
immediately and sent little geysers of steam into the air.

Emma unzipped her parka, took off her hat, and looked at
me solemnly. "You know Gil, we can't let these eggs hatch. We
have to go in there and destroy them before they mature." She
turned her hat inside out and back again.

"What do you mean we?" I stammered. "I'm on my way
to Central America. I've got no stake in this horror movie. As a
matter of fact, I'm not sure if I even believe it. Sure, I might have
been raped by a gaggle of screwball women last night, but
nobody is going to believe it was rape. You said so yourself. So
who do you think is going to believe this cock-and-bull story you
just told me?"

"I can prove it, Gil. Go visit Catherine today and kiss her
goodbye; kiss her on her neck just below her ear. You'll see a
small slit behind her earlobe. That's a gill slit. You'll see it move
as she breathes normally. If that doesn't convince you, come
with me tomorrow night and we'll witness the ritual of the egg
passing. If we don't destroy the eggs, you will become a
soldier."

I shifted in my seat and straightened my back. "That's

another thing. What is all this soldier nonsense? I'm more of the draft dodger kind of guy, and yet I'm hearing <u>soldier</u> this and <u>soldier</u> that. What's the--?"

'The soldiers protect the sisterhood, and breeds with them, just as they did for hundreds of years." She grabbed my arm and pulled herself closer. "Catherine wants you to become a soldier."

I was trying to think of some excuse so that I could forget this <u>Twilight Zone</u> story and go wiggle my toes in the Caribbean sand. "How are you going to witness this ritual? I thought you were scared of these people. What's your stake in this, Emma?"

Emma sighed. She closed her eyes and tried to conceal teardrops that threatened to spill on to her cheeks. The lines in her face grew deeper, "Gil, my brother was killed by those monsters five years ago while diving near Blakely Harbor and I'll not rest until I destroy the Sisterhood, or it destroys me."

"I'm sorry about your brother, I--"

"As to how, I've been a diver for thirty-years now. The captain and I began the first dive shop, and worked together for twenty years."

"Our dive boat captain?" I smiled. "No..."

"The same. He was a different man back then." She poked a finger in my chest. "Shut up and listen. I'm a qualified re-breather diver, and I can teach you. We can go into the broch underwater, undetected. I've done it often. That's why I know so much about the Sisterhood." She punctuated her words with her finger on my chest.

Still looking for a way out I said, "So, why not take the captain with you?" I folded her fingers into a fist, wrapped my hands around it and held it tightly against my chest. Can she feel my heart beat faster and faster, I wondered?

"The captain's a soldier now," she whispered. She pulled

her hand away, turned in her seat and looked out the back window.

"The old captain's a soldier?" I turned sideways in the car. "No, no, no. You can't --"

She swung her head back to face me. "You better believe it, Gil." She was quiet for a moment. "Don't underestimate that old man."

I told Emma I would think about what she told me, but in the meantime, I wanted to pay off the captain and the dive boat for our trips. I dropped Emma off at her place on the way. She lived in an old-style Victorian on five acres of pastures and evergreen trees. Snow blanketed her home in a Christmas-card setting. Horses stabled in a barn adjacent to the house rushed out to greet us as we drove in. The two black and white Appaloosa's romped in the snow like children.

"They're my babies." Emma smiled although she looked exhausted.

I took her by the arm and helped her up the front stairs, kicking away the drifted snow to make a pathway. She slipped, her knees buckled and I caught her up in my arms like a child.

The house was warm and I laid her on the couch and propped her head against the armrest. "Are you alright?" I knelt by her side and placed my hand on her forehead.

"Just tired, I haven't slept much in three days. Leave me here. I'll take a nap and be as good as new." She turned on her side, "Wouldn't you know I'd let a man bring me home and I'd fall asleep even before I'd gotten him to bed." She mumbled, "Unassembled snow..."

"What did you say?" I pulled off her cap and smelled the warm wool on her hair.

She looked up at me through half closed eyes. "My brother used to say that when it snowed, the snowflakes fell from heaven as unassembled snowmen."

I shook my head and watched her eyes close. "I'll stop by later and check on you." I stood up to leave and heard her whisper.

"Be very careful, Gil. Don't trust them."

She sighed deeply and then became still. I pulled the blanket from the back of the couch and tucked it tightly around her. I closed the front door quietly as I left and looking up, I smiled at her unassembled snowmen.

Chapter 17

The road was treacherous and wound down out of the wooded forest, then into the flats next to Eagle Harbor. Driving took up all my attention, which left little time to think about the Sisterhood.

The road terminated at the entrance to Eagledale marina where the captain kept his boat and office. A locked iron gate kept non-members out. I reached through the bars and managed to grasp the handle on the opposite side and open the gate. The captain's boathouse was the first one in a series of covered boathouses attached to a wooden dock. All of them were ram-shackled and oil-stained. The captain's boathouse had a high-peaked roof and unpainted, rough weathered gray siding. I knocked on the door, then as I let myself in; rusty hinges sang out in protest.

The interior was well lit and neat and as put together as the Spirit. The little dive boat fit inside the boathouse like a hand in a glove. A light burned inside the boat's cabin and I climbed over the gunwale, knocked loudly on the side of the house and announced myself. "Permission to come aboard?"

"Come on aboard," hailed the captain. He pushed open the cabin door with a shoulder and stepped out onto the wet deck.

He was covered with oil and grease; his left hand brandished a dirty filter. He wore ragged coveralls with <u>Spirit</u>, written across the front in black marker. A baseball cap was perched on his head with the bill turned backwards, as oily as his coveralls.

The boat shifted gently under my weight as I climbed aboard then righted herself as I stepped into the wet deck. The captain smelled like scotch and diesel fuel.

"How about a cup of coffee, Sonny?" He grinned at me and raised his eyebrows.

"Thank you Captain, that would be good." I followed him as he turned and walked through the cabin hatch.

"The diesel heater keeps her pretty warm when she gets to percolatin'. Toss your jacket on the seat there." He pointed to the captain's seat and then sat the filter next to the open engine hatch cover. "Black?"

"Perfect, thanks." A four-foot by three-foot wooden hatch had been removed inside the cabin floor and the top of the engine was exposed. I tiptoed around the opening and took off my jacket, stretched and lay it across the seat. "Big job today?" I stepped around the greasy rags that carpeted the deck.

"Watch you don't slip on the wrenches and o-rings." He wiped at the condensation on the windows. "This coffee's been cookin' awhile. Might be a bit strong." He reached up and took down a white ceramic cup, which he proceeded to fill with coffee and a liberal dose of scotch. "Here you go," and handed it to me, and poured straight scotch into his own mug.

"I knew it was gonna fuckin' snow. Didn't I say so the other day?" He picked up the used filter and tossed it into a plastic bucket and took a long swallow from his cup. "We're not diving today. I don't think we're set 'til tomorrow, so what do you need?"

"We're done diving for now, Captain, until the wolf eels hatch. There's nothing more we need." I took a sip of coffee and gagged and let the mouthful drain back into the cup.

The captain's eyebrows waggled happily.

"I thought I'd pay you and Catherine off. Steve and I are booked on a four-thirty flight today to Belize. If you would, when the hatching begins, call me in Belize, and I'll fly out for a quick photo session to finish up."

"Sure, I can do that. Write the phone number on the ship's log. Did you talk to Catherine yet? The diving part of the charters is kind of up to her." He pointed to the green book next to the steering wheel. "Right in front of you."

"I've got time to do that. Where can I find her today?" The scotch and coffee slid down roughly, setting fire to my lungs. I sat the coffee next to the logbook and scribbled the number to the resort.

"She'll be at the dive shop today. I think she said she would be working on some regulators or tank valves, or some fuckin' thing. Anyway, get over there and see her before you take off." He sat the cup down, plucked his hat off with one hand and ran his free hand through his long hair before he replaced the cap.

I handed him the half empty cup and watched a smile begin at the corners of his moustache. "The dive shop gets the charter money, right?"

"That should work." The smile had grown and pushed up the moustache hairs so that they stood straight out. "More coffee, Sonny?"

"How about the tip?" My wallet was in my hand when I heard him growl.

"I don't work for no fuckin' tips. Do I look like a fuckin' waiter to you? You pay your fare; you get your dive trip, simple as that."

"Yes, Sir." I left quietly and heard the captain mutter and bang tools as he climbed back down alongside the engine.

The roads on the way back were churned up from traffic and made the drive much trickier. The snow stopped and the temperature was now above freezing. Snow slid off the trees, dropped heavily and often took the branches with them. I was told power outages on the island were a way of life, and preparations in town were well under way.

I found Catherine in her workshop with a regulator held in place on the workbench by an old iron vise. A kerosene stove and lanterns provided the heat and light for the entire store. Unlike the captain's boat, the workshop was chaotic, dive gear hung from doorknobs and nails. A wetsuit hung over a half wall and dripped water next to the computer. Tools were strewn across the workbench helter-skelter. I fought my way through the shop to Catherine.

"Hey kid, how's it going today?" I wrapped my arms around her waist, lowered my lips to the back of her neck and kissed her behind the left ear. I froze for an instant when I saw it-- a slit in the skin just below her earlobe. It moved. I recovered rapidly, and then kissed her quickly on the lips to hide my dismay.

She pushed the regulator aside and hugged me back. "Hey, Soldier. It's going well. You ready to dive tomorrow?" She was dressed in blue jeans and a tight red sweatshirt, and when she smiled her face flushed bright pink.

"That's what I came to talk to you about. I'm leaving this afternoon for Belize with Steve. Something has come up and we won't be able to stay." I was sure she could hear my heart race and I tried to relax.

She looked at me wide-eyed with a hint of a smile on her lips. "Why are you zipping your jacket up and down?"

"What?" I closed my hands into fists. "Cold, I guess."

"Come closer, I'll warm you up, Soldier." She slid her arms around my waist and pulled me close. My eyes were inches from the gill slits and I closed them. "Better?"

"Yes, thanks," I stumbled. "I spoke with the captain earlier and he'll keep me informed about the hatching, so I can fly back here for a photo shoot."

"Whatever works," She said releasing her hold on me. She stared past my shoulder with a far off look in her eyes. She turned back to her regulator and tightened a nut, then loosened the handle on the vise and jerked the regulator up and out of the vise. She reached over and hung it on a nail in the wall then turned to face me. "Hold on a minute, and I'll get your bill updated."

As we walked out of the workshop into the main store, the front door opened and admitted a tall, slim, woman. She glided through the door as if her hips and shoulders were unattached, and I thought of a cat, ready to pounce. This was the same woman I had seen from the track and from Devil's Boulder. She looked at me, and grinned. "Hi there Soldier. How's the knee?"

Catherine, at the computer, looked up and introduced us. "Gil, this is Lois. Lois, Gil. He's on his way to Belize. Gil is leaving the island during the most beautiful time of the year."

As Lois and I shook hands, I noticed the gold pendant hanging around her neck. "We've met before, twice actually." I held on to her hand a long moment and held her gaze.

"The necklace was mine!" She purred and winked at me

139

mischievously.

"What?" My jaw dropped and I looked to see if Catherine had heard the exchange. She was turned away from us and as I twisted back, Lois leaned in close and licked my upper lip. I jerked back. "What did you say?"

She ignored me, sat on the corner of the desk and proceeded to remove her rubber boots. Slush still clung to the sides of the soles, dripped dirty water onto the floor. She nodded to Catherine then removed her coat and draped it across a white plastic chair.

I was lost momentarily in a fog. When the dive shops air compressor rumbled like an old steam train and began vibrating in the adjacent room, it brought me back to reality. I watched Lois attach hoses to unfilled air tanks and wondered if it was possible that a woman like Lois, who could pass for a fashion model could in-fact be feeding on human flesh. I quickly dismissed the notion. It was not possible.

The computer whirred then spat out a white sheet of paper.

"Okay Gil, here's what you owe the store, this column is the boat's due." She bent over the account with me and pointed to the various charges. "Do you know the captain's view on tips?"

"I've just learned. Do you feel the same way?"

"If you weren't so beautiful Gil, I'd take all the money you wanted to give me, but no. No tips."

We finished our business and said our good byes. I walked out into the cold day and shivered more from the idea that I may be dealing with monsters than the actual temperature. As I walked past the plate glass window toward my car I saw Catherine and Lois in a heated discussion.

I drove back to Emma's house. The sun reflected on the

snow in blinding brilliance. Picture postcard farms were framed behind stock fences; white fields and tree branches bent double and nearly touched the ground.

Her front door was ajar. I mounted the steps two at a time and pushed at the open door. "Emma?" My voice rang hollow, echoing back to me. I stepped inside and looked around the doorway to the living room where I had left her asleep. The couch was upended, a side table overturned nearby and the lamp was shattered across the floor. The blanket that had covered Emma now lay tossed across the television set in the corner. Scuffmarks and melted slush dirtied the otherwise shiny hardwood floor.

I reached for the telephone to dial 911 but found the line had been wrenched from the jack. I searched through the other rooms on the main floor, but found no other damage. Adjacent to the range in the kitchen a door stood ajar and led down into the basement. The light was on and I called out, "Emma?"

The stairway led down a full story without handrails to a cement floor. On the last stair I turned right and encountered a lighted full basement workshop dedicated to diving. An air compressor the size of a large refrigerator stood at the entrance of a full service dive shop. The white-painted plywood walls were covered with tools, arranged by sets and size. On the workbenches beneath, tools were stainless steel and gleamed under fluorescent lights. Across the room, another workbench held two backpacks, each with a small canister of compressed air and large bladders on either side.

"These must be the re-breather units Emma used to spy on the Sisterhood."

As I looked around the basement and listened to the silence

of Emma's house, I could imagine what had happened. The Sisterhood had decided to silence her, and if what Emma had told me, was correct, the sisters would need fresh meat for their egg laying. Emma could still be alive, held prisoner for the evening's ceremonies. There was only one thing I could do: learn to use a re-breather and go and find her. As I assembled all the gear I would need, I hoped the sisterhood had alternative plans for dinner this evening. Emma was coming home with me.

Chapter 18

Steve was standing in the living room dressed in a Hawaiian shirt and matching trunks as I crashed through the front door. "Sit down, Steve."

"What the…?" He backed away quickly and tripped over the coffee table. He landed hard between the couch and the table. "Why the Hell are you flying in here like that?" He kicked the coffee table away and lay flat on the floor.

I closed the front door and helped him to the couch. "We've got another problem, Partner."

"The only problem you're going to have is how to walk after I kick your ass." He saw that I wasn't smiling. "Problem? We don't need any more problems." He squinted and looked around.

His glasses had skittered across the room. I picked them up and handed them over.

"Sorry, Partner. I didn't mean to startle you."

"What the--?" He jammed the glasses on and looked up at me.

"Just listen." I sat down across from him and relayed the story of the mermaids.

Steve looked at and cleaned his glasses on his shirttail.

"Okay, you're either nuts or the story is true. Either way, there is only one course of action for us. Let's get the fuck out of here." He stood up, grabbed his suitcase off the kitchen table, and headed for the front door.

"Steve, Emma's in trouble and may die because of me. We have to try and get her out of this."

He stopped, turned around and set down his case. "For Christ's sake, Gil, call the goddamn cops! This isn't something we do. We're not Navy Seals. Call the cops and tell them you know where this woman is being held. Gil. Hello, it's their job." Through his tirade he waved his arms at an imaginary orchestra.

"We can't call the cops, Steve; we don't know if any cops are involved as soldiers. And, if they're not involved, how are we going to convince them that some of their wealthy, beautiful citizens are flesh eating monsters?"

Steve sat on the arm of the couch. "You're right. I'm not sure I believe this story." He sanded his hands together. "And, I know you!"

"Look, I only brought one re-breather unit. I'll slip in the water across from that old house in Blakely Harbor, swim across, to try and find her. If I can't find her, I'll get away and then we can get the hell out of here. Come on, Steve, one quick dive, and then we go." I walked into the kitchen and poured myself a half glass of scotch. "You want one?" I raised a glass towards him.

"Shit, shit, shit! That's the most idiotic plan I've ever heard." He wiggled his hand for me to pour him a drink. "First of all, you don't know where you're going. You don't know where you'll end up." He started ticking the reasons off on his fingers. "If you find this cavern, and what's- her-name _is_ there, you don't know how you're going to get her out." He went over to the couch and sat down again. "If this Sisterhood finds out, you're dead. And lastly, if you dive, you'll need to wait twelve hours to level out your nitrogen levels before you can fly." He held his hand out for the glass.

I took a deep swallow, walked over and handed him his drink "Don't be so negative. It's a cinch, you can delay our flight until tomorrow. Trust me. Have I ever led you astray?" My hands shook as I finished my drink.

"Stupid, stupid, stupid!" He drained the last of the scotch out of his glass. "You're not falling for this, this whatever her name is, are you?"

"Her name's Emma," I sat next to him on the couch. "I might be." I inspected the contents of my glass, "Are you with me on this?"

He nodded his head. "Ohhh, shit!"

* * *

The time of the hatching arrived. Steam escaped as the temperature stabilized at one hundred degrees, the temperature necessary to release the eggs. Visibility decreased to less than fifteen feet. The stone floor had been washed; the excess water flowed into the black pool in the far corner of the broch. The delivery of the eggs would take place separately upon the altar attended by the core of the Sisterhood. Three eggs would be placed in the protection of the Sisterhood this day, each fathered by McCrae sperm. It would be an historical day for the Sisterhood. The mood was festive as the women entered the broch and removed their robes, uncovering their long tresses. Also, revealed was the evidence of some members need for fresh meat. Patches of skin on their necks and shoulders began to peel away and displayed the slick and scaly skin of their marine cousins.

The host flesh was tied to an iron ring embedded in stone at the side of the broch just outside of a pool of light. The feeding would be frenzied.

Chapter 19

Steve parked the car off the main road on a muddy track surrounded by fir trees. A meager trail wound down a wooded ravine to the water. The wind returned and brought with it more clouds and rain. It was deathly quiet. Heavy brush covered with wet snow muffled the rest of the world. We spoke in whispers afraid to disturb the peace.

"Zip up my dry suit," I struggled into my gear next to the car.

Steve pulled the zipper closed across the back of my shoulders. "Okay, you're tight." He slapped me on the back and said, "I'll grab your tank and weight belt and drag it down to the water." He unloaded the dive gear and closed the trunk. "Can you manage the rest of the gear?"

"Yeah, I got it. Let's go." I picked up my fins, mask and dive light and followed him down the slope. Steve crouched in heavy brush ten feet from the water's edge. He swiped at the accumulated snow from the backpack and turned on my air. I tapped him on the shoulder, "That's Catherine's house directly across the harbor. Do you see it?"

"Yeah, yeah, I see it. Hurry up and get in the water before I lose my nerve." He slapped at the tank assembly one last time.

"How do you want to do this?"

"I have a tentative plan." He looked at the sky and back at me. "It'll work, don't worry." I sat down beside him in the snow. "I want to limit my exposure on the beach, so I'll put on the gear once I'm in the water and descend. I'll swim underwater the quarter mile over and locate the caves, then I'll figure the rest out."

"Stupid, stupid, stupid fucking plan." Steve's hands shook. "What if they see you coming?"

"I'm using the re-breather. No bubbles. They can't see me coming." I slapped him on the shoulder. "Come on; help me get this tank over the bank."

"Stupid fucking plan." He said under his breath as he checked the valves on the tank again.

"You know, Steve, you're starting to sound like the captain. I'm going to wash your mouth out with hot sauce when we get to Belize."

"If you meet the captain down there, you won't be going to Belize." He pointed to the water, twisted the valve, "Okay, you got air."

The beach I was standing on was not exactly a beach, but a black, rocky reef that climbed out of the water onto the dirt bank. There was a three-foot drop from the bank to the rocks, and then three more feet to the water. It was high tide. I dropped into the water and gave Steve the thumbs-up sign. I set my compass so that my approach to the house could be accomplished entirely underwater. We exchanged a last look, and he dropped the tank assemble over the bank.

I looked across the harbor to the brick-and-stone building and almost lost my nerve. The house was dark and rose out of the ground like a tombstone. Towers on either side of the main structure ascended three stories high and as the clouds raced across the sky they were obscured behind the torrential rain. The hairs on the back of my neck stood up as I thought of what I was about to do. I knew that if Emma were taken to this house she might be somewhere inside one of those towers. Steve's words, "Stupid, stupid, stupid," rang in my ears.

Steve leaned over the bank and said, "Okay Gil, do it, but goddamn it, be careful. Don't take any chances. I'll be right here when you get out."

I slid quietly under water and descended. At thirty feet the bottom was gray silt, but visibility remained a constant twenty feet. The bottom gradually sloped down to ninety feet, before it began to climb again. I followed my compass bearing and held my flashlight continuously on the dial. The re-breather was quiet, without the normal exhalation noise created by bubbles from my usual regulator. It was harder to suck in air, and I slowed down to keep from tiring.

The bottom was featureless, a few starfish, and some sea pens. I could see the outlines of old bottles. Other than a bit of debris, there was nothing to guide me but my compass. The bottom changed as I headed into sixty feet of water. Large boulders appeared which indicated the rocky reef ahead. Then a vertical wall blocked my path. I looked up from its base and saw it rise above me unbroken, supporting a crop of large, white, plumose anemone that clung to the wall for as far as I could see. They created a flowing, waving carpet of illumination as their tendrils swept the waters for food. I found it nearly impossible to see the rock wall itself through the bodies of its inhabitants.

As I swam the length of the wall, I pushed aside these rubbery creatures. I peered behind them looking for an opening. Thirty minutes under the water already and the added exertion taxed my energy. I stopped for a moment to rest and sank to the bottom. As I looked up and to my right, I noticed an area darker than its surroundings. I swam up to it and shined my light into a deep recess. This was the opening I was looking for.

The cavern was large enough to drive a truck through, but tapered significantly as it angled and twisted upwards. Twenty feet into the cave and in thirty feet of black water, the cave turned into a tunnel less than three feet across. The sides were smooth like the inside of fine pottery. I turned off my light; afraid its luminosity could be detected from above, and found myself in utter blackness. I clipped the light to my weight belt and slid my hands up the rock tunnel on either side of me, feeling for any change of dimension that would indicate a decreasing circumference or a dead end. I hope this is the right tunnel

I ascended slowly, twenty feet, fifteen. The numbers on the luminescent dial glowed in the murky darkness. Ahead and above me was the barest perception of light. At ten feet the light became apparent, then brighter still. I slowed my ascent and drifted toward the light. I broke the surface of a small pool with a ripple and found myself inside a massive cavern, lit with kerosene lanterns affixed to the stone walls. I knew this place. This was the where the Sisterhood had raped me. A shallow area to the left afforded me a ledge where I could crawl up onto without being seen over the lip of the pool's enclosure.

I only removed my backpack, mask and fins. I peered over the lip of the pool and looked into the cavern. Steam filled the enclosure like a heavy fog bank and limited my visibility, even more so near the saltwater pool as it condensed over the cold water. I began to perspire inside my dry suit, and for a brief moment entertained the thought of removing it, but then I figured a quick exit might prove my only escape.

The steam was a creature itself, inside the cavern. It swirled in one direction then another before it moved upward or laterally, then spilled from above like a waterfall. I could see the altar by the far doorway one moment, then the fog concealed it the next. The upper recesses of the cavern were not visible, neither was the doorway.

A low hum commenced near the altar. The drone sounded like a high-pitched-metered chant, poetic. There were no words I could understand, but it continued to increase in volume. Another voice joined in, very low. It accented the first voice, before long many voices combined and the enclosure was filled with a beautiful chorus that reverberated and echoed around the chamber. The fog swirled and danced ever faster, it kept time with the incantation. I could not see the choir through the vapor. I thought the best time to move would be now, the chant would cover any noise and the mist would conceal me.

I edged forward on my stomach; the lead weights on my belt scraped against the stone until I was over the lip of the pool. The stone floor was wet and slippery from the steam; I felt like a salamander. I slithered across to a point alongside the wall opposite the altar and the chanting. Within fifteen feet of the altar I was secluded within the steam and darkness, I lifted my head each time the mist cleared and made out as many as eleven women cloaked in black, positioned in a semicircle around the altar. Each woman's head was raised toward the ceiling. The steam obscured their legs and feet, and their black hoods obscured their faces. At the head of the altar stood a woman considerably shorter than the others with raised arms leading the chant, the conductor. Catherine?

The chant ceased suddenly and the women dropped their heads to look upon the altar. The focus of their attention was a

151

woman who lay on her back, legs spread, back arched, and hands that gripped the sides of the altar. The woman was naked but lay upon a black cloak. I lay there horrified, yet entranced, camouflaged in my black dry suit in a black corner of the cavern, watching this ancient ceremony. The kerosene lanterns hissed and labored to keep their flame intact as the steam formed a halo around their diminished light.

As I watched, the fog lifted at the same moment the woman's body contracted. Legs were splayed wide and she arched her back and lifted her buttocks off the stone altar. Her flesh trembled and vibrated in waves from head to toe. Her face was contorted into a mask of pain. As she mouthed a long silent groan, she pushed out a grapefruit-sized brilliant white orb. The egg splashed forth, trailing red from between her legs. One sister snatched up the egg and held it aloft, as if in triumph. The chant began again. The women raised their arms high above their heads and their chant boomed through the cavern, an evil, bone-shaking cacophony tempered only by the muffling effects of the steam.

I tried to make myself smaller as this dirge ricocheted from one side of the cavern to the other. I covered my ears and felt like a rabbit caught in a headlight, as if the chant would bounce off my body and expose me. Sweat from the room and my own fear soaked my woolies worn under my dry suit. I looked around me and noticed a fissure in the wall above and to the left of me. The crack looked large enough for me to conceal myself in and afford me better visibility. The women seemed intent on the ceremony so I slowly stood and moved sideways to melt into the crack in the stone.

From this new position, I could see not only the altar, but also the doorway on the other side of the cavern. I felt better camouflaged and took stock of my surroundings. The woman on the altar was being helped up, her robe draped around her stooped shoulders. She was assisted by two sisters and led from the cavern. The chorus had subsided to an intimate whisper and the sisters followed one another through the doorway and out of the cavern.

As the last one exited the cavern, I slid from my concealment to gain a better view of the enclosure. To my right, and adjacent to the altar along the far side of the cavern, something moved. I froze against the wall, a kerosene lantern on a ledge two feet above my head sputtered. The movement continued. I inched my way until I could make out a shape against the stone wall. Her arms were stretched over her head and her hands tied with rope to an iron ring mounted in the wall. She was naked. Her face and head were encased in a hood, a drawstring tied around her neck. Although her feet were free to move, she was too short to reach the floor except on her toes, and so she hung there like a carcass ready to butcher.

Her body was lithe and athletic with small breasts and hips that glistened from the condensing steam. Tiny rivulets of water streamed down her body, and then trickled down her toes. Her muscles quivered, and chest, nipples erect, heaved from the strain of her bonds. Her hands were white. I reached out and touched her shoulder. She whimpered, "No, no," and withered at my touch.

I placed my hand over her mouth, and whispered, "Be quiet, it's me." I kept my hand against the sack until the tremors decreased, then untied the drawstring from around her neck and lifted the hood up over her head and threw it to the floor.

She blinked and then looked at me wide-eyed. Tears streamed down her face. She jerked her head in the direction of the altar. "The--"

I placed my finger to her lips. "Shhhh, we're not out of this yet." My hands shook as I pulled my dive knife from its scabbard; it slipped from my grasp and skittered to the stone floor. The knife sounded like an alarm clock in my mind and I dropped to my knees, splashed along the floor with my hands and snatched it up, then stood and flattened myself against the wall again. I took a deep breath, turned and looked toward the doorway. Nobody seemed to have heard. I sliced through the rope ties and grasped Emma as she dropped to the floor.

I gathered her up, she was like putty, and it was all I could do to hold her to my chest to and keep her from sliding to the floor. I crab-walked, my back to the stone wall, eyes toward the doorway. I put her down next to the lip of the pond. "Okay. What now," I muttered to myself.

"What are we going to do, Gil," she whispered. .

"I'm working on it." I pulled her down so that she was closer to the water and out of sight. Her foot touched the water in the opening and she shivered.

"Emma, listen to me." I took her by the shoulders and shook her. "I'm going to have to leave you here and go get help. I can't swim with you and get you out of here alive. Lie down right here next to the pond and, I'll be back as soon as I can."

She stiffened and threw her arms around my neck. "No Gil, don't leave me here, they'll kill me. I can make it with you. We can breathe off the same regulator. I'm okay."

"I've got no way to keep you warm, Emma. You'll freeze in the water." I placed my lips next to her ear. "Do you understand?"

"At least I'll have a chance with you. If you leave me now, you'll never see me again," she cried. "Please, don't leave me."

"Okay kid, just hang on tight." I knew she was right.
Her voice quivered. "I'm ready."

"I'll take a breath first and then hand you the regulator." I
pulled her face in close to mine and made her look me in the
eyes. "You ready to do this?" She looked like a panicked deer. I
grasped her face in both hands and brought her, nose to nose with
me. "Come on, Girl, you're the instructor. Are you ready?"

She blinked her eyes and nodded. "Gil," She grasped my
shoulders when I let go of her face. "My body temperature will
drop and I will become hypothermic. You'll have to hold me
tightly and swim for the both of us."

I looked over her shoulder and then back into her eyes.

"We'll manage." She smiled. "The other problem is that
the re-breather is a double hose assembly. You'll have to
manipulate both hoses so that we can share the air, especially,
when I lose consciousness." She cocked her head to one side.

I grimaced, then smiled, "How come I have to do all the
work?" I pinched her shoulder. "Come on, let's go."

I strapped on my tank assembly and put on my mask and
fins. Without looking back I took Emma in my arms and
dropped into the water. I heard her gasp as the cold water
engulfed her naked body. She clung to me like life itself. I swam
hard, straight down as fast as my fins would propel me to the
tunnel entrance. As we touched bottom I took the regulator out
of my mouth and pushed it into hers.

She took it hungrily, breathed in deeply twice, and handed
it back. I held her close to me and wrapped my right arm around
her waist; I made the exchange with my left. My compass was
also strapped to my left wrist. I needed to surface near where
Steve waited. The water was black, and my compass was hard to

see. I switched the dive light on to charge my compass dial and checked ahead for any obstructions. We swam twenty yards or so, then stopped to exchange breaths. Emma became weaker and no longer gripped me as tightly.

I swam with Emma suspended beneath me, often dragging her legs in the silt and over sunken logs and rocks as if I were in a marathon. My body ached, but I forced my muscles to continue. I forced the regulator back into Emma's mouth and held it there until I needed another breath. I couldn't take the time to check and see if Emma was actually breathing. She had completely relaxed her grip on me now. Kick, breathe, kick, breathe, and get the job done. My legs had lost all feeling; I knew that to slow down now would mean certain death for Emma. She counted on me and I would not let her down.

Emma's muscles were in constant spasm in their attempt to warm the body. I held her closer and hoped my rubber suit would radiate warmth into her frigid limbs. Her eyes were closed; her tight curly hair straightened in the dark water past her shoulders and picked up tendrils of seaweed. The small flashlight I used to see my compass reflected off her body. She radiated a blue-white luminescence like a corpse.

I began to suffer double vision, a sure sign of oxygen deprivation. I would either have to slow down or I would black out underwater. I checked my compass bearing for the twentieth time, on course.

Suddenly I careened into a rock and lost my grip on Emma. I pulled her to me and stood on a rock to get a better purchase. My head was out of water. Emma was listless in my arms. We were three feet from shore. Steve ran into the water toward us. I thought Emma was dead. That I failed. "No, no, no," I cried out and railed against the water with my fist.

Steve grabbed Emma around the waist, then lifted her up onto his shoulder and carried her up the bank.

I sat in the water and sucked in the fresh air as I removed my fins and mask. Then, I followed Steve into the underbrush. Steve was not in the cover of the woods and I limped up the trail we had come down on earlier and found the car was running; the windows were fogged. I tossed my gear in the trunk and hurried to the side door. I flung it open and hoped to find Steve administering CPR.

Emma was ensconced in a red blanket in the back seat. She smiled as her teeth clicked together and waved a shaking finger at me. "Hey," she managed.

I laughed. "Yes! We did it!" My knees quivered with relief.

"Get in! Shut the goddamn door, and let's get the hell out of here!" Steve shuddered with excitement.

I climbed into the back next to Emma while Steve guided the car back onto the surfaced road, and we made our getaway. The tires spun and threw clumps of dirt and leaves into the snow behind us. We careened sideways until the car's wheels found purchase on the hard surface.

"How you doing, Girl?" I asked gently and pulled the blanket tighter around her neck.

"F-ff-fine. Th-th-thanks," she stuttered.

"I knew we'd make it all along." I lied. "No problem." I wrapped my arms around her and held her close again. I could see Steve's eyes in the rear view mirror.

"You're my hero," she whispered. She closed her eyes. Her body shivered uncontrollably and I rubbed her skin vigorously through the blanket. She relaxed and sighed, "I think I love you," before she collapsed in my arms and slept.

Teardrops glistened on my cheeks, I pulled her closer and I laid my head against hers. "Ditto," I whispered.

Chapter 20

I woke up in the car, wet, clammy, and alone. The windows were fogged and the car vibrated. My muscles ached and my mouth was cotton-dry. I swiped a circle in the fog at the side window and looked out. Land passed by through the porthole in the car deck as the ferry made its turn out of the harbor.

The zipper that ran across the back of my shoulders, and sealed me in the wet suit was, thankfully, unzipped. I peeled out of the suit and changed into the sweats Steve left beside me in the car.

In the silence the rescue of Emma and the swim with her under Blakely Harbor washed over me. Waves of adrenaline splashed over my tired muscles and made me tremble as I laced up my shoes. I ran my fingers through my hair and then went in search of my friends.

Steve and Emma were in the coffee shop sipping lattes in a side booth in the galley. She was dressed in his clothes and Steve was still wet from the waist down. I bought a coffee, slipped in next to her and exchanged my hot coffee for her cold hand.

"You two are quite a pair," I said.

"Hey, sleepyhead." She squeezed my hand and managed a

smile. "How do you feel?" She pulled her hand free and picked small segments of seaweed that still clung to her curls like last years Christmas ornaments.

"Tired." I looked at Steve. "How about you, Partner?"

Steve sipped his coffee and then sighed. "I'm okay, but…" He stared at the table.

"But what?" I gulped my coffee and stretched my shoulders. "I am sore, but damn it all we did it, didn't we?" I smiled and looked at their sober faces and said, "What's wrong?" I put the cup down.

"Look, Gil, uh--" Steve looked at me with his mouth open.

"Okay," I cracked my knuckles and leaned forward. What's going on? Do we have a plan, or another problem?"

Silence. Steve took off his glasses and held them up to the light of the window.

"Well?"

"We need to go back and destroy those eggs," Emma said in a small voice. "They'll take the eggs back to Lois' house. They tend the eggs in the basement. We can do it, Gil." Her voice became louder. She twisted around in her seat, grabbed me by the shoulders and shook. "We must do it."

"Fuck that," I glared at her. "We're goddammed lucky to be alive--especially you!" I looked at Steve. "Are you crazy?"

"Quiet." Steve shushed us and looked around the galley as people turned their heads. "Emma wants to go back and destroy the eggs. I already told her how dangerous that might be," Steve began.

I looked Emma in the eye and pointed my finger in her face. She slapped my hand aside. "You have a bounty on your head, Woman. They'll kill you if they see you again, and probably me now, too."

"Me, maybe, but they have no way of knowing you had anything to do with my escape. Besides, I can take care of myself." She poked her finger into my shoulder on each word.

"Hello?" I grabbed her poking hand and held it on the table. "Are you on the same fucking page we're on, or even the same book? You were about to become the main course for dinner on an all you can eat buffet. Do you even know what time it is? I'll tell you what time it is. It's time to get the hell out of Dodge." I shook my head and looked at Steve. He shrugged, sat back, sipped his coffee

The ferry maneuvered to line up with the entrance into Seattle Harbor. Other passengers finished their coffee and started to gather up their belongings. A waitress moved among the tables and cleaned up coffee spills and picked up trash. A little boy rushed past with a teddy bear clutched under his arm.

"I've booked the three of us on the seven-ten to Dallas." Steve said. He stood up and pulled his jacket over his sweatshirt. "Let's talk on the way to the airport."

Emma and I sat and glared at each other like two siblings ready to argue over who gets to ride in the front seat. I stood up and offered her my hand. "Okay, I'm sorry Emma. Come on, let's talk about it."

She grimaced and allowed me to help her out of the booth. We followed Steve to the auto deck.

During the thirty-minute drive from downtown Seattle to the Seattle-Tacoma airport, we discussed the situation. Emma was wedged between us in the front seat, her arms folded stiffly across her breasts.

"Look, Emma." I patted her right leg.

She jerked away, I held on. "Don't, Gil, Goddammit. I know what needs to be done. Don't try and pacify me." Her voice rose an octave and tears dripped from the corners of her eyes. "You just don't know what--"

"I believe you, Emma. I really do, but now is not the time to climb back into that hornets nest." I could feel muscles vibrate through her sweatpants. I reached into the glove box, found a tissue and handed it to her.

Steve slammed on the brakes at a red light. "Gil's right, Emma."

She sniffled and wiped at her eyes. "I know, but--"

He sped onto the freeway as the light turned green, and then said cheerily. "Look, let's let this all settle down a bit and when we come back for the photo shoot we can make new plans." He patted her left leg. "Much more sensible. What do you think?"

She sighed and slumped in the seat. "Yeah, maybe you're right. I guess so." She dropped her hand on top of Steve's and squeezed. "You know we shouldn't fly for at least twelve hours."

He turned his head. The car sped into the right lane and he jerked the car left and slid on the wet pavement. "Shit! Hang on. What?"

I slammed my shoulder against the window. "Whoa, Partner. Watch the driving."

"Sorry.' He had the car slowed down and under control. "I just—"

"We talked about that earlier; remember waiting twelve hours after a dive to keep from getting the bends." I looked at Emma. "I think it will be okay." I squeezed her leg. "What do you think?"

"Well," She placed her hand on mine. "I think that would give us time to go back, destroy the eggs, and then fly." She looked up at me and fluttered her eyelashes.

I tightened my grip. "No, that's not an option. Look, we've--"

"Okay, okay, I get the point. Let go of my leg." She shifted them toward Steve. "It's all problematic anyway. The plane is pressurized and as long as we don't lose cabin pressure, we shouldn't have a problem. We'll need to drink lots of water though," she smirked, "Without the scotch, hotshot."

Steve sighed and looked through the rain. "She is one complicated woman."

"No shit," I agreed.

The headlights reflected off the blackened roadway as we turned into the Avis rental return lot. Emma headed for the ladies room with hopes that a comb and a paper towel would make her presentable for the flight to Dallas.

"Hurry up, Girl, we're tight on our schedule," I called after her.

In the terminal, Steve shuffled and Emma tried to run in her oversize pants while I trotted behind. "It's a good thing we'll have time in Dallas to buy some clothes." I glanced at my traveling companions. "I hope nobody thinks you're with me." I laughed and slapped Steve on the shoulder.

He wheezed and looked back at me. "You're one to talk."

My camera case banged against my legs as we ran down the concourse, the last to board the 747. The flight attendants gave us a quick once-over.

"Here we are," I pointed, "seats one, two and three, first class." The attendant raised her eyebrows. Thank you National Geographic, I thought.

I awoke as we hit the runway in Dallas. Emma was still asleep, her head lolled against my shoulder. She smelled of saltwater. Her shirt had come unbuttoned and an unfettered breast lay against my right arm; I tucked her back in. I buttoned her shirt, but she woke, grinned at me and closed her eyes again. Steve was asleep across the aisle. The young woman who sat next to him, plugged in her headphones and turned up the volume to drown out the noise.

We purchased some decent clothing in the airport, hurried out the door and headed for concourse three. Emma grabbed my arm and pushed me against the wall.
"What--?"
She jammed her face next to mine and whispered, "Did you see her?"
I looked around. "See who?" I slipped my arms around her back and held her tight.
She shivered against me and for a moment couldn't speak. "The woman by the drinking fountain."
"I don't see anyone." I pushed her to arms length. "Emma, what the hell is going on?"
She pushed my arms down and turned to look across the busy concourse. "Nothing, I guess, sorry, I just--" Tears ran down her cheeks. "I thought--"
"It's okay. We left the monsters far away." I put my arm around her shoulder. "Come on, we have a plane to catch, and Steve is probably going nuts at the counter." I pulled her back out in traffic, looked around again and shivered.

Chapter 21

The flight would take three hours. "Where in the world is Belize, anyway," she said.

I reached over and pulled the brim of her hat down over her eyes. "It's a long way from the cold Pacific Northwest." I laughed as she pulled off the multi colored thing and swatted me with it.

"I'm serious, Gil. I know its somewhere in Central America, but I've never been that far south." She folded the hat and stuffed it next to the armrest.

I released my seatbelt and turned toward her. "It's just south of Mexico, here look." I pulled out the dog-eared in-flight magazine and pointed to the map. "See, here it is."

"And, why are we going to Belize?"

I traced a line down her leg from the bottom of her white shorts to the top of her ankle. "It's kind of a hangout for me and Steve. The sun always shines; the beaches have real sand, not of the rocky beaches you're used to, and the diving is world-class. We vacation down there almost every year. You'll love it."

She turned toward me, pulled the armrest up, kicked off her sandals and put her feet in my lap. She closed her eyes while I massaged her toes. "I'm loving it already," she sighed.

A short cab ride from the airport delivered us to the city docks in downtown Belize City.

Steve's rubber sandals stuck to the dock with each step. "Jesus H. Christ, it must be ninety-five degrees in the shade," he grumbled. "But look at that blue sky." He waddled ahead of us down the dock with three little Belizean boys in tow who pulled the luggage across the rough wooden planks. "Come on boys," he yelled back at them playfully. "We don't have all day."

I pulled Emma into the shade of a large trawler. "Let's have a shade rest for a minute. Okay?" I scooped her up from behind and licked the back of her neck. "Yum, you taste salty."

She danced out of my arms and into the sun, twirled like a ballerina, hat in hand. "You sit in the shade like an old man if you want. I'm gonna soak up as much sun as I can." She laughed and bounded down the dock, "Steve, wait up."

After resting a moment I trudged down the dock and caught up with them, parked my plastic camera case between them and sat on it. Steve was lecturing Emma.

"She's a forty foot oceangoing aluminum dive boat with two diesel engines; and she can almost fly," he bragged as if the boat were his.

Emma spread her arms wide and exclaimed, "Wow," and winked at me.

"She has a walk-through transom and can be piloted from the fly-bridge," Steve continued

"Wow!" Emma clapped her hands and spun in a circle. "I'm so excited."

He pulled his glasses off, took a handkerchief from his pocket and wiped at the sweat from his forehead. Steve turned to her and smiled, sheepishly. "You're screwing with me, aren't you, Little Lady."

She laughed, threw her arms around his neck and planted a kiss on his cheek. "I love it when you lecture, Steve."

Dave Kincade stood up on the flying bridge, leaned over the railing and called out, "Come on aboard." He swung over the railing and landed neatly on the deck near the open hatch. The hair on his massive belly sparkled with sweat and his long toes curled over the decks edge.

Emma stepped back and leaned toward me. "Who is that?"

"That gorilla," I gave her an affectionate swat and said, "is our host. He operates Winfred resort and he doesn't bite. At least I don't think he does." I waved. "Permission to come aboard, Captain."

He bellowed at the baggage boys. "Come on you two; get my ol' friend's gawd-damn luggage on board." He leaped onto the dock, plucked the suitcases from the youngsters and heaved them onto the deck. He spun and picked Steve up in a bear hug. "My buddy," he boomed. "I am so glad you're here."

"Easy, big guy! You're not half as glad as I am." Steve wriggled from the grip and stepped onto the boat.

"And you." He stared and then stopped in his tracks when he saw Emma by my side. "Whoa, and who is this lovely little thing?" His enormous paw pressed against my chest and I stumbled backwards and grabbed a light stanchion to catch my balance. Emma's hands were dwarfed inside his other paw, and she flushed, as he looked her up and down. His belly jiggled when he laughed and he said, "Young Lady, you take some advice from an old sailor like me and stay away from this bilge rat you're standing next to." He jabbed his thumb in my direction, "Big Dave here will take care of you."

I cleared my throat, "Dave, I would like to intro--"

He dismissed me with a wave, his attention never leaving Emma. "You can ride with me, Young Lady." He took her by the arm and helped her board. "We'll ride on the fly bridge and let the riffraff ride steerage."

"Well thank you, Dave." Emma curtseyed and stepped aside to make room beside her. "I am so tired of traveling with these here, boys." She batted her eyelashes in her best Scarlet O'Hara imitation.

A large brown pelican landed neatly on the rail beside our host and Dave chucked it under the beak and said, "Okay, Petey, you can ride with me and the lady on the fly bridge." He motioned Emma to the ladder to the top of the boat, seized the bird under his arm and said, "Petey, I would like to introduce you to, uh--"

Emma turned at the top of the ladder as Dave and the pelican began their ascent. She reached down and patted the bird on the head and said, "Hello Petey, I'm Emma. It's good to make your acquaintance."

Dave bounded up the remaining rungs. "Emma, Emma, Emma. A name right off the pages of the bible, I'm sure." He bowed, kissed the bird on top of its head and said, "Well, little lady, me and Petey are mighty happy to meet you." He dropped the bird on the settee behind the steering station, turned toward the dock and boomed, "Gil, Steve, you got all your gear stowed?" We nodded. "Alright, let those lines go."

Dave started the engines and we were off in a cloud of black smoke. The boat roared out of the harbor as Dave swung the boat right and left to avoid the coral reefs. I climbed the ladder to the fly bridge and sat with Emma beneath the bimini top while Dave kept a close watch on his course.

Emma leaned close to my ear. "Where did you meet this man?"

I cupped my hand behind her neck and said, "Steve and I met Dave many years earlier in El Paso, Texas. He was selling cars in a used car lot when we were passing through. Dave put the hustle on us to buy a used van. He had noticed our rental car filled up with our usual dive gear and persuaded us to take a look at the great deal he would make us on the van. To make a long story short, we didn't buy the van, but became fast friends with Dave."

"He looks like a native, except maybe for all that hair on his back." She fought the wind to keep her hat. The pelican dropped to the deck and stood between Dave's legs.

"He does now, but when we met him, he was a fat and broke with one foot in debtor's prison and the other on a wet banana peel. His ex-wife threatened to impound what little he did own. He begged us to take him to the Gulf with us, and we did." I held on to the seat stanchion with one hand as the boat bounced through the teal blue water.

Her hat still flapping, she gave up, and pushed it between the seat cushions before sitting on it. "So, how did he end up here?"

"Dave's a mechanical whiz. I got him a job with a friend in commercial diving and he just blossomed. He lost fifty pounds and now runs the resort."

The boat left the calm waters of the harbor and began its passage through the deep waters between the mainland and the reef islands. The swells built and whitecaps burst as the boat crushed them and sprayed warm Caribbean water over us. We held each other tightly as the boat broke free over the tops. I screamed into Emma's ear and pointed at the horizon. "Those are the Belize atolls, there. Can you see them?"

Grabbing her hat, she half stood and then was forced to sit and hang on. She nodded.

It wasn't long before the protection of the atolls smoothed the water and the boat rode easy. Emma stood, hat in hand and moved to stand with Dave. I eased myself down onto the hot deck behind them and closed my eyes. I tasted the salt on my lips and tried to forget where we'd recently come from. I felt warm and safe, but the thought of Catherine and sex pervaded my conscious daydream. I drifted back for just a moment to the Pacific Northwest--to cold rain, warm sex, and the smell of seawater and honeysuckle. I shook my head, opened my eyes, and looked up to see Emma looking down at me, smiling. Can all women read my mind I wondered? She turned back, dropped her hat to the deck, stood on the brim and listened to Dave.

Dave draped a muscular, brown arm around Emma's shoulder, and pointed toward his right. "Don't look at that deadhead; look a bit to starboard." He was jabbed a thick index finger to the right.

Emma shaded her eyes against the sun and squinted. "What am I supposed to be looking at?

"That's the Turneff Island group. Twenty miles of shoal water, configured like an hourglass. And, see over there?" He turned her head gently with the palm of his hand. "That's Winfred Island, about two points on your starboard."

"That's right?" She wrinkled her eyebrows and patted the side of her nose with her finger.

"No, it's called Winfred. Oh—you mean the direction? Yeah, starboard's right and port's left."

He looked at her and smiled mischievously. "I thought you great North westerners knew that kind of shit—pardon my

French." He laughed at her game. "Don't you worry your pretty little head, I'll take care of you." He pointed. "Look, dead ahead; that's the channel we need to stay in, to avoid the coral heads."

As I watched Emma, I could see the magical change that had taken place. The warm sunshine and easy company relaxed her, and took her mind off the problems we had left behind. She put her arm around Dave's neck and pulled his face down near hers and planted a wet kiss on his bushy cheek. "Where's our island, Dave?"

"See that little piss-ant harbor with the wooden dock, just ahead?"

"The island with the water tower?" The wind tossed her curls, and her hair shimmered off the many colored tresses.

"That's home, Baby."

Dave throttled down the powerful diesel engines and approached the dock slowly, then thumped against it. A dozen young, black men grabbed lines, swarmed aboard and began carrying supplies to the main resort. Steve slept through the hour-long trip, and now stood and stretched on the wet deck.

Dave shouted orders to his workmen. "Eli, I want the refrigerated stores carried up first and put away."

Eli, a young man, thick and swarthy, winked at us, then looked at Dave and scowled.

"He's my oldest," Dave's chest swelled, "but he thinks he's smarter than his old man. He could actually run the entire operation without me, but I'd never tell him that." Dave climbed down the ladder first. He offered Emma his hand. "Let's see if we can find y'all a place to bunk." His thick Texas accent rolled like sorghum.

Conch shells bordered the path that led from the boat dock to the main lodge. Mature coconut palms shaded the grounds and competed with lush bougainvillea awash in red and purple blossoms. The sand was white and swept clean. The spicy odor of cilantro, molasses and red-hot chilies floated out from the open door of the dining room. My stomach growled.

Emma stretched on tiptoe, nose in the air, like a hungry bear sniffing blueberries. "What is that wonderful smell?"

"Jerk chicken fried in coconut oil, new potatoes, fresh baked Belizean bread, with hot salsa and chips on the side." Dave proclaimed and rubbed his hands together.

Steve raced to the open door ahead of the rest of us.

"How about an ice cold Bombay and tonic on the veranda before dinner? We can catch up and then you can let me know what you require," Dave said as he guided Emma up the stairs to the veranda. "Step into the plastic wash water first, Emma."

Emma glanced at her feet quickly, and then at the three of us as. "This a joke?"

"Just an old Belizean custom, Sweetie." Dave pushed her to the side and stood in the plastic pan of water. "Keeps the sand on the beach, and off the floors."

We all stepped into the plastic pan, then stepped through the entry to the covered veranda and sat in wicker chairs. Ice-cold glasses were set before us and we all drank deeply.

"I think I'm in heaven," Emma whispered.

Dave belched, took another long swallow. "The resort's between bookings now and I've held two spacious rooms above the dining room, just in case we filled up early. The rooms share a common balcony and look out to sea." He belched again and said, "Will that work?"

"Two rooms will be perfect." I winked at Emma.

"Yes" she said. "I hope you boys enjoy sleeping together."

After dinner and too many gin and tonics, I slept the sleep

of the dead.

Steve was in the cot across the room. "Wake up, Partner," I called out, leaning up on my elbows. "Fresh bread and hot coffee; come on." He snorted and rolled over. I lay back in bed, draped in a sheet, wishing I were next door. I dreamt during the night, and although I didn't remember the dreams, the smell of seawater and honeysuckle permeated my senses. My body was covered with sweat, and as I pulled the sheet away, I half expected to find a mucus coating on my skin. I showered away the night memories, climbed into a pair of shorts, and joined Dave downstairs for coffee.

Steve and I planned to get organized in our combination workshop and office while Dave took Emma on a dive tour. A room behind the bar had been readied for me to print and systemize my photo collection for Steve's article. Steve planned to write and collate his notes on the balcony.

"Good morning, Gil. Grab yourself a cup o' Joe and sit down here." Dave said. He had on the shorts he wore the night before and puffed on a long fat cigar as he drank his coffee. I ambled toward the coffeepot and he called after me. "Emma's gone to the dive shop to pick out some gear. After breakfast we'll shoot over to Lost Cay and dive on the wall there."

"I'm jealous," I carried my coffee out on the veranda to join him.

"That little heifer has got some looks, my friend. And the way she tells it, she's a hell of a diver," he said. He leaned his head back and blew cigar smoke like a steam locomotive. "I might have to get a little closer and teach her some rope tricks or something, that is, if you don't mind." He gestured with his thumb and forefinger held in a circle. His lascivious smile stretched from ear to ear.

"It's okay with me, Dave, but I'll bet your mamma would cut off your balls and serve them to you, fried, for dinner if she found out."

The mention of his wife made him sit up straight and whisper. "Ain't that a fact? She'd cut off my balls if she ever caught me smoking, these here Havana's," he shrugged, "but a little dreaming never hurt nobody." He looked in the direction of the dive shop, "Here comes Emma now, and don't that wiggle just set your heart afire?" He tapped ash off the cigar.

Emma jogged down the beach toward us. She wore loose-fitting short-shorts and a brilliant blue tank top, which bounced wildly. She waved as she approached.

"Hey, Gil, I thought you guys were going to sleep all day. Where's Steve?" She stepped into the rinse water and climbed the steps to the deck as Steve walked out onto the veranda.

"Speaking of the Devil are we, lady and gentlemen?" Steve entered the room and sat down across from Dave. He stretched, then took off his glasses and cleaned them on the tail of his unbuttoned shirt. His stomach hung over his shorts and continued to vibrate after the rest of him became still.

Emma leaned over and kissed him on the cheek. "Coffee, Dear?"

"Yes Emma, please, and will you marry me?"

"Okay, but only if you're a virgin." She strolled into the kitchen and the screen door slammed behind her.

Dave piped in, "He may not be a virgin, but he's the closest thing you'll find around here; I goddamn guarantee." We could hear her chuckle in the kitchen. "After one more cup of coffee, Girl, we'll get to the boat."

The morning air was balmy. White, puffy cumulous clouds sailed across the blue sky. We would have a good day to start our work. Our yesterdays mercifully began to fade.

* * *

Work went well that day and continued through the next ten days. We settled into a routine. Steve, Emma, and I used Dave's twenty-foot open skiff to explore the reef around the Turneff group in the mornings, then worked in the afternoons. In the evenings we traded sea stories with the guests and drank anything alcoholic.

The diving was spectacular. Vertical walls plunged hundreds of feet and teemed with life, then disappeared into blackness. Sharks, barracuda, eagle rays, and sea turtles were our daily companions in eighty-six-degree water. Diving too deep was easy, and we had to monitor our dive computers continuously. I could lie on the bottom at 130 feet and still see the outline of the boat.

One day as Steve and I floated on the surface, I turned to him. "Emma is the most comfortable diver I have ever seen. She swims rings around us, dives deeper faster, and her underwater buoyancy is flawless."

"Yeah, I've been watching her." He rolled in the water and then floated on his back and looked at the sky. "She has been diving a lot longer than either of us, you know."

I rolled over onto my back. "She reminds me of a dolphin when she swims. You notice how she holds her legs together? I wish I could do that." I took off my mask. "I'd swear she's made of rubber." As I floated there in the balmy water, I began picturing images of those legs in the clouds and what I'd do with

175

them.

On one morning dive, we followed a large loggerhead turtle that swam lazily between coral heads. It dipped and then spiraled upward and used its flippers as if they were wings on an airplane. The barrel and basket sponges that sprouted from the side of the vertical wall were brilliant orange and green, some large enough that Emma would hide in them. Giant, green, moray eels slithered in and out of holes in the coral and dared us to catch them. In the deep water we could make out the shadowy black tip sharks that circled about in the deep, as if to decide whether or not we would make a good meal. Blue and green parrotfish argued with one another and their neighbors while they nibbled at the coral.

Steve discovered a rock structure he wanted to explore. Emma and I hovered at sixty feet and watched him. The structure was deep, and we had already been under water for forty minutes. Then, Steve was in trouble. He clasped his regulator in his hands and began shaking it, then looked at us and gave the out-of-air signal. Emma dove immediately, signaling me to wait. She dove straight to one hundred forty feet in seconds, thrust her spare regulator into Steve's mouth, and then helped him with a controlled ascent. They breathed off the same tank of air. My air was already low, but I stood by in the water in case they ran out of air from Emma's tank.

As they ascended, Steve's eyes were wide with the knowledge of what might have happened. I stayed close and drifted to the surface with them. Emma had the situation well under control.

Later that night as Steve and I worked on the article, Steve said to me in a quiet voice, "It was my good fortune to have

Emma with us today. I might have ended up as shark shit if she didn't have enough air to share with me."

"She was a dive instructor for years, Steve. She was operating on instinct. You're probably not the first one she's pulled up."

"My tank was empty, and that makes me stupid. I'm still kicking myself, but how much air did you come up with?" He had his glasses in hand, and wiped at them vigorously.

"I had two hundred pounds, why?" I shifted in my chair.

"Emma had <u>twenty-five</u> <u>hundred</u> pounds left after we surfaced." He looked away.

"That's impossible. You must have read the gauge wrong." I looked back at him and shook my head. "Oh no, Steve, you're jumping to conclusions. We saved her from that group, remember?"

Steve relented. "I could have read the gauge wrong. I was scared, even after we were back aboard, so, I guess it is possible."

"Goddammit, let's not borrow trouble, Steve. We're in paradise, man." I slapped him on the back. "I'll check for gill-slits behind her ears and write you up a report."

Steve stopped typing and turned to me. "Really? You'd do that?"

"No, no, I was kidding on the square, for Christ's sake. Relax."

However, I knew that I wouldn't be able to relax until I did.

Chapter 22

That night I made love to Emma on the polished wood floor in her room. We sat on the balcony with our gin and tonic; feet propped up on the railing, and talked about nothing and everything. The night was still; the moon hung in the sky as if suspended by God from a necklace of golden stars. Emma wore a long, silk shirt held together by two buttons; her exposed skin glistened. My blue shorts were damp from the humid air, and I shifted in my chair uncomfortably.

I took a sip of my drink and used the glass as a pointer as I lectured about the constellations. "Have you ever seen so many stars in one place?" I asked, condensation dripped from my glass and created a puddle on the railing.

"Never." She pulled the shirttails from between her legs, fanned them, and then let them settled over the top of her legs. She pointed to the sky with her glass and whispered, "I can almost see where the night sky touches the ocean." She shook her glass. The ice cubes clicked like barracuda teeth. "See, right there."

"Ummm," I rocked back on my chair and pointed to the moon. "You see how the crescent moon lies on its back and forms a perfect bowl."

She drank deeply and the moonbeams sparkled in the glass. "Yes, it does." She turned to me. "So?"

"That means it won't rain tomorrow." She cocked her head. "It's true. If the crescent were tipped so that its point were up or down, the bowl would not be able to hold water, and it would rain." I peeked over my glass at her.

She looked back up at the moon for a moment and then smiled. "I think that moon-bowl may not hold water tonight, but it may hold a lot of bullshit." She glanced at the moon and then looked at me. "You're kind of a romantic, Mr. McCrae, aren't you?"

"If we could read our future in the stars, it would go on forever." I swallowed the icy gin and sat the glass back on the railing.

Emma was more interested in the present. She placed her drink down next to the chair, stood and straddled my lap. I dropped my feet to the floor; gently placed my hands on her back and pulled her closer. She laid her head on my shoulder, licked my neck, and hummed in my ear softly. Her breasts pressed against my chest and I could feel the nipples harden. Her skin was moist, slippery, and smelled sweet. I kissed her ear and suckled on the lobe, my hand wound tightly in her soft curls.

"Looking for something behind my ear, Gil? You won't find it, but if you come into my room I'll show you everything I do have." Her voice was quiet and seductive. She took my hand, slid off my lap, pulled me up, and led me into her room. The fan circulated the air and caressed our bodies as we stood directly beneath it. I moved my hand in circular motions on her back in time to the rotation of the fan blades and kissed her eyes and nose and savored the sweet scent of her fluid skin. Her silk-covered breasts triggered goose bumps on the back of my neck as she stroked the hairs on my chest with her erect nipples.

"Undress me." She whispered so softly that her words were barely audible.

I unbuttoned her shirt and let it drop to the floor, then kneeled in front of her. I took a hardened nipple into my mouth and suckled on it. She grasped me by both ears and rotated her hips into my chest. She hummed again in time with her movement and thrust her hips, increasing the tempo; the hum became louder, and more agitated. With both hands I squeezed her buttocks; she collapsed into my lap and together we fell to the floor.

"Make love to me, Gil," she cried out. "Oh, God, I need you." She tore at my shorts. "Hurry, Gil. I need you inside me, now."

We slipped in the sweat that pooled beneath our bodied as we tried to find purchase on the wood floor. Somehow my shorts were at my knees. I kicked them off. My mind lost its focus and my body desperately tried to find solace in the dark recesses of Emma's body.

"Yes, yes," I cried out as her hand guided me into her. Silky legs encircled my waist and I was forced deep inside. She bucked and thrust herself on my shaft again and again, as her moans changed to breathless gasps. Abruptly she stiffened, tightened her legs around me, and wailed, "McCrae" in a long, drawn out exhalation of pure pleasure.

I was wracked with waves of ecstasy as I filled her with my hot seed.

We lay on the floor in the center of the room for a long time, content to let the ceiling fan dry the sweat from our bodies. The moonlight danced on our skin and we lay entwined; one body still connected flesh to flesh, wet with each other's desire.

"Don't leave me," she whispered. She scratched my back in tender circular motions until I sighed and closed my eyes. She hummed in time with her motions and I felt her jaw vibrate against my shoulder. "McCrae, she purred; what shall become of us?"

I pulled out of her and rolled to my back and groaned, "I'm not going anywhere."

"Oh, no. No. I told you not to leave me." She curled onto her side, away from me and folded her hands between her legs. She giggled and then straightened before she turned over toward me and laid her arm across my chest. "That was fun. Can we do it again?" She grabbed one of the scattered pillows and placed it under my head. "Right now?"

I exhaled. "Give me a couple minutes." I leaned toward her and kissed her on the nose. "Maybe later," I reached around her and traced my finger along the curve of her back. She stiffened.

"What are you looking for now, Gil, scales?" She pushed my arm away.

"I'm sorry. You're a bit touchy. I was just--"

"You just what? You just thought maybe I was one of those monsters?" Her voice shook. "I don't think you completely understand what we're dealing with here." She turned her back to me. Those women are cold-blooded killers."

"I said I was sorry, Emma." I tried to pull her to me, but she shoved my hands away, and then rolled away from me. She stood and then sat on the edge of the bed.

"You just don't understand." Elbows on her knees, she brushed the curls from her eyes.

I sat up and clenched my hands into fists. You're right, I don't fucking understand. Like I don't understand how you came

181

up with 2500 pounds of air, and Steve's cylinder was empty? I also don't understand why these mermaids need to consume human flesh." I stood and walked in front of her. I placed my hands on my hips and glared. "Tell me!"

She looked at me all traces of anger gone, and then began to laugh.

"What's so funny?" Arms wide, I stepped back She continued to laugh.

"What?"

"If you only could see yourself." Her gentle laugh had turned into a belly laugh. She pointed a finger at my mid-section and howled.

I moved forward, grabbed her by the shoulders and shook her, but she only laughed harder. "What is it?" I cried. Realization dawned; I let go of Emma, covered my groin with both hands and began to laugh. "What am I laughing for?" I plopped onto the bed beside her and continued to chuckle.

She gasped for air and then doubled over and held her stomach, her breasts bounced like puppies on a trampoline. "If you could have just seen…"

I pushed her backwards on the bed so she lay on to her side and swatted her butt.

"I'm sorry, Gil, but you looked so funny." Her breathing had slowed, but her smile threatened to bring on more laughter. "Gil, when you were standing in front of me, with your hands on you hips, and your dick bouncing in front of my eyes; I just couldn't stay serious. I wish you could have seen it."

I lay down next to her and said, "I'm glad I didn't." We watched the moonlight shimmer through the louvered window at the foot of the bed, and play across our naked skin. I lifted my head and licked the salty nipple. She shivered and pulled away.

She took a deep breath. "Look Gil, the Sisterhood on Bainbridge Island is just one chapter of descendants of the original Scottish Sisterhood. There are others in England and Western Europe, as well as a small chapter in Vermont, I believe."

"Are they all alike, with a--you know, scales and such?"

"I believe that the Sisterhood is basically the same everywhere. The main difference is Catherine." She propped her head on her elbow and looked toward the louvered window. Moonbeams painted zebra stripes across her face and then she lay back down. "Catherine came to the island five years ago from somewhere in Great Britain."

"I didn't notice an accent, or--"

"No one seems to know where she actually came from. The Sisterhood on Bainbridge consisted of a few women who had the capability to become mermaids, but had lost the skills to practice their arts. When Catherine moved to the island, she identified the women and began to show them where their potential lay. It wasn't long before the chapter was in full swing. The women worship her."

"How do you know all this? I mean-- the Sisterhood is some kind of secret society, isn't it?" A cloud covered the moon and in the darkness I moved closer to her. "I feel like a kid listening to a ghost story, around the campfire. Did these women tell you they were mermaids, or what?" I ran a finger up and down her arm.

Emma spoke in a whisper, and I leaned in closer. She smelled of sex, and it excited me.

"I told you that the captain and I co-owned the dive shop. We knew that some of the women divers were exceptional. They could do things underwater that I never dreamed of. There were three women who lived together, had very well paying jobs, but seemed uninterested in dating men. I simply thought they were lesbians." She raised her leg and lay it across mine. "You met Lois. She was one of the original divers that I thought was extraordinary. We became friends. She told me about the Sisterhood, and the changing and all the rest of it. Like you, I thought it was a bunch of nonsense. It was none of my business." Emma shimmied across the bed, stood and walked to the balcony then leaned against the railing, and looked out at the stars.

I stood, moved behind her and nestled her in my arms. "What about the captain?"

"The captain is a Scot. He grew up on one of the offshore islands in Scotland and he knew of the legends of the Sisterhood. When Catherine moved in, she immediately sought him out. Before I knew what was happening, the captain was sleeping with Catherine and the other women. She bought out his interest in the dive shop and forced me to sell my half."

"Forced you, how?"

Emma sighed. "She offered to buy me out. Said if I didn't sell, she would start a new shop and take the captain with her. Made me an offer I couldn't refuse." Her laugh was dry.

"So the captain's a McCrae?" I nibbled on her neck.

"Don't start feeling too special just yet, Mister McCrae. The captain's blood was good enough for breeding, something about the characteristics of the Scot's blood, but they needed to enhance the bloodline to increase the strength in their offspring." She turned around. "That's where you come in." She wriggled against me and sighed as I pulled her tight to me.

"It's good to know I'm special." I moved my hands up to her breasts and played with her still-hard nipples. She pulled my hands away and down to her waist and held them tight.

"The other reason, that you were a godsend to Catherine and the Sisterhood is because the captain was getting old." She brushed her palms up my arms "He was getting tired of screwing the women, and wanted out. There was a rumor he had some prostate problems and I think he was just ready to retire. The Sisterhood needed a new soldier, and you were going to be that new soldier." She yawned and stretched. Her muscles rippled in the near-darkness as I pressed against her. The railing creaked and the onshore wind ruffled the palms. Coconuts cracked against each other before they thumped to the hard packed sand below. The wind carried the warm sweet smell of tropical saltwater. I inhaled deeply.

"What about the killing," I asked.

She loosened her grip and turned toward the freshening wind and gazed out to sea. "The taking of human flesh is an old Druid notion. It signifies that when you eat the heart of your enemy, you gain his strength, becoming twice as strong. Catherine either believes that eating human flesh is beneficial, or she has simply developed a taste for murder.

Her delicious bottom rubbed against me and interrupted my thought processes. I moved back slightly and gulped in the warm air.

She cocked her head. "The little head thinking again?" She giggled and continued. "The women of the Sisterhood have the gene that gives them the ability to become mermaids. They don't need to eat human flesh. None of the other modern-day chapters that I know of take human life." She arched her body back against me, placed her lips to my ear. "Don't let them take you. I think I'm in love with you."

I kissed her nose then scooped her up and brought her back to the bed where I laid her gently down in the center. I kissed her lips, her neck and then moved down until I made contact with her breasts. "You're so beautiful," I whispered.

"Mmmm. Not now," she whispered. She pushed me aside and stood up, then reached down for my hand to pull me up. "Shower time, Big Guy," she declared. As I stood, she grabbed onto my erection and tittered, "Maybe a cold shower for the little guy. What do you think?"

* * *

The next morning at breakfast we received the message I had hoped in the back of my mind would never come.

"The hatchlings are showing signs of imminent release. Within three days, they will all be out. Expect to see you soon. Love, Catherine." The note was an e-mail and was deposited on my plate before breakfast. I read it twice and then handed it to Steve. He read it glumly, handed it back, and finished his eggs.

"We need those hatchling pictures pretty bad, don't we, Steve? I said.

"Yes we do, but I don't think we need them bad enough to put your life in jeopardy. We can hire a local photographer out of Seattle for a quick photo job." Steve set down his fork.

"No, Partner, I have to finish this job. There's no reason for anyone to believe that I'm connected to Emma. No one saw us escape. I'll jump on a flight tonight, be on the island tomorrow evening and shoot Wednesday, and if necessary, Thursday. I can be back here by Saturday with all the photos to finish the project. Piece of cake." I swallowed my coffee in one gulp.

Steve wiped his lips with his napkin and then began on his glasses. "I'll go with you and keep your sorry butt out of trouble,"

"No, no, no" I argued. "You'll just be in the way, and besides you have a ton of text to finish up. By the time I'm back we should be ready to put this whole thing together. Then we can relax and put this all behind us. Besides, aren't the kids due here on the fifteenth?"

"The seventeenth. Are you sure you'll be all right?" He searched for something in his coffee cup and avoided my eyes.

"I'm serious Steve; I'll shoot the hatchlings and be back on Saturday."

"What about Emma?" He shook his head. "She's going to be one pissed off woman."

I reached across the table for some toast. "Oh, don't worry about her. We have an understanding." I picked up my knife. "Would you pass me the butter?"

* * *

"You're going to fly back to the island over my dead body!" Emma screamed at me as she flew down the beach.

Her hands balled into fists as she neared me, and I backed into the water. She had slept late and was fresh from the shower, her hair still dripping, a terrycloth robe tied hurriedly around her middle. She waded right into the water, grabbed my shoulders, and thrust her face into mine and whispered, "They don't need you, Gil, but they need your sperm and they will do anything they need to in order to have access to a fresh supply. They are building up the Sisterhood and they can't afford to let you leave again." She quieted down, but her body trembled. "There will be no arguing with me on this point."

"Okay," I said. "I won't go today and we can discuss a

new plan at dinner. Maybe we can figure out another way to get those shots. I'm not keen to get back into forty-six-degree water." I patted her on the shoulder and walked her back to the resort.

Once in our room, she turned to me and said, "I'm sorry I jumped you. I am just so scared. Promise me you'll wait until we can plan a little better." She moved close and wrapped her arms around my back. I slipped my hands beneath the wet robe. Her skin was cool and silky. She squirmed away. "Later."

"Okay, you go get dressed, and I'll go get to work." I left her sitting in front of the mirror. I went down to the dock and jumped on the re-supply boat headed for Belize City.

***

I felt guilty all the way and worried that Steve would feel the brunt of her anger when she discovered I was gone. I wasn't used to explaining myself to women, and in this case, I concluded I knew best. Emma would have demanded that she accompany me to Bainbridge Island, and would have become a liability.

I couldn't stand the thought of her in the hands of the Sisterhood. The Sisterhood knew that she was their enemy, but knew very little about me.

I believed that if all the facts were to come to light, this Sisterhood would prove to be a women's organization like any other but that they went to some extremes in order to keep it interesting. What was the harm? There were the missing divers, but divers go missing all the time. The women got together and held their little rituals, tied a man up, conjured up a little kinky sex. Emma explained to me herself that a jury would laugh me right out of court if I had the bad sense to take it that far. I rationalized it was too many women on one small island fighting amongst themselves, that was probably the answer. In retrospect, I really should have known better.

The boat landed hard against the dock. The captain screamed at his deckhands as I jumped to the dock and hailed a cab. I would have plenty of time to consider the sisterhood problem, on the plane ride back to Seattle, and even more time to dream of Emma.

Chapter 23

The two-hour flight from Belize to Miami arrived with enough time to catch the red-eye out. The jet rumbled into the night sky and I fell asleep on the flight to Seattle. At touchdown, we were greeted by forty-degree weather and light rain.

It was late so I rented a car and drove two hours through the night. I entered the island on the north end via Agate Pass Bridge. Once checked into the only motel on the island, I shivered to sleep dreaming of white sandy beaches and cold English gin.

I awoke at nine-thirty to more rain and wind, pulled the frayed blankets over my head and tried to re-kindle my warm water dreams. Raindrops pelted the window and I sat up, kicked off the blankets and groaned when my feet hit the cold floor. "Coffee; I need coffee." I bundled up and ran to the coffee shop across the parking lot.

"Coffee, Sir?"

"Yes please, black." The wind and rain held my attention through the window. The waitress mumbled something and hurried away. I pulled off the windbreaker and jammed it between the wall of the booth and my leg, felt the cushion sag and twisted my head around as Catherine sat down beside me.

"Hey, soldier, you ready to dive yet?" She took off a red baseball cap. "Nice day today, don't you think?"

My heart skipped a beat. "Hey, Girl, does it ever stop raining here?" I pulled my windbreaker out and tossed it to the seat opposite, scooted over and turned in the booth to face her. "How did you know I'd be here?"

She leaned in, kissed me on the cheek and winked. "Drumbeats," she whispered.

"Hmmm, I'll bet. Coffee?"

She shook her hair like an Irish setter and sprayed me with cold droplets. The gray-blue color in her eyes sparkled and she grinned a crooked smile. "No, thanks." I felt her vibrate when her shoulder came into contact with mine. "I can't tell you how exciting the hatching has been," she said out of breath. "I bet I look a fright." She grabbed a napkin and wiped at the flush in her face.

"Are you alright?" I touched her hand. "Damn, Catherine, you feel as if you have a fever." I placed my hand on her forehead. "You're burning up."

She pushed my hand away. "No, no, I'm just excited about showing you the babies." Hurry and finish your coffee."

"The baby wolf eels?'

She nodded.

The coffee arrived and I took a quick swallow. Her excitement was contagious. "Okay, just a little--"

"Finish your coffee, and get your act together. You should be able to get a lot of shots of the hatching today." She brushed the hair out of her eyes. The weather had transformed it into a brier patch. I thought I saw tiny pieces of seaweed clinging to the curls. "Bad hair day." She said.

"It looks good," I lied. "A new do?" She ignored me.

"The boat's ready whenever you are. I've got gear on board and the captain's sober." She looked into my eyes for a moment. "It's good to see you back." She placed her hand on my leg and squeezed.

I was so enthralled, I forgot all about the tales of mermaids and kidnapping. I just wanted to dive and see this miracle myself and capture it on film.

"I'll just finish breakfast, grab my camera gear from the motel, and meet you at the dock."

"Yes, we must dive today, and I'll make you dinner tonight. Okay?"

"Deal," I agreed. Electricity sparkled from her fingertips.

She was up and gone as quickly as she had arrived and left behind a residual aroma of honeysuckle and seawater. She waved from outside, and then disappeared into the gray mist. I looked out the window again half expecting her to be standing there again. A sensation coursed through me and made me uneasy, but I couldn't quite put my finger on it. I sensed she was near and that impression lingered on through breakfast. Something itched inside the back of my skull.

***

I picked up my camera gear and hurried to the public dock. Even the relentless rain didn't dampen my enthusiasm for the upcoming dive and photo shoot. The Spirit waited as I parked my car beneath the canopy of an enormous Madrona tree. Except for the dive boat, the dock was vacant. Little wisps of blue smoke puffed out of her stack as she stood, bending from side to side. Like Catherine, the Spirit radiated life and enthusiasm. I could feel her beckon me to come aboard and begin a new adventure. I slung my camera gear on my shoulder and stepped over the transom.

"Permission to come aboard," I sang out, ducked my head and sidestepped forward under the cabin top. The gear Catherine told me about was onboard, neatly arranged.

The captain eased himself through the cabin door and called out. "Welcome aboard. What the fuck took you so long?" He smiled amicably and grabbed my upper arm and propelled me into the heated cabin. "Good to see you. Sit down and have a cup o' Joe and tell me some lies about diving in Belize." He hoisted himself into the captain's chair and handed me a cup of black, thick mud and continued before I had a chance to speak. "Catherine went up to the store to get some bread because she was too busy to bake any last night." He spit into a plastic cup that teetered on the dashboard.

"How'd you even know I'd be in town today?" I took a tentative sip of coffee. "I didn't have time to notify you when I'd arrive." I winced and put the cup next to the stove to cool down. "Drumbeats?"

The captain laughed. "There's not much goes on around this fuckin' island that Catherine don't know about."

I swallowed hard. "So, how's the Spirit?" Coffee grounds adhered to the tip of my tongue.

"Just got her out of dry-dock. Painted her bottom up good, changed zincs, and changed fuel filters. She's a happy little girl." A big grin crossed his face as he patted the cabin bulkhead. "She was feeling a little down, what with the barnacles growing on her bottom and a fouled filter. We're a hundred percent now."

The captain's speech was animated when he spoke of his boat, as if she was an extension of his own being. An eerie feeling surfaced in my mind at that moment, that if the Spirit ever sank, her captain might die. He loved the boat and treated her as if his life depended on it.

"Ahoy there, you dive rats! Let's get this show on the road." Catherine bounded over the transom with fresh bread cradled in her arms like a newborn baby.

The captain sighed and stood, "Hold that spring line, Catherine, so's we can motor her out of here in the wind."

I hurried aft and let go the stern line while the captain worked the boat ahead and into deeper waters. Catherine jumped next to me, kissed me on the cheek, and disappeared into the galley with her bread. Moments later as the boat turned and headed out of the harbor she danced out of the galley with two fresh cups of coffee.

"Here, try this." She winked.

I watched her accelerate from one end of the wet deck to the other, coffee cup in hand as she checked quickly through the gear and then sat across from me and put her cup on the bench. I took a deep breath for her. "We all set?"

"Here's the dive plan," She said matter-of-factly. "We'll be back on the Devil's Boulder today. We want to take it slow and easy so we don't frighten Mom, Dad and the kids. We'll hang on to the anchor line and descend, check our buoyancy, and then drift slowly up to the den. I guess I don't need to tell you what your camera settings should be, but don't shoot until I tell you to." Her knit cap was a size too large and slipped forward and covered her eyes. She pushed it back with a quick flip of her hand. "We'll have plenty of time to shoot, so you can pick your shots. We start back up with five hundred pounds. Got all that?" She took the hat off, tossed it aside, and pulled her hair through an elastic tie.

"Got it," I said. "What about current?"

She sipped her coffee and looked over the brim. "Don't worry about anything except your photos." She looked passed me and nodded. "I'll take care of you."

We suited up as the boat rounded the entrance buoy that marked the turn out of the harbor. The rain fell and beat a tattoo on the cabin roof. Although the wind had settled, swells lifted the boat up and then gently sat her back down again. A ferryboat passed on our port side. Her car deck loaded and created a bow wake that she pushed ahead of her. The Spirit climbed up the ferry's wake and dropped noisily down into the trough.

I could hear the captain muttering, "Slow that cocksucker down, for Christ's sake."

Soon the boat hung easily on her anchor. She drifted smoothly in a circle and found a comfortable place to settle. I looked up at the gray clouds as the captain hoisted my tank assembly onto my back.

"Don't worry; it's not raining down there. And while you're gone, I'll talk to God and see if we can't get some sunshine up here for you when you get back aboard. I'll tell him you pussy divers from the South Seas just can't stand the cold weather." He laughed, spat tobacco juice onto the dive step, and slapped me on the back. "You're all set, Son."

I plunged into the cold, black water, and then bobbed to the surface to await Catherine. She pitched in headfirst and signaled me to follow her to the anchor line. "Damn, this water's cold," I whined to myself. My face burned then grew numb as we descended. I held tight to the anchor line and slid my hands over its rough surface.

We had dropped only thirty feet and I could make out the rocky formations outlining this majestic underwater city. Free falling in slow motion, I watched the city grow larger as we descended into its bowels. An enormous gray lingcod eyed us suspiciously as we came too close to her egg case. A chubby capezon lumbered by, intent on getting someplace quickly in this slowed-down world. Catherine glided ahead of me and casually negotiated around rocky corners and colonies of massive white anemone.

We dropped onto the ledge that led into a dark tunnel, and she stopped and lowered herself onto the black rock. She turned her halogen light on and signaled me to follow her in, as before, like a blind man who must pick his way along a crowded cobblestone street. Her light was my only guide. I sensed that other eyes followed our progress through this nightscape and could not shake the sensation. We entered into the main cavern, and Catherine's powerful light illuminated the enclosure. My eyes encountered a scene that I had never witnessed, nor was I sure I ever would again. At least two-dozen young, wolf eels, reddish-orange in color, swam in zigzag circular patterns. The parent eels extended half way out of their den. They weaved, gyrated, and danced to silent music as their young swam between them. I was repulsed and fascinated, for they reminded me of snakes slithering among one another so I retreated. Catherine swam up to the den, pulled out her goodie bag and was immediately engulfed in eels that squirmed and sashayed, their jaws snapping up morsels. To my surprise, the parent eels receded into the edge of their den and let the young feed while they watched. Catherine signaled for me to begin shooting. I moved in and framed my shots. When I finished my roll, I switched to camera number two. Catherine pointed to the backside of an escarpment in the cavern. I swam up to it, and looked over the top. Two giant eels instantly challenged me. Their jaws opened and snapped inches from my face. Catherine swam between us and embraced the eels. She motioned for me to look closely, and to be ready to shoot. Behind the escarpment, attached to the rock, was an egg case containing hundreds of light gray eggs the size of marbles. I could see where many at the top of the case had already hatched, the tiny eggs broken and uninhabited. In as many as a dozen eggs I could see movement where the eggs were transparent and new life was imminent. I shot again and again until the roll was finished and Catherine tugged on my arm. I wished I could linger, if not to photograph the rest of the hatching, at least to witness it, but it was time to ascend.

We surfaced together near the <u>Spirit</u>, signaled the captain we were all right, and swam to the dive step. Once on the boat I could not contain my excitement as the reality of what I had witnessed washed over me. "I can't believe I shot those hatchlings interacting with the parent eels." I laughed and danced around the wet deck with my camera cradled in my arms. "Steve won't believe this. We had no idea we would be able to photograph the eels together in a goddamn family portrait. It's like winning the lottery for a photographer." I slipped and then caught my balance.

"Here, give me that fuckin' camera before you drop it." The captain pried the camera from my arms and submersed it in fresh water. "Let's see if we can keep the salt from eating it."

"I thought Mama was going to bite my head off when I looked at her egg case," I grinned so hard my face hurt. I bent and checked my dive computer. "We were only down there twenty minutes." I stood. " It seemed like an hour. Wow."

The captain leaned over the side of the boat and spit into the water. He slapped me on the back and said, "Relax a minute, Son, I'll put on the soup so's you'll have strength for the next dive."

I sat back on the bench, wedged my elbows over the gunwale and stretched out my back. Catherine quietly changed our tanks.

"You're awfully quiet, is everything okay, Catherine? You look beat." I twisted my head from side to side.

"What's that?" She jerked her head around. "I'm sorry, I was light years away." She finished my tank and clipped it into the tank holder on the stern.

I leaned forward with my arms on my knees. I said, "You look beat. Is everything all right?"

"Yes, I'm okay. I was just thinking how proud the parents were of their little family. I wish I could have stayed a bit longer, you know. It's nice to be part of a family; it makes you feel kind of warm. Does that make sense to you? Maybe it's just my biological clock ticking." She stood on the deck, hands on hips and stared intently at me when the captain walked out with a tray filled with bowls of soup.

"Bean and bacon soup for a cold day." The captain beamed as he placed the tray between us on the wet deck. "Eat two bowls and it'll keep you warm tonight, too." He started to laugh, choked on his tobacco, and spat it over the side with, "Goddamn it to hell anyway."

The soup was hot, spicy, and delicious. He served it with warm honey wheat bread that dripped with butter. We ate in silence under the covered deck and looked out into the gray day and calm water. The rain had abated and the swells calmed, but mountainous clouds promised downpours later.

"Piss on a platter." The captain spoke quietly, looking to the east.

"What's that?" I looked up at the captain.

"That's when the water gets that oily look before a big storm. Piss on a platter, no doubt about it."

Catherine smiled and shook her head. She stood up, grabbed the captain by the mustache. Then nose-to-nose she declared loudly, "You know, Cap, one day we're going to get a high class client on this boat and they're going to have a heart attack and fall over dead the first time you open your mouth." She let go and kissed him on the forehead.

"What the fuck did I say now?" He twisted his mustache. He continued to mumble and picked up the empty dishes and stomped into the galley.

Catherine sat back down. "Okay, Soldier, we've got about twenty more minutes of surface time until we get wet again. Let's go over the dive plan. We won't bother the family again, but I've got another jewel for you. I've been watching a female octopus on her eggs, and they've started to hatch." She removed her hair tie, rung out the water and replaced it. "You can get some great shots today. I know you're here for the eels, but we can't disturb them again today--maybe tomorrow." She grabbed a towel from the bench and tossed it near the stack. "That okay with you?"

"Okay by me, so what's the plan?" I stood and looked over the stern.

"The plan is to dive the same site and give you a tour of what the Devil's Boulder is really all about. Simple plan; follow me; start up to the surface at five hundred pounds. Make sure you increase your strobe power if you can because we'll be going into some dark holes." She skipped into the galley, then back out on the wet deck with a cup of coffee for me.

We stepped into the water for our second dive. I noticed little wavelets had begun to form on the surface of the heretofore, calm water.

The captain leaned over the gunwale and shouted to us before we descended. "Don't you stay down there forever! Wind's picking up; it's going to start blowin', soon."

"We'll be up in forty minutes or less," Catherine shouted, and then we dropped.

Catherine was inverted and dove without a pause. She righted herself with a forward flip and contacted the bottom and touched neatly on the tips of her fins. I arrived beside her and looked at my depth gauge—130 feet. I said to myself. "Do this right, Gil, or you'll make a long decompression stop on the way back."

We stood on a rock that was as large as a garage. Catherine kicked off and I followed her across a boulder field that resembled a giant's marble playground. As we swam around and over them, I marveled at the abundance of fish, much like those found in an aquarium, so plentiful they bumped into each other. This must be a spear fisherman's paradise, I thought; or if the stories had any truth, a spear fisherman's graveyard. I shivered involuntarily. The large, white, plumose anemone decorated the tops of the boulders and waved their long, stocky bodies in unison with the movement of the current. Orange sea pens nodded at us from the silty bottom and red and white scallops clapped their shells and flew like butterflies between the pens, then up and over the monolithic boulders.

As we approached the 'city' from the north, the rocky reef soared sixty feet over our heads. Some of the rocky inclines were vertical; others rose in plateaus or obtuse angles, forming wide cracks. We ascended halfway up to one of the plateaus to a small cave; its maw opened and invited us to enter.

The interior was black and Catherine turned on her light and swam in. She summoned me to follow, so I swallowed the lump in my throat and proceeded into the cave entrance. My throat was dry, and I thought a cold beer would taste pretty good.

The cave was a tunnel that twisted and turned; other branches led off in different directions. I lost sight of the glow of Catherine's light as she turned, but picked it up again when the tunnel straightened. The tunnel ended in a massive cavern, and as Catherine swung her light in a 360-degree circle, it reminded me of an enormous book repository with hundreds of ledges; each ledge harbored a small cave; a resident octopus occupied each cave. We were in octopus heaven.

Catherine knelt on the floor of the cave and waved me to her. She had already explained on the Spirit that my flash would have to be concentrated in a small area. To shoot photos with my flash in the center of this cavern occupied by hundreds of octopus would invite trouble. I had already learned that octopuses were easily agitated by a strobe. She pointed to a ledge high on the wall and motioned me to follow her.

We slowly ascended to a niche that I thought was unoccupied; stones covered the entrance. Catherine moved the stones with care, so that a three-foot hole was revealed into the entrance of yet another cave. She signaled for me to look inside and prepare to shoot. I took her light and edged forward to peer over the lip.

Inside, lurked an enormous octopus, which occupied the entire space. Its tentacles stretched about one another in constant movement. Hooked to the ceiling in the center of the cave hung thousands of rice-size, white eggs strung together. The female octopus waved her tentacles and circulated water around the eggs. She ignored me while I watched her. I shot timidly once, and then peered in again to see what her reaction might be. She was unconcerned and concentrated on the care of her eggs.

I noticed hundreds of tiny, fully formed octopuses that swam helter-skelter around the eggs. They were no more than one-half-inch long. I knew that the mother octopus would soon die, starved to death, after her offspring hatched. The sight of the beautiful tiny octopus was awesome and I snapped off another roll of film.

As I shot, I recalled sitting in on a lecture given by Steve, sponsored by National Geographic. He spoke of octopus that could reach sizes of up to twenty-feet in length and weighed over two hundred pounds. I looked about with trepidation, and wondered if one of those giants lurked nearby. He'd said that, "The octopus lives only six or seven years and that the female usually dies after the eggs hatch. They feed on crabs and other shellfish." I saw no evidence of their prey here.

I looked behind me to see Catherine levitating in mid-water tapping her gauges. It was time to go. She followed another tunnel out of the main cavern. My shoulders scraped the sides as we moved through the passageway. This way was much shorter than the tunnel we had entered through. We exited on the side of a vertical wall, sixty feet from the surface. I had five hundred pounds of air left. We had spent considerable time at depth, so stopped for a mandatory safety stop at fifteen feet to off-gas any residual nitrogen in our bloodstream.

While we were suspended, I watched Catherine's regulator exhaust. Very few bubbles trickled from her regulator, which meant that she either wasn't breathing, or that she was out of air. I took her gauges in my hand, as she watched. Her gauge read 2800 pounds. My gauge read 250 pounds. I looked into her eyes, dropped her gauges and proceeded to surface.

     I did not mention the air discrepancy to her on the trip back to the dock. What could be said, after all.

     "I'll pick you up for dinner at eight, casual." She winked at me as the <u>Spirit</u> left me on the dock and chugged happily home.

Chapter 24

Back in the motel room, I lay down exhausted on the lumpy bed. It was only five o'clock but I needed to close my eyes for ten minutes or so I switched on the bathroom fan and opened the tiny window above the tub. "Must be a smoking room," I grumbled and fanned the door a couple of times. Raindrops drummed against the window and headlights flickered against the heavy, maroon draperies as cars passed through the parking lot.

I awoke startled as two tiny hands shook my shoulders and a voice beseeched me, "Wake up, nap time is over, dinner's waiting."

"Emma?" I struggled to sit up and rubbed my eyes.

"No, Baby, it's only me." Catherine smiled her crooked smile. She swatted me. "You trying to hurt my feelings?"

"What time is it?" I said. My eyes were filled with gravel. I pushed her arms away and swung my feet to the floor.

"It's time for you to take a shower, Soldier, you stink. Hurry up. I'll bring you a cup of coffee." She stood and headed for the door.

When she was outside, I stripped off my clothes. She was

right and a shower, sounded good.

****

We headed out of town in Catherine's Jeep Cherokee. The evergreen landscape on the south end of the island looked as if it might drown. Large tree limbs hung heavy, saturated with moisture; green needles turned black. Puddles in the road surface marked potholes the Cherokee seemed unable to avoid. Traffic was light and soon the two-lane road narrowed to a gravel drive that sloped down toward the water. The trees trunks, as big around as the Cherokee lined the road on either side.

"I thought you were cooking dinner tonight?" I said. I looked around and saw nothing but forest. "Where are we going?"

"Some of the local divers are having a little potluck dinner to celebrate winter solstice tonight. I thought you'd like to join in. That's okay with you, isn't it?" She kept her eyes on the narrow track as it twisted through the old growth forest.

"Yeah, sure, I suppose so. Who are the other divers?" I kept my voice steady.

"A women's dive club from the island," she said sweetly. "I think you might have met some of the members." She shifted into low gear.

I reached for the ignition key, but in the same instant her hand snaked around my wrist and held it a steel vise. "This is not a great idea, Catherine." I tried to break her grip, but it was no use.

She sighed and released me. "Don't do this, Gil."

I massaged my wrist and stared out the window. "I thought we were having dinner together. I don't like surprises."

205

She stopped the car and turned off the ignition, turned toward me and said, "Relax Gil, you're in no danger. The house we're having dinner at is the safest place in the world for you." She drummed her fingers on the steering wheel. "I know the stories you must have been told and I know that you are afraid right now. Relax, have dinner with us, and listen to my sisters this evening. Ask any questions and they'll be answered truthfully. Trust me, Gil, if I had wanted you hurt I would have let you drown this morning in the tunnels." She removed her right hand from the steering wheel, placed it in my lap and looked at me. "You're a McCrae; I'll protect you with my life."

I was still apprehensive as we continued down a driveway, which eventually terminated in front of a large, two-story home. The home was part of a waterfront estate.

"This is where Lois lives," Catherine explained. "You met her at the shop; she also untangled an octopus from around you." She patted my leg. "Do you remember?"

I nodded. We got out of the Cherokee and walked through the rain to the front entrance. Lois opened the door wide and before I could retreat, surrounded me with her arms, planted a long, wet kiss on my startled mouth.

"Welcome to my web, said the spider to the fly." She pulled me through the door into a two-story foyer.

"Don't start, Lois." Catherine said through her crooked smile. "He's ready to bolt at the drop of a hat."

Lois ushered me into a large, formal living area carpeted in dark blue. The alabaster walls were textured stucco, trimmed in dark mahogany. Two long, overstuffed couches covered in red, green, and black tartan dominated the center of the room. We passed through an archway to the left toward a paneled library filled with books floor to ceiling in mahogany bookshelves. A round, wooden table occupied the center of the room and sat close to the floor, surrounded by five children's chairs. To the right and down two steps was the kitchen that led to the dining room, where half a dozen women sat around the table.

The women were dressed casually and spoke in hushed tones. Five young girls that I guessed were about six years old stood in the background with their hands folded and watched the older women intently.

As we walked into the dining room, all conversation ceased and all heads turned in our direction. Lois propelled me ahead of her and called out, "Come over here, Ladies, and give this man a kiss and make him feel at home."

The women pressed against me and stroked me like cats competing for attention. They kissed, hugged, and I thought, left their scent on me. When they returned to their seats, the five young girls approached, curtsied and shook my hand, then returned to their places against the wall.

"Sit down at the head of the table, Gil." Catherine guided me to a seat that faced the water, and sat on my right. "We can all eat and you can ask questions of anyone at the table."

Lois clapped her hands and the five young girls scurried into the kitchen. They returned with plates, silverware, and napkins, which they arranged around the table.

"I feel like a speaker who had lost his notes," I mumbled. I looked from face to face at the young women and wondered; could these women be killers? They could have been contestants in a beauty contest or young fashion models, but not killers. Emma was so sure, and had I not saved her from certain death at the hands of these beautiful monsters?

It was ominously quiet in the room except for the clatter of dinner being served.

"I'm not sure where to start," I began.

I had no idea what to ask these women that would not sound ridiculous, so I kept my mouth shut. If I told these women what Emma had confided in me and it was true I might find myself strapped to the wall in the cavern as the next night's meal.

From my chair I could make a run for it through the glass, out into the backyard and then off through the woods before they could scramble to catch me. Being a runner, a scared runner, they would never be able to keep up with me.

"You'd never make it, Gil." Lois smiled at me from across the table. "We're much faster and stronger than you are."

"Can you read my mind, too?" I tried to blank my thoughts.

"No, but I can read your body language." She inhaled deeply. "And, I can almost smell what you're thinking." She winked at me and sipped her wine.

Catherine wagged a finger at Lois. "Lois, no." She then turned to me. "Relax, Gil, I told you that you are safer here than anywhere else in the world. Nothing will happen to you, I promise. You are free to leave right now if you want. However, you won't find your answers by running." She placed her hand on my arm and squeezed. "Have some dinner and ask your questions."

One of the young servers plopped a fat salmon steak on my plate.

"Let me help you get started, Gil. We know you took Emma from the broch; took her onto the ferry and then to the airport, and to Belize." She removed her hand from my arm and picked up her wine glass.

I stared at her. "How— " My fork froze midway to my plate.

Catherine frowned at my surprise and continued. "She told you stories about the Sisterhood and you believe those stories. Correct so far?" She cut into her fish, speared a chunk and then laid her fork down.

"How'd you know?" My hands began to sweat and I dropped my fork.

Lois giggled, swallowed a bite of fish and said, "We watched you."

The other women giggled and Catherine shushed them with a motion from her hand. "You were very good Gil, but awfully noisy. You are brave, but we'll have to work on your stealth. You'll make a good soldier, if you choose to be one."

"Did you really think Emma was in danger?" Catherine asked and then picked up her knife and fork again and glanced at her plate.

"She was stripped naked, tied to a stone wall, unconscious. That made a pretty good impression on me," I shot back. My stomach grumbled at the smell of the fish under my nose.

Catherine's forehead wrinkled. "Did Emma bother to tell you that she broke into the broch to try and kill our babies?" The muscles in her neck and shoulders stiffened. Her fingers gripped the silverware, her knuckles white. Her voice was soft, but her words tumbled out in staccato bursts. "Did she tell you that she was ready to smash our eggs and kill our little babies that lay inside unprotected? Did she tell you the truth, Gil, of why she wants to hurt us?" Catherine stood and looked down at me. Tears glistened from the corner of her eyes, her utensils held like weapons. I leaned back in my chair.

Lois came around the table, put her arm around Catherine, and eased her into her seat.. Quiet prevailed around the table and in the house. I could see the reflection of the table and the women in the window that had become a mirror as the night turned darker. The other women watched Lois and Catherine tensely until both were seated once more.

"I don't know what the truth is," I said with a shrug. "I was never interested in the truth. I'm only a photographer trying to do my job. Why didn't you just leave me alone?"

"We couldn't leave you alone, Gil. You are a McCrae with the gene we require to strengthen our future children." Catherine wiped at the tears from her eyes.

Lois stood, a natural teacher, "The last remaining McCrae we have access to is no longer able to produce the sperm we need with the appropriate gene." She held a wine glass in her hand and sipped as she spoke. "The gene we require is many faceted. It increases the body temperature so we can survive in cold waters and it provides the nucleus for the production of gills in our children. There are other subtle transformations that take place that the gene is responsible for, and without it our children will be unable to survive as the Sisterhood." She sat down and motioned Michelle to continue.

Michelle's voice was soft. She looked at me through eyes that seemed too large for her slender face. Her hands floated in front of her as she spoke and prompted the blue, silk shift she wore to shiver like a hummingbird's wing. I leaned forward. "It was as if the gods sent you here, Gil, just at a time when we needed to strengthen the Sisterhood. We were prepared to send a delegation to the Isle of Skye and petition the Sisterhood there to provide us with a liaison, but then you arrived." She took a deep breath. "Heaven sent, it would seem."

Catherine interrupted "We made some mistakes, or I should say I made some mistakes. We should have dealt with you honestly and openly, but I was so excited and taken with you that, well, you know what happened." She stared at me and her eyes darkened. "Would you have believed me, Gil, had I told you the truth?"

"No," I said, "and I'm not sure that I believe you now." I looked at the fish on my plate, took a bite. It was cold.

The women suspended their dinner and conferred with one another with hand signals. The little girls who served us peeked out of the kitchen doorway and pulled at their dresses.

"I'm sorry, Gil, we were speaking behind your back. Stay the evening with us and you'll leave believing," Catherine sipped her wine, her food untouched.

I looked into Catherine's eyes and said, "Tell me you don't eat human flesh."

Catherine groaned and was silent a moment. "Not anymore, Gil, but in the beginning it was thought that consumption of human flesh gave us the powers we were just acquiring, but that was hundreds of years ago. Good god, is that what you thought?" She sat her glass down too quickly and slopped wine onto the tablecloth and ordered, "Girls, clean this up."

"I'm trying to understand. Emma told me that the Sisterhood killed and devoured her brother. You have to admit that there've been some strange comings and goings that I don't understand." I paused, sipped at my wine and looked at each of the women.

Catherine started to speak. "Well--"

"For example," I interrupted, "what happened to Professor Griffin? The young girl wiped at the spilled wine and gaped at me wide-eyed.

Lois stood, and placed her hands on her hips. "I don't know a doctor Griffin. At least I don't recall the name.

211

Catherine, do you know a Dr. Griffin?" Before Catherine could respond, Lois asked, "What has this doctor to do with anything anyway?"

"He was a friend," I lied. "He drove his car off a cliff into the water and the cops never found his body."

"We can't tell you what we don't know Gil," Catherine offered.

"What do you know about me being pulled underwater and nearly drowned next to the houseboat?" I swirled the wine in my glass.

"Maybe you fell in the water and nearly drowned, it was an accident. My goodness Gil, if I had wanted to drown you, I could certainly found an easier way to do it; don't you think?" She smiled. "Come on, Gil, look at the facts." Catherine poured more wine into her glass.

Lois sat down. She twirled her pendant necklace between thumb and forefinger. It twinkled in the candlelight and sparkled off her perfect teeth as she smiled at me. She slipped the pendant into her shirt, and purred. "I think I remember saving your life, Soldier."

I lifted my glass in a toast. "And I thank you, Lois. But, please don't call me Soldier." She nodded. I tried to think of a way to examine the necklace to see if the markings were on the back of the necklace she wore.

She pulled the necklace from out of her shirt again and dangled it from her hand. "This necklace symbolizes the Sisterhood. It's my prize possession; do you like it?" Her eyes were closed and then opened slowly.

I played with my cold fish while Lois filled in details on the anatomical differences between humans and the Sisterhood. She stood and ambled around the table and gestured like an attorney before a jury. "We have evolved over hundreds of years as a coadunation of human, marine mammal, and marine fish. We're a much more complex organism than a human or a fish, with abilities to live comfortably on land or in the water completely submerged." She stood behind me and massaged my shoulders. "Because our body temperature is much higher than that of a human, we are not prone to illnesses associated with the human population, and our metabolic rate is so low, we age much slower as well."

I took a sip of wine. "What about--"

"Sex, I thought you'd get to that." The women laughed and signed excitedly to one another. She rubbed her hands through my hair and moved further down the table. "We lay eggs and give birth to females only. This enables us to limit the penalties of procreation, long pregnancies etcetera, and to raise children conformable to the Sisterhood. Our mission in life is the protection of marine life for a sustainable harvest, without endangering those animals and fish species that are not necessary for human survival. How we physically accomplish this, you will be able to witness later."

Lois drank deeply from her wine goblet and continued. "The drawback to belonging to the Sisterhood is that we must belong to both worlds. That is to say, we must become a marine animal to keep from losing the ability to live underwater, and a land animal to be able to live among humans. If we breed with an ordinary man we produce monsters that are unable to live in either world."

She reached her place at the table, sat back in her chair and studied me for a moment. "Do you understand that to us you are not an ordinary man; that you possess in your chromosome makeup the gene that helps us survive?"

I shook my head, and pushed the plate of salmon away from me. Neither my brain nor my stomach seemed inclined to come to any conclusions. "You all are beautiful women, Lois, but this is simply a story to me--fanciful and imaginative--but a fairytale all the same."

"The man's a skeptic, Catherine." Lois threw up her arms in mock surrender.

Catherine stood and took me by the hand, "If everyone is finished with dinner, let's take Gil to the pool house. Children, clean up here and meet us in thirty minutes." Catherine spat out her orders with military precision.

We walked out onto the deck, then downstairs to the pathway that led to the pool house and the beach beyond. I looked back at the house from this side and was surprised that it loomed three stories high. A stone door led to the basement. The rain ceased, but the night was cold and frost began to form on the bricks. I could see stars through the clouds. In the channel a ferryboat glided by, lit up like a gigantic birthday cake; its reflection in the water like a mirror that trembled.

Lois unlocked the pool house door and we stepped through into a carpeted classroom. The women removed their coats and stacked them on the low table in the center of the room. The classroom was warm, and the windows that faced the beach, fogged over. The pool was adjacent to the classroom and utilized three quarters of the space in the building. The underwater lights illuminated the water within the pool and created a bluish iridescence that rippled on the walls. I leaned down and submerged my hand in the water; it was icy cold, perhaps fifty degrees.

"What, no heated pool?" I jerked my hand out of the water.

"The water temperature is perfect for us, Gil. Go ahead, shuck those clothes and dive in." Lois' hands went to my shirt buttons and I pushed them away. "Oh, come on," she pleaded.

"No way are you getting me in that cold water." I backed away from the side of the pool.

"Come over here into the classroom, Gil; where your instruction begins." Catherine stood with the other women and waited for me. "Watch."

I stood transfixed as Lois and three of the women removed their clothes. They stood naked, their blue-white skin contrasted with their auburn tresses. They circled me and held hands and stepped sidewise in a slow dance around me.

Lois whispered in my ear as she passed. "Watch closely."

I did not know what to watch for, when simultaneously their skin seemed to melt and flowed over their body like lava down a hillside. I gasped, repulsed, and tried to break through the circle. As I brushed against Michelle, I jerked my arm back when I came into contact with a slippery, gel-like substance. The circle held and I wrapped my arms around my body to try and make myself smaller, but was unable to take my eyes from this spectacle.

After a minute or so, the women were swathed with a lustrous new skin, with fish-like scales that reflected the light from the pool as they continued to circle. When they stopped, as one, they dropped to the floor. I looked down in horror as their legs began to meld together. Two legs formed one appendage. They became, in front of my eyes, mermaids.

Catherine stepped into the circle, pulled me down onto my knees, took my hand, and said, "Feel their new skin, Gil."

She placed my hand on Lois's shoulder then guided it over her breasts and stomach, then down onto the new appendage.

The scales were smooth, slippery, and cold and were still covered with the mucous material. Their upper body appeared normal, except their mouths, which seemed to have swollen into a pout. When I tried to elicit conversation from Lois, I was met with silence.

"They can't speak, Gil. Their tracheas are blocked so that water can't enter their digestive system but is re-directed into their gills. That's another reason we have become adept at signing. The mouth, if you look closely, is enlarged so that they can accommodate their new teeth, and if you look closely at their eyes, they are covered with a third eyelid to protect them from the saltwater."

"I don't believe it," I croaked. I stood and stared as the women rolled into the pool and began to swim lengths. I was mesmerized by the transformation of these women, who were still beautiful, though no longer human. Were they animals, or fish? I wasn't sure.

"Say something." Catherine took my hand and said, "Are they not remarkable?"

I was speechless. I knelt next to the pool and let my hand trace the body of one of the women as she neared the surface.

After a moment my voice returned. "They remind me of the dolphins I petted in the Caribbean," I said and looked up at Catherine. "You understand?"

She nodded.

This was the same feeling. These women's sheer power invoked the true definition of freedom to live and breathe underwater, or to live on land. It was their choice. This was unprecedented, and I was a part of it. I began to see the significance of my role in the legacy of the Sisterhood, and I began to feel the first inclinations of responsibility to these women. Maybe I felt a little pride in the fact that I was one man in millions who could alter the genetic code that existed between man and the animals on the earth to better the species. On the other hand, was it really my role to increase the numbers of monsters that existed in this shadow world?

I looked up from the water as the five little girls entered the classroom. They wore identical white robes and gathered around Catherine. At a nod of her head, the five girls dropped their robes. Like children anywhere they ran for the pool and dove in. Unlike children anywhere, these little girls stayed underwater. I saw them swim and bump and push one another. They reminded me of puppies roughhousing.

"Neophytes?" I asked as I stood on the side of the pool. I held my breath as they played.

"Exactly." Catherine beamed at her girls. "These are the last batch from our long-time donor. Gorgeous, aren't they?" She clasped her hands to her breast and smiled.

The play in the pool had expanded as the older women joined in. They swam to the surface and I moved away from the side to keep from getting drenched.

"They remind me of seal pups," I remarked.

"That may be, Gil, but you must remember that they're not animals. The women of the Sisterhood are quite remarkable in many ways, not the least of which is their minds. These five little girls could compete intellectually in college, today!" She looked past me and signed to a woman near the door. I turned and looked. The three women not participating in the pool stood strategically around the pool area.

Catherine pointed, "You noticed that those women seem to be guarding, don't you?"

I looked around. "Yes?"

"The sisters are most vulnerable during the transformations. If they were to be attacked at that time, they would have no defenses. A soldier is always nearby during transformation. We all have our own soldiers as bodyguards. You will rarely see one, but they are there." She placed a hand on my shoulder.

"The Captain?" I queried.

"Yes, of course. I knew you would put that together soon enough. The captain and I have been together many years." She turned to the three women who were still dry and signed to them. "It's time to get out and get dry," she shouted to the revelers in the pool. The three women stacked towels next to the pool.

The alteration back to human form was equally remarkable. The mucous membrane dried and cracked and left the white, flawless skin intact.

"Our five young ladies will not be able to complete the transformation process until they are older," Catherine said, as she dried a little girl off. "They can withstand the cool water and are able to breathe underwater, but to become one with the sea will take a few more years.

Soon everyone was fully dressed and we all headed back to the main house.

Catherine held my arm as we traversed the pathway to the main house. The five girls ran on ahead of us. They pushed and shoved one another, squealing and signing as if they had not decided which language to use.

I watched the little girls play, "What kind of future do these young girls have? Do they realize what they're getting into?"

Catherine stopped on the path and turned toward me. "I'll answer your last question first. They are not 'getting into' anything. They are what they are, and they know that. They are not little human children; they are part of the Sisterhood, and that makes them different. They attend private school here on the island, taught by the Sisterhood." She took my hand and pulled me. "When they are old enough, they will attend college, closely supervised by the Sisterhood. They will never marry, and will breed only with those who will be able to provide the appropriate gene. They understand our mission."

"Will they remain on the island after college?" I shivered and pushed my other hand into my pocket.

"Some will; others will be sent where their skills are needed. You see, the Sisterhood is an international family and is run like any international conglomerate. Our girls will study the sciences, law, business, whatever it takes to keep the family tuned to its objective," Catherine explained. "Come; let's have a drink in the living room. You must be freezing."

We passed through the dining room and entered a large living room. The women from the pool house occupied couches positioned around a fireplace. They lounged in pairs, drank wine and talked in hushed tones. While Catherine moved to pour me a scotch I sat with Lois who immediately snuggled close and rubbed against me sensuously. She closed her eyes, and seemed content, yet I could feel her muscles vibrate. Her fingers played absently with the pendant. She wound it around her finger and then unwound it. Each time it paused, I could see scratches in the metal. I bent my head closer and squinted. It was the tiny cross. A chill ran down my spine.

"Your drink." Catherine offered me a whiskey glass. I accepted the scotch with numb hands. "Are you still a skeptic, Gil? I have one more little surprise for you." At that moment one of the five neophytes bounded into the room. She looked at me as if she were confused, then ran to Catherine and whispered into her ear. The other women in the room knew the content of the whisper and immediately left the room.

I sat up straight. "What's going on Catherine?" Lois disentangled herself and followed the other women.

Catherine, aglow in electric energy, rose off the couch, and pulled me up with her. I could feel a shudder as she held my shoulders and said quietly, "How would you like to come down and meet your daughters, Gil?"

I smiled weakly. "Daughters? I've never had children, Catherine."

"Well, you do now, Daddy. Follow me." She turned and left the room; I stood in a daze by the couch.

My brain had not contacted my legs, and by the time I had decided that I could move, Catherine was gone. I hurried to the doorway that led into the kitchen. Next to the refrigerator, the pantry door had been left open. I looked inside and saw a stairway leading down. I heard the little girls and the women's voices echo up the stairway. Down the flight of stairs I found myself in a daylight basement. I discovered another doorway and yet another stairway leading deeper. The voices were clearer, so I descended.

The room was dark at the bottom of the stairs, I stood a moment and blinked. I was in a room that was half as large as the entire house. The cavernous ceilings soared fifteen feet high Steam billowed and swirled like in the broch that held Emma. This cavern was a series of arched ceilings connected to brick pillars. The light source was provided by electric lamps recessed into the brick walls, which dimly illuminated the enclosure. As I advanced, I walked through pools of light circles, then darkness.

The echo effect was stronger here, and I was unable to

understand what was being said. I could see the women gathered and saw that they peered down at something. As I approached, a sulfur odor pervaded the area. I coughed and Catherine turned. She signaled me to come closer.

I stood between Catherine and Lois, against the side of an enclosure three feet wide and fifteen feet long. A trough built of the same red bricks, but curved to form a half-circular sluice box from one end to the other, filled with water. The trough was no more than twelve inches deep, and the water moved from right to left in a sluggish stream. Steam rose from the trough and inside the trough lay three oblong-shaped spheres resembling small, dark brown watermelons, leathery and stiff.

The women murmured to the neophytes, and pointed at the objects in the water. Shadows cast from the women danced over the trough and created the appearance of movement within the spheres. Two of them were split lengthwise and small puffs of steam hissed from the cracks, which caused the women to comment anxiously as to the condition of what seemed to be an imminent event.

"Do you think you're ready for this, Gil?" Lois said, not turning her attention from the trough.

"The hatching," I whispered.

"Of course," Catherine murmured, "The birthing of our children has commenced tonight. You will witness something few humans have ever seen."

"You said I would be meeting my daughters tonight. Are you telling me that those brown watermelons have something to do with me? Are these the eggs produced by your sisters?" I wrinkled my nose, confused and repulsed that I could have anything to do with the production of anything so hideous. I was having a nightmare; I was hoping I would awaken in my lumpy bed at the motel any minute.

"Trust me, and watch as your questions evaporate and your daughters spring into life." Catherine smiled, and then, a transformation began that lifted the hairs on the back of my neck.

Catherine's face melted and then to reformed into a larger replica of itself. Her jaws grew lumpy and exaggerated; her nose flared and reformed elongated and jutted from her face. Her lower half remained unchanged, which doubled the horrific affect. She lifted her arms and her hands altered into long, claw-like appendages and then leaned into the trough and positioned one of the eggs so that the longitudinal crack was at a right angle to her. She inserted one hook-shaped claw into the crack and drew the claw toward her splitting the egg lengthwise.

The other spectators were stone statues bent forward, their mouths open, looks of veneration in their eyes as their future asserted itself in this ceremony.

My knees shook as the first egg was laid open. After the crack was widened, Catherine used her hooked claws and grasped the egg from opposite sides and pried it open. It came apart with a loud, wrenching sound and a hiss of sulfurous gas and then fell to either side of the trough. Inside the egg was a sack of pink tissue with convoluted, intertwining, blood vessels; each vessel pulsated like a beating heart. Again, the claw was introduced into the tissue, but this time with the first prick, a thick, red-brown liquid spewed from the wound and cascaded down into the trough. Catherine reached into the opened sack and pulled forth a writhing, pink infant covered in fluid.

"Oh my God, the smell." I cried out. I covered my nose, turned away for a moment and retched.

"Quiet!" Lois turned to me. "Watch this."

I held my nose and turned back.

It was quiet in the cavern and Catherine grasped the infant gently and then submerged it into the water and washed it clean. She then lifted it clear of the water and the baby began to cry lightly at first, and then howled. The women and young girls let out a cheer as Catherine turned toward me and planted the infant into my arms.

I felt as if I were holding live warm Jell-O. I sank to my knees and juggled the baby in my arms. My call for help was met with laughter. The baby looked like any newborn, wrinkled, wet, and beautiful only to its mother. I did not like to hold babies, but this one seemed less brittle than most, less likely to fall apart. I looked into her blue-gray eyes and she looked directly back at me, focused and aware. I felt something I had never felt before a filial relationship to a child I thought I would never have. She needed my protection. Yet, there was so much more depth to this child, as if she already knew where she belonged.

The women gathered around the newborn in my arms. There were tears in my eyes as they took her from me and passed her around, each woman held the child, then each little girl took her turn and mimicked the older women. Finally, the baby was handed to Lois who immediately bared a breast and began to feed the child. Catherine, silent, looked on, and began to open the next egg.

The next baby was brought into the Sisterhood in a similar fashion. Emily took the second child to breast and Catherine signed that the births for this evening were concluded. She slid to the wet brick floor, covered her face, and began the transformation to human form. It took only moments, and when she looked up at me from the floor, exhausted. I held my hand to her, and once standing she had to lean on me for support.

"What do you think of your new family so far?" She said. Her voice was ragged. She reached for a robe and pulled it across her shoulders.

"I'm speechless. They're beautiful, absolutely beautiful." Slime from Catherine's transformation oozed under my feet and I slipped. "Whoa, hang on." I regained my feet and paused a moment, against the wall.

I heard the women ascending the steps; the little girls tittered and talked excitedly. Catherine leaned into me and I held her close; I wrinkled my nose at the odor of sulfur that clung to her.

She noticed me turn my head away and said, "Would you mind helping me upstairs and into a shower?" She stumbled as we turned.

I carried her up the stairs and into the bathroom. "I think maybe that I'm too tired to stand in the shower. Would you run me a bath instead?"

I laid her in the tub, pulled off the robe and turned on the tap. I found a washcloth and held under the tap and then bathed her as if she were a baby. Bits and pieces of scales that still clung to her washed down the drain.

She laid her head against the back of the tub while I ministered to her. I scrubbed her skin until it was bright pink and then plugged the drain and let the tub fill. "Oh, that feels so good. I'm going to have to keep you around, Soldier."

I felt a bulge in my pants begin to swell and moved back and sat on the toilet seat. "Tell me about the birthing process." I crossed my legs and leaned back.

Catherine ducked her head beneath the rising waters and rinsed her hair. She draped a leg over the side of the tub and began. "For centuries the Sisterhood has celebrated the birthing of its children in the same manner as you watched this evening. My transformation is as natural to me as shaving is to you, but demands more from me physically."

"No kidding?" I chuckled.

She locked her fingers behind her head and stretched. "The marine animal takes over during a birth and is impossible for me to control. My strength doubles and affords more protection for the babies, and my marine brain has instinctual memories I don't possess in human form. These memories tell me when the babies can be taken from their shells, and in which direction to open the shell."

The bathtub was full and I leaned over and turned off the valve. She closed her eyes and I straightened and turned to leave.

"Gil?"

I turned toward her. Her eyes were still closed. "I'm here."

"Those two little babies you saw tonight are as much yours as they are ours. They are your flesh and blood."

"Yes, they're beautiful." I smiled and shook my head. "My little girls."

Catherine's eyes opened. "But remember this; the babies will remain with the sisterhood for their entire life." She sat up and rested her arms on the side of the tub. "You do understand that, don't you?"

I looked at her for a long moment and nodded my head, turned and left. With the door closed, I shivered involuntarily. I stood at the closed door a moment and then ambled down to the living room.

The women and little girls alternately nursed and played with the newborn babies. It didn't seem possible that these tiny, pink beings could someday change into such an alien being that I witnessed at the pool.

"Do they have all their fingers and toes?" I asked.

"Come look for yourself, Gil." Lois waved me over." Five fingers on each hand, five toes on each foot, and two perfect gill slits."

Normalcy was relative, and in this group, my little daughters were normal. I plopped down onto the couch next to Michelle and watched the young girls play with the babies. Lois sat on the armrest and stroked Michelle's hair and stared at me. I nodded to her and she closed her eyes, licked her lips, and turned her head to the ceiling. I watched, repulsed as her nostrils twitched as if she had caught scent of her prey.

The clock struck midnight when Catherine joined the group in the living room again. I suffered jet lag and could barely hold my head up. It was warm and cozy and I looked into the night sky as a storm raged through. The wind surged against the side of the house and pelted the windows with rain. I rested on the couch with a baby tucked under one arm and tried to stay awake. In the reflection of the window, I saw Catherine fresh out of a bath, as her shadow cast itself over me.

She smiled down at me then reached over the couch and plucked the baby out of my arms. "You look tired, Soldier. We have a guest room you can use." She rocked the baby and looked down at me. "It must have been a long day for you."

The guest room seemed too far to travel and I stretched out on the cushions and listened to the quiet babble and thought of Emma. Was she nearby? I licked my lips and tasted the sweet gin flavor of her breath. As I drifted to sleep, I wondered too, if Catherine knew about the necklace, and the chance that Lois could be a killer in their midst? Should I be the person to bring up the subject?

That night, I dreamed I was back in the safety of the Caribbean.

Chapter 25

By eight-o-clock in the morning I had showered, shaved and was ready for breakfast. I followed my nose and found three young girls in the kitchen.

"Good morning, Ladies, smells like bacon and eggs in here." I took the smallest of the three and danced a little two-step around the kitchen.

"Good morning, Soldier, coffee's on the porch," she giggled.

The sun flooded the dining room. I opened the French doors and walked out onto the porch. The Olympic mountain range to the west was lit so brilliantly the peaks were on fire. A light breeze ruffled the waves in front of the pool house and the cold, winter sun danced on the water. I looked around at the forest and shades of green dripped raindrops from the storm the night before. A dozen rainbows arched their bodies and sprang to life above the trees.

I shook my head, "Hard to believe that the calendar says there are five days until Christmas." I muttered.

I sat down at the table and poured myself a cup of coffee. Catherine glided through the doorway noiselessly, dressed in a peach-colored morning robe buttoned to the neck. No hint of the previous night's fatigue show in her face.

She smiled. "Good morning, Gil," stretched, held her arms wide, and threw her head back, "I slept like a baby. Did you?"

"I don't even remember falling asleep," I yawned. "Coffee?"

"Yes, please." She sat in the chair opposite me and I poured her a cup and heated mine up. "I'm leaving tomorrow evening for Belize, Catherine. I promised Steve that I would finish the photo shoot as soon as I could and bring back the finished product." Her hand paused for an instant as she took a sip of coffee. "I'd like to come back and see the babies again, if that's possible."

Catherine put her cup down, pushed it away and looked at me. "These babies are yours to see whenever you choose. I would like you to return and stay with us forever, but I think you already know that. You do what you need to do, Gil. I won't pressure you to stay." She tilted her head and combed her locks with her fingers.

The eggs and bacon arrived. As tiny Erin stretched across the table to settle the platter in the center of the table, her elbow touched the hot coffeepot. She jerked her arm away and the dish clattered to the table.

She cried and clutched her elbow.

"Are you all right?" I pushed my chair back and took the little girl's arm and pulled up the sleeve. "Good, there is no burn, you'll live." I patted her on the shoulder.

"I know I'll live." She sighed, pulled her sleeve down and looked in my eyes. "Will you be my soldier too someday?"

"You go on back to the kitchen, Young Lady." Catherine turned to me as the girl scampered back inside. "They learn quickly. There aren't enough soldiers to go around. Sometimes a soldier will have three or even four women to watch over." She stood and scooped eggs and bacon from the platter, scraped the remainder onto my plate and sat it down in front of me. "Eat."

"I'll help Steve finish up the project, probably in a week or so, then I'll fly back here and we'll see." I munched on bacon and smacked my lips.

"Hmm," Catherine mumbled between bites.

A cloud floated across the sky and trailed its shadow in the water, and disappeared.

"We got some great shots the other day. I don't think I'll need any more. I sent Steve some samples. I think he died and went to heaven. He's very excited."

Catherine concentrated on her eggs, the bacon and finally the toast. She finished and looked at me. "You were saying?"

I spoke without looking up, "Steve also mentioned that Emma left Belize." I picked at my breakfast.

"I know." Catherine shrugged. "She's on the island now. I'm having her watched."

My fork was frozen in place, "Watched? Why? I don't understand how Emma could be so wrong. Did you explain to her what it is that you do or did you try to find out how her brother was killed? She's seems very knowledgeable about the Sisterhood, and she's intelligent. It doesn't make sense." A warning flag fluttered in my brain. I didn't want Catherine to know how much I cared for Emma. "But then again, how would I know."

"As to why? Emma was a member of the Sisterhood for many years," Catherine explained. "She was a product of a breeding error and never developed the physical abilities to adapt to life underwater. She's a throwback to ancient times when a sister merely held her breath, before the gene pool was strong and the physical changes began to take place. Don't be mistaken, Emma is a powerful woman in her own right, but she can't breed or bear the eggs for children. She became very morose and bitter as the other women bore the future of the Sisterhood and Emma was relegated to duties outside the broch." She spread apart a napkin and wiped her mouth.

I dipped my toast into the yolk and listened.

"She rebelled and called for a change in the ceremonies and in the very way we conducted our lives. We had no choice but to exclude her from functions and soon, from the Sisterhood itself. Emma has been a thorn in our side for many years, even though she has never brought violence directly against any of our members. We were planning to ship her back to Skye until you intervened. Be wary of her Gil, she could be dangerous." She balled up the napkin and tossed it onto her plate. "She can be a violent woman. I don't think you--"

I shook my head. "I still don't think you're being fair to her, Catherine." I sipped my coffee and thought for a moment. "Emma's still upset. After all, she lost her brother," I persisted.

"You're not listening to me, Gil; Emma could never have a brother. I told you, she's a product of the Sisterhood."

I put my toast down.

A door opened somewhere in the house and admitted a whisper of cold air that brushed against my skin like sandpaper. I shook my head and then finished breakfast without another word. Catherine watched me while she sipped her coffee.

"Would you like a ride to your motel?" She stood and pulled the robe tightly around her.

"Yes, do you mind?" I gulped the rest of my coffee and stood. "I need to collate my notes and I thought I would stop in and see the captain on my out of town." After the last sip, I put my cup down. "I will be back for dinner tonight though, if that's alright."

"Sure. Give me a minute to change." She turned, then stopped, "Change into appropriate <u>clothes</u>, I mean."

"Very funny." I laughed, and she disappeared into the house.

***

I opened my motel door and found Emma sitting cross-legged in the center of my bed like a Buddhist monk. She was wrapped in the motels off-white robe, her hair wet, the skin on her face pulled taut in a grimace that made her eyes seem unusually large. She sat and peeled nail polish off her toes as I closed the door. She looked beautiful and needy and I wanted nothing more than to hold her in my arms. I made a quick survey of the room and noticed her suitcase was open, her clothes scattered on the floor. I took off my jacket, pulled out a chair and then sat down facing her. She continued to look at her nails and then shook her wet hair and looked at me. Steam swirled from the open bathroom door.

"Did I tell you that I love you yet today?" I whispered.

"You lied to me, Gil." Her voice cracked and she cleared her throat. "You told me you wouldn't leave Belize until we discussed it."

"I'm sorry; I just wanted to protect you. I--"

"No, Gil. Listen to me." She sniffed and rubbed her nose on the sleeve of the robe, "I can't believe anything you tell me now." Tears coursed down her cheeks and she tried to erase them with her thumbs. She pushed the tears to the side. Her eyes were closed as she tilted her face to the ceiling; the tears changed course and ran down her neck. "Why, Gil? Why did you lie to me? What the fuck did I do to make you lose your trust in me?" Her voice became louder; her hands and shoulders shook. She leaned back against the headboard, opened her eyes, and screamed at me. "You lied to me, Goddammit! You just couldn't wait to get back here and fuck Catherine. Is that it? Am I right?"

"Emma, listen." I stood and walked to the side of the bed.

She buried her face in the terrycloth folds between her knees and wept; her back heaved as she gasped for air. I sat next to her and took her in my arms.

"I'm so sorry, Emma. Look, I've fallen in love with you and I don't want you to get hurt. I'm truly sorry I lied to you, but listen; I did not have sex with Catherine last night. I swear to you." She leaned against me, and then threw her arms around my neck, her cheek next to mine and sobbed. Her tears wet my face and I felt a lump grow larger in my throat. I rubbed her back and said, "Don't worry, Babe, we'll work it out."

"Work it out? We'll work it out?" Emma stiffened in my arms, and drew back to look at me. "There's nothing to work out for God's sake! What the hell do you think you're talking about? We'll work it out? Jesus Christ Gil, we're talking about monsters that must be destroyed, and you want to work something out?" Emma raised herself to her knees and pushed me away.

"Quiet down Emma." I looked around. "You'll bring the cops in here."

She stood at the side of the bed now, and pointed her finger at me; the robe fell open. "Have they got to you, Gil? Goddammit, tell me right now so I'll know where I stand."

"Look, Emma, I held my baby daughter last night, my

baby daughter. Can you understand?" I sat on the side of the bed and took her face in my hands and tried to erase the tears on her cheek with my thumbs. "This is just a misunderstanding. You could be part of the Sisterhood again, we can work it all out." I opened my arms to her.

She looked down, searched for the belt and re-tied the robe with a jerk. The tears began again, "Oh, Gil, I'm so sad for you, and I'm sad for myself too. I thought I had a partner I could depend on to get rid of these monsters. They got to you. I was so afraid they would." She walked around to the other side of the bed near her suitcase, turned and looked at me. My heart constricted. "The daughter you think you have is just another monster, Gil, a monster in a pretty disguise."

"Emma, please don't do this, you're wrong. They're only babies." I stood and again reached my arms out to her. "Come with me now. I'll prove it to you." My voice rose as I pleaded with her. "I can take you to the house and show them to you."

She disrobed and began to dress in jeans and a gray sweatshirt.

I went around the bed and grabbed her by the shoulders. "Look me in the eye, Emma."

She pushed me aside and finished getting dressed. "Stay away from me, Soldier." Her eyes turned dark and I shuddered. "Go back to your Sisterhood, and remember my warning. Stay clear of me!"

She hurled the rest of her clothes into the suitcase and never looked back as she slammed the door.

"Damn, damn, damn." I threw on my jacket, grabbed my keys and left the motel room. She was gone.

**

The day was still early. I drove the road around the harbor to the boathouse. I knew I would be most likely to catch the captain as he worked on his boat this time of day. The sun continued to gain strength and had dried the street and left the side of the road muddy.

A storm drain had over-filled, water washed over the street and the entrance of the small marina. The floating walkway no longer hid debris under a mantle of snow, but displayed them openly. Old coils of rope, rotten from exposure mixed with rusted engine blocks and empty oil cans, made for a treacherous hike to the boathouse. On either side of the walkway skiffs lay tied alongside, half-filled with water, their lines stretched taut.

The door to the captain's boathouse was ajar and I let myself in. It was still neat and tidy inside and around the Spirit; the water was black and calm.

"Captain, permission to come aboard," I called out.

I heard a muffled reply from within and stepped over the gunwale into the wet deck. Boxes of grocery items were stacked on the deck and the cabin door that led to the galley was open.

"Hey, Gil, good to see you. Lend a hand for a minute, will you?" The captain shouldered his way out of the galley. He was dressed in black canvas work pants and a wool plaid shirt; the tails hung over his pockets. His gray-blond hair hung limp on his forehead. He brushed the hair aside and reached down for a box.

"Grab that box on top on the port side there, and haul her inside." He turned and stepped down into the galley and continued forward.

I found the box marked Coffee, and followed him into the

hatch. "Looks like a lot of groceries Cap. You have some big charters coming up?"

He wasn't in the galley, but deeper inside the hull of the boat through a small hatch behind the galley stove; a storeroom of sorts.

"What'd you say?" His voice was garbled.

I rounded a sharp turn and he stood before an open shelf five feet high and as wide, partially stocked with groceries. "I said, what's all the food for?"

He looked at me with a wicked grin and said, "Well, Sonny, now that you're fuckin' the sisters, I'm gonna fuckin' retire. Me and the Spirit are headin' north, up into British Columbia to do some explorin'."

"What are you talking about?" I sat my box down.

"What the fuck do you think I'm talkin' about? I'm talking about retirin', gettin' the hell out of here. No more dumb-shit charters and especially no more women. Hand me that box of coffee." He stood sideways, arms outstretched.

"I thought you were Catherine's soldier. Why are you going to quit that?" I picked the box up and handed it to him.

"Fuckin' A, Sonny, that's why you're here, to take my place. I've put a lot of time in for Catherine, and she's paid me well for it. I've fucked all her sisters and generally had a good time. But it's time to retire when you get tired of fuckin' pretty women. Now, don't you agree?" He chuckled, finished stocking the coffee and pushed me in the direction of the galley.

"So you're just 'Captain McCrae', right?"

"In about a week I'll be Captain Fuckin' Retired McCrae. Now, help me with the box of canned goods. Then we can take a break." He levered the end of a large box up off the deck and waited for me to pick up my end.

Back in the larder, I helped him stack cans of food in neat, straight rows. His shelves were numbered to accommodate the foodstuffs he would be consuming on each particular day. You can't judge a book by its cover, entered my mind as I helped him.

"Okay, let's have a cup of Joe, and you can tell me why you came down to visit, cause I know it's not for my charmin' personality." He turned to the coffeepot.

I noticed his cup rack contained white, ceramic cups, each with a name stenciled on its side. The captain's cup was stenciled with Captain and next to his was Catherine, and so on down in a descending order of seniority, ending with Emily's. He took a rag from his pocket and wiped at an already clean cup.

"What I wanted to talk to you about, was Emma," I began.

"That cunt," he snarled.

I blinked.

"I don't know what's going on between her and the rest of the family, but I figured you would be able to give me a heads-up. Maybe I can help heal some bad blood." He handed me the cup with Emma's name scratched out. I touched her name and my heart beat faster.

"You think you're going to understand women politics? You're out of your fuckin' mind. My advice to you is do your job and keep your mouth shut." He threw back his head and drank deeply. "When they want some protection, you protect. When they want to fuck, you fuck them. See, it's simple. Don't go and make it all complicated. That's what women are for. Just do your job and you'll be all right." He finished his speech and saluted me.

I sat back in a galley chair and sipped my coffee and

pondered the captain's advice. The galley was warm with the door closed; heat from the stove condensed on the round hatch windows that lead to the wet deck. Remnant smells of the morning's breakfast lingered.

I sat and sipped my coffee in silence as the captain tended to a pump behind the stove and listened to the heartbeat of the Spirit, little noises that went unnoticed when she was working. An automatic bilge pump expelled water over the side. The battery charger whirred. The Spirit was alive and I could feel her excitement as she readied for a trip into northern waters. The captain was a different person as he began a narrative of his upcoming trip.

"We leave here on the seventh of January on the morning ebb. I figure it'll take about ten hours to reach Friday Harbor. We'll anchor up in the harbor a couple days, then set out for the Queen Charlottes. I expect we'll spend most of the winter gunkholin' in the Charlottes, fishin' and crabbin'. We can pretty much live off the sea once we get up there." He sat his cup next to the stove. "There must be three hundred islands we can lose ourselves in. No people, no women, just the two of us." He patted the woodwork, looked at me and winked.

"You keep saying we, Cap. Who's going with you?" I handed him my empty cup.

"Why, the Spirit of course. Who the fuck did you think I meant?"

"You talk about the boat as if she were a person. I'm sorry; but I thought--"

"The Spirit is my lady. We've been together for twenty years now, and she never once lied to me. She, don't bullshit me. It's hard to explain, but she knows that I'll take care of her, and she'll take care of me. She's not complicated like most women.

She's comfortable, and if you ever find a woman like that, don't let her go."

I thought of Emma and smiled.

He jabbed me in the chest with his middle finger. "Now cut out that day dreamin', I got to get back to work. You're welcome to stay and shoot the shit, but you'll have to work, too."

"No, but thanks. I've got to go finish up the data for Steve, then have dinner with the ladies this evening. I still don't know how I should handle this thing with Emma. Well, I better get going." I stood and opened the galley door.

"Remember what I said. Keep your nose out of their politics and just do your fuckin' job." He turned back into the larder. I heard him chortle as he made his way into the bowels of the boat.

"Fuckin' job. Ha, ha, ha. That's a good one."

* * *

I parked under a naked maple tree at Lois's house. Every window on the two sides of the house I could see, glowed brightly. The rain had held off all day and with the clear skies the night promised to be cold. Six o-clock and already frost began to form on the brick pathway. The front door opened on my approach and Emily filled the gap. She was dressed in a white, lacy dress that swept the floor when she moved and fit like a glove.

"Welcome home, Soldier." She wrapped her arms around me in a hug, stood on her toes and kissed me on the cheek.

"Hi Emily. You look beautiful tonight. You remind me of my little sister."

She screwed up her nose. "Thanks."

"What's for dinner?"

"Steamed king crab legs and French bread, and my mouth is already atwitter." She took my hand and pulled me through the door. "Come on, the fire is hot and cozy."

A plump woman I had spoken to on the ferry, stood guard at the kitchen doorway, a stained white apron stretched tightly across her middle. She looked at me coldly and then turned back to the stove.

"She the cook," I asked?

Emily nodded and whispered, "and the housekeeper," and then hurried ahead of me, but did not turn around.

We went directly into the living room where six women were seated by a fire. My daughters lay asleep on the carpet between Lois and Mary. The babies were dressed in teal jumpsuits and pink booties and were the focus of attention. I heard the little girls in the kitchen; their high-pitched voices intermingled with the clang of pots and pans. Lois moved aside and patted the couch; her long, green dress was glued to her skin. I hadn't intended to sit with Lois and looked around for another invitation.

"Sit," Lois commanded, grabbed my wrist and pulled me. I collapsed at her side and brushed at my wrinkled pants.

"I feel underdressed," I said to no one in particular. I'd worn the same clothes on the flight from Belize.

"We always dress on Fridays, Gil, but I guess with all the excitement no one told you. It's not a problem; you look perfect." Lois patted my knee. My muscles tensed and I made myself relax.

A drink was brought to me and we all sat and talked for the better part of an hour. The babies stirred and woke up twice, but someone was always ready to pick them up and nurse them or to rock them back to sleep.

The women took turns with me, and as the evening wore along, I grew to know all of them better. They seemed like such well-adjusted young women, easygoing, thoughtful, and completely relaxed. When they moved to stand or sit down, their muscles rippled like those of a great cat. They were athletes, aware of their strength, and very comfortable in that knowledge.

The warm house, a drink, and the pleasant company lolled me into comfortable conversation with these beautiful women. They asked me about photography and traveling, about Steve and working with <u>National Geographic</u>. They wanted to know about my ex-wife and about the relationship I'd had with her, and why there were no children. I then realized these women were not worldly, not connected to the mainstream way of life because of their special circumstances. They were a community unto themselves with rituals, secrets and even ideals completely foreign to their neighbors. I was a new source of information for them, a new book to read. I was a bridge to gap the distance between them and mainstream humanity. They not only needed me for my seed, they needed me for my humanity, to make them feel a part of the race.

Dinner was on the table and the little girls called us to eat. Everyone but Catherine was present, her seat at the head of the table conspicuously vacant. It was a sumptuous meal with crab legs ten inches long and as big around as Emily's wrist. Loaves of hot, French bread were strewn down the table like elongated footballs. The girls brought out bowls of green salad, and distributed them next to the plates of crab. We all wore bibs, cracked the legs and sucked out the succulent white crabmeat and bit off chunks of French bread which melted in our mouths. It was a feast accompanied by music from Beethoven and Mozart, the sound turned up to drown out the crunching carapace as we devoured all the crab on the table.

"Catherine is missing a great meal. Where is she?" I looked around the table, but no one volunteered an answer. I turned to Lois. "Will she be here tonight?"

Lois sucked a crab leg dry, placed the empty carcass on her plate and shrugged. "Maybe; maybe not."

"Is that a yes or a no?" I bit my lip. "Lois?"

Lois' head jerked in my direction, her eyes dilated and her nostrils twitched as if she smelled something repugnant. Her eyes focused again and she nodded. "That was a maybe."

I clenched my fists, relaxed my muscles and finished my dinner.

We retired into the living room and sat by the crackling fire. Catherine still hadn't shown up. I drank another scotch and fell asleep on the carpet next to the fire. I awoke sometime in the middle of the night to a dead fire and a warm body snuggled up spoon fashion in front of me beneath a comforter. My pants and shirt had vanished and the blackness of night, through the windows, told me it was not close to dawn. My neck hurt. The pillow someone placed under my head slipped out and my head lay at an angle. When I pulled the pillow back, Catherine moved in tighter to me and wrapped my arm around her just below her breasts. I wondered what she would think if she knew that I wished it was Emma lying here beside me. Catherine's long, silky robe rubbed against my thigh and my mind, along with my male ego, regained consciousness. She grasped my arm and whispered, "Don't even think about it, Soldier. Go back to sleep."

Through the window I could see the crescent moon.

I fell asleep and dreamed I was with Emma on a sandy beach, under a full Caribbean moon.

Chapter 26

I was wrapped up tightly in a down comforter, my sleeping partner missing. The smell of fresh brewed coffee wafted into the living room.

"What time do you fly out today, Gil?" Lois sat on the carpet in a patch of sunshine and rocked one of the babies.

"Good morning," I groaned and stretched my back. "What time is it?"

The baby began to whimper and Lois opened her shirt and directed a nipple into its mouth. Little fingers pushed at the base of the full breast and it suckled noisily.

"Quarter past nine. I'll be running you to the airport today." She looked at me, closed her eyes and sighed.

"No need for that." I sat up and untangled the blanket. "I've got to return the rental car to the airport anyway, but thanks. The flight leaves at midnight so I'll catch the ten-o'clock ferry off the island. Where's the rest of the gang?"

"I think Catherine is having coffee on the porch with the captain." The baby sputtered and Lois popped the nipple from its mouth and patted its back.

I walked into the kitchen and poured a cup of coffee. One of the young girls pulled on my shirttail. "Breakfast will be ready in about," she sucked in her bottom lip, "--in a little while," she said.

The porch was as warm as the living room and so I left the door ajar, stepped into the brilliant splash of sunshine and set my cup on the railing. Two chairs were pulled out from the table and two half-full cups still steamed. A coffee carafe sat in the center of the table. I sipped my coffee and looked around the grounds for Catherine and the captain. The water was flat calm and the sun had risen high enough to reflect on its surface, creating a firestorm mid-channel. A ferry entered the glare, disappeared for a moment, then re-emerged and continued its passage. Seagulls floated above the ferry like kites tethered to the superstructure.

On the porch, patches of ice hid in the shade, glistened and fought off the sun. A squirrel chirped noisily at me from a safe perch on a fir branch high above. Movement by the side of the pool house brought Catherine and the captain into view. They walked hand in hand, lovers relishing one more day together. Each wore blue jeans and green canvas jackets. He walked on the downhill side of her and made up most of the difference in their height. Her hair was twisted into a three-strand braid, which fell down the middle of her back. As she turned away from the sun the strands of auburn hair caught fire in the sunlight.

Walking gingerly up the grassy slope, Catherine looked up and waved. I waved back, poured myself another cup of coffee, and started down the stairs to meet them. Halfway down I noticed a movement to my left inside the tree line, at least thirty yards from the house. A swatch of blue near the trunk of a fir tree distracted me momentarily and caused me to slip on the stairs. Probably nothing, I thought; a stellar jay, perhaps?

"Good morning, Catherine, and to you good captain." I called out. Another movement behind them caused me to stop and look closer. I was almost to the bottom of the stairs when a figure materialized out of the wood line. The person, dressed in a blue rain suit stood in the clearing with something metallic held in their arms.

I thought I recognized the blue slicker. "Emma?" I said, "What are you--"

The captain and Catherine saw the look on my face then turned and faced in the direction of my gaze. The figure took two steps, raised a spear gun and fired.

"Catherine, watch out! I shouted. It was too late. The spear had been loosed and sped toward her. "No!" I cried out.

Catherine stood her ground wide-eyed, as the steel shaft raced toward her heart.

In a blur of motion, the captain launched his body in front of Catherine, pushing her out of the way. The shaft hit him in the chest like a baseball bat connecting with a fastball. The captain gasped as the spear ripped through him, propelled him backwards and pinned him against the side of the house; its sharp point driving into the redwood siding. He hung there for a moment until his weight wrenched the spear point out and he crumpled to the wet ground. The shooter disappeared.

Catherine screamed and threw herself on top of him. Her scream changed into a howl of pain-filled rage. The spear penetrated the captain's chest and a geyser of blood erupted from his wound and spewed out onto Catherine's coat and into her braid as it lay across the wound. I rushed to them. "Catherine, move aside. We've got to stop the bleeding." I pulled her away and pushed the captain onto his side. The barbed spear point was screwed onto the shaft and protruded from his back.

"Pull it out," Catherine screamed. She sat on her knees and reached for the spear.

I grabbed her hand. "No, Catherine, It'll make it worse. He'll have a chance if we leave it in." I tried to pull her hand away.

"No, no, no. I want that 'thing' out of him. Get it out, now." Her hand was on the shaft.

I held her wrists and squeezed. "Okay, let me do it." I unscrewed the barb and backed the shaft out. The captain groaned.

The blood continued to spurt unabated and I pushed my hand tight against the wound. The blood trickled up through my fingers. "Catherine, call 911 and get me some towels." She stared at me blankly. "Now!" I screamed at her.

Shaking her head, she pushed my hands away from the wound. "It's too late," she said quietly.

The captain closed his eyes and said clearly, "Catherine, I lost the keys to the Spirit." He relaxed in her arms and she held his head to her breast. His legs and his left arm continued to seize, but they soon relaxed as the blood slowed its exit and the captain lay still in her arms.

"What did he mean, Catherine…what keys?"

Her face was streaked with tears, "He was telling me," she choked back a sob, "that he was dying."

Catherine moved and gently rested the captain on the ground. She then lay cuddled up to the full length of his body, her face burrowed alongside his and wept like a child. Between sobs, she whispered, "I'll keep my captain warm."

I stood above them. My own tears welled up within me. A cloud had blotted out the sun and turned the landscaping into shadows and altered the color of the blood from red to dark brown.

Lois barged upon us and pushed me away. "What happened?" She looked at the captain and then turned to me. Her pants were muddy where she must have fallen in her rush from the house. She grabbed my shoulder and screamed, "What did you do?"

"Not me," I gasped. I wrenched myself from her and pointed toward the wood line. "Over there. It came from over there"

She stepped into me and knocked me to one side, gazed toward the beach and growled. Saliva dripped from her lips.

I looked and saw a small skiff speeding away. "There," I pointed.

The other women gathered around the captain and Catherine. Their faces displayed the devastation we all felt. Catherine lay quietly atop the captain. Then with a howl of despair, she slowly got to her feet. Her clothing was saturated with blood. She turned to me with a face that might have been chiseled from granite. "Pick him up. Help Mary take him to the house and clean him up." Then she turned to the other six women present and signed to them.

Without a word all seven ran to the beach, letting their clothes drop to the sand, they began their transformation. Within minutes they had disappeared under the waters gray surface. The cloud that brought the shadow now brought a light rain, and made me think that God may have been crying for the captain, too. It was not his time to go; he had an appointment with British Columbia, and all waters north.

I wondered what type of hold Catherine had on the captain that he would so unselfishly lay down his life for her.

Maybe he was in love with her
although, his only professed love was his <u>Spirit</u>. Maybe on
another level he didn't even realize, he loved Catherine. Then
again, maybe he was just doing his job.

    I looked once more at the captain and thought that Emma
could not have wanted this; would not have committed this
crime. I would have sworn it was her that stepped from the
brush. I also knew she certainly had a motive. And yet?

    Mary stood at the captain's side and looked for me to
give her some direction. She shuffled her feet and wiped at her
eyes.

    "Pick up his feet, Mary-- not his feet actually, but maybe
his knees so we don't drag him on the stairs."

    The captain was heavy, and we advanced a step at a time
until we were on the porch, we laid him down gently. We left a
trail of blood up the stairs that the rain already had begun to wash
away. The little girls stood at the top of the stairs and unrolled a
plastic sheet in the dining room to lay the captain on.

    "Girls, run down to the beach and bring up the women's
clothing before they get too wet." They looked at Mary.

    "Hurry," I said.

    The little girls did as I told them while Mary and I pulled
the captain through the doorway and onto the plastic sheet. I
covered him with a blanket and tucked it around him as if he
were a child at naptime.

    "Where's the phone, Mary? We need to get the police
here as soon as possible." I walked toward the kitchen and Mary
stopped me.

    "No police, Gil. Catherine said we were not to call the
police; that she would take care of everything."

    Mary stood and wrung her hands, and I remembered the

captain's voice, "Keep your mouth shut and do your job."
Maybe he was right.

"Okay, Mary, let's get the captain's clothes off and clean him up the best we can. Do you have spare clothing we can put on him?"

"He keeps a room here and has a closet full. I'll run and get something."

An hour later we had cleaned and dressed the captain. We tried to hurry, as neither of us knew how long it took a body to become stiff. As he lay there looking up at us through dead eyes, I thought of what he said as he lay dying, something about keys. He'd lost his keys and I know we hadn't discovered them on him. I walked outside to where the murder occurred and searched the ground. On the grass I saw a ring of keys, and a little plastic float to keep keys from sinking if they were ever dropped in the water. His keys. I picked them up, surprised at their weight. Brass keys can endure the salt air, like the captain, I imagined. I slipped them in my pocket and planned to check on the Spirit later in the day knowing that the captain would appreciate it.

I looked toward the beach and hoped to see Catherine and the rest of the women returning, but found none. The wind picked up and the rain cascaded down on the brick walkway. Most of the stains on the side of the house had been washed clean, and the rain would take care of the rest. I had become an accomplice to covering up evidence, maybe even an accomplice to murder. Who was I protecting-- Emma or Catherine?

I picked up the spear and wiped it as clean as I could on the wet grass, then carried it back to the house with me. I was now soaked and cold. "I'll be back in an hour, Mary. Tell Catherine I'll be at the captain's boat if she gets back before I do."

As I drove I wondered where Emma might be and what she was thinking. I was worried about her and knew that the sisterhood would be on her trail. I felt guilty because they may not have suspected her as the shooter if I hadn't called out her name. I slapped the steering wheel. "How could I have been so stupid?

I felt compelled to check on the Spirit on the captain's behalf and thought in the back of my mind that the captain may have kept a log which could reveal to me what I may be getting myself into. Any details he might have written about the Sisterhood would be helpful to me.

I parked my car as close to the gate of the marina as I could and raced down the dock. I fumbled for the right key to the boathouse. I opened the door and stumbled across the threshold, slammed it closed and locked it. I turned around toward the boat but it was gone. I thought maybe the Spirit had been moved to another dock. I rushed back out and checked the other boathouses. Most had locked doors, but vents in the side of the boathouses allowed me to peek inside. The Spirit was nowhere in the marina.

I stood beneath an extended roofline of one of the boathouses out of the rain and looked across the harbor. The public dock was empty. As I turned to go back to the captain's boathouse; two small otters slithered up on the dock across from me and growled. I jumped backwards, then the otters pitched back into the dirty water.

Looking around inside the boathouse, I noted everything was the same as it had been when I visited the captain the day before. The locker with the dive gear seemed untouched. I was stumped. With my hands on my hips, I peered down into the black water where the day before the Spirit was docked, and detected a flash of silver beyond my own reflection. I bent down and looked closer. The flash of silver was the top of the masthead light. I lay down on the dock and cupped my hands over my eyes and leaned nearly into the water.

The Spirit was at the bottom of the harbor beneath the boathouse. She was in twenty feet of water, buried, just as the captain would be buried the next day. As I looked a trickle of bubbles escaped; the Spirit would breathe no more. The lights in the cabin were still lit, but they dimmed and as I watched, they blinked out. The Spirit was as dead as her captain.

I shed my tears for the Spirit, as I had for the captain, but I found some solace in knowing they would be together soon, someplace. I mused that she must have died when the captain drew his last breath, as the two seemed so connected. She could not survive without him. I thought It would have been the same scenario in reverse had the Spirit been murdered. I took the ignition keys off the ring and dropped them into the water. I watched them settle on the cabin roof, knowing that the captain would have approved. I slipped the floater from the key ring into my pocket, said my farewells and left.

As I turned away from the corner Emma stepped from the shadows, into my path. Startled, I stepped back, lost my balance and fell toward the water. I grabbed for the corner of the boathouse, but it was too far away. Emma snatched my arm and pulled me back.

"Gil," she whispered. "I need your help."

"Jesus H. Christ, you scared the living shit, right out of me." I held on to her arm, until I had regained my balance. I shook loose, stepped back and looked at her. "You need help alright, Girl, but the kind of help you need right now is of the legal-type help."

She tried to comb her hair with her fingers, but the entanglements proved too tough. Pieces of brush and thorns were caught up in her hair. "The Sisterhood won't call the authorities. There's too much at stake for them. So I won't need a lawyer." Her face was streaked with mud. "Please, Gil, help me?"

I pulled her into my arms and squeezed her. She laid her cheek next to mine. I whispered, "What am I going to do with you?"

"Just hold me a minute." She held me tight and shivered. "Will you help me, Gil?"

"Help you to escape?" I pushed her away and held her at arms length. "Emma, tell me you didn't do it."

"Gil, you have to listen--"

I made my fingers into a mock pistol, and pointed at her and then to the Spirit. "Or maybe we could sink another boat or two, before nightfall." I shook my head. "Please." I cupped her chin in my hands. "Tell me you didn't do it."

She sighed, "Gil, I--"

"No, don't lie." I dropped my hands and turned away from her.

She pulled me back around and shook her head. "I didn't do it."

"You were there. I can see it in your eyes. I knew it." I turned my back on her again. "Damn, damn."

"Yes, I was there. Gil, I went to kill the rest of those eggs, before they hatch," she said softly and rubbed her hand along the length of my arm. "Will you help me?"

I spun back around. "You must be the craziest, lunatic woman I have ever met," I scoffed. "The Sisterhood will be on your ass soon, and this time there won't be a stupid photographer around to help you out. You killed the captain for Christ's sake." I leaned close, touched her ear with my lips and smelled the sweat and the fear, then lowered my voice to a whisper. "You killed the captain." The wooden dock creaked and moaned under our feet as a yacht passed by.

"I didn't kill him. Lois killed him." She grasped the front of my shirt. "I was there, yes, but to destroy the eggs." She looked around. "Gil, you have to believe me." She threw her arms around my neck and squeezed. "Please, believe me."

The wind blew out of the south and brought with it an increased rainfall. Waves broke over the wood dock planking and splashed our feet with cold water. I pulled Emma toward me, opened the boathouse door, and we stepped in out of the weather.

"You killed the captain, Emma. It doesn't matter that you were trying to kill, Catherine, and you missed your target. The fact is, the Sisterhood is pissed, and they're out looking for you right now." I held her by the shoulders and shook her.

She pushed me away. "Look, Gil, you have to believe me. I was hiding in the brush ready to break in, find the eggs and destroy them when Lois stepped from behind a tree and shot the spear gun." She balled her hands and struck the wall of the boathouse. "She had a blue raincoat on and left it next to the tree. Go find it. You'll see."

I remembered the muddy, pants Lois had on. "Goddammit, that doesn't make sense. Why would Lois shoot the captain?"

Emma squatted and exhaled. "She wasn't shooting at the captain." She looked up at me, and a tear rolled down her cheek. "It's simple politics. She wanted to kill Catherine! Lois wants to be the leader. Lois knew I was on the island and could blame the murder on me." "Gil, don't you believe me?" Her hands were cold as she took mine and pulled herself up and then clenched my hands between her breasts. "Not yet?" She pleaded.

I jammed my hands in my pockets. "Well, I don't know. I just don't know what to believe anymore. What about the sisterhood?"

"Fuck the Sisterhood, and fuck you too. While you were rocking the little monsters on your knee, another egg is ready to hatch. Go back to your baby monsters, Mister Clueless. I know what I have to do."

Emma pressed me against the wall of the boathouse, and pushed her index finger into my chest. I tried to back away, but there was nowhere to go. I grabbed her by the shoulders and shouted to her, "I'd like to help you, but Goddammit, you don't stop and think. No! You jump right in with both feet, and forget to bring your brain along."

"If I'd waited for you to--"

"You listen to me." I turned her around, so that her back was now to the wall. "We're going to get your ass into my rental car. Then we're getting the hell off this island, before the Sisterhood invites you over for dinner." I backed away. "I don't care what you did or didn't do."

For a few moments, we stood toe-to-toe and gazed at one another. A tear overflowed from the corner of my eye. "I love you."

"Fuck you!" She pushed my hands away and stepped toward the door. "You want me to run away? If you had seen what was left of my little brother, after the Sisterhood was finished with him, you wouldn't act like such a coward." She reached for the doorknob.

I stepped between Emma and the door, and placed my

hand on her arm. "Catherine told me you were a member of the Sisterhood, and never had a brother. She said you lied to me about having a brother."

"Take your hand off my arm, Gil." She pushed me away, pulled the door open and stepped out into rain. Before she closed the door, she leaned inside and said, "I'll bet she lied about eating human flesh too."

I stood alone inside the boathouse with my thoughts and my confusion. Now, I wasn't sure who killed who, or why. The captain was dead, and his boat lay on the bottom of the bay. If I didn't stop Emma, she was bound to be next.

I turned the doorknob and heard a strangled cry. I pushed the door open wide and vaulted outside. Two figures stood at the end of the walkway, their arms around each other. If I didn't know better, I'd have sworn they were dancing. I ran down and then halted five feet from the end.

Emma cried out, "Get away, Gil, get away!"

I tried to move in closer, but the monster swung a claw-filled fist at my head and missed my face by inches. I fell back, my hands slid on the wet boards.

The monster gripped Emma to its chest. I could hear Emma gasp for breath. She tried to call out to me a second time, but her voice was inaudible.

"Lois?" I called out. The creature turned its head, "Lois. Don't do this. Let her go." I stood and moved slowly toward the monster.

I was not sure that this thing was Lois, but I thought I might as well take a chance. The mermaid stood on the end of its tail, well over six-feet tall. The body was covered with iridescent, overlapping, scales. Mucous trickled down, streaked the scales, and deposited oily droplets on the rain-streaked dock.

256

I knew I had seen this substance before, on my negatives. As I watched, the creature moved to the end of the dock, the mouth opened and closed, rhythmically. Teeth, shiny and white reflected the lights of the darkening day.

"Wait," I called out. "Leave her and you can have me instead. Let Emma live and I'll be your soldier." I held out my hand. "Please, Lois, don't hurt her."

The mermaid's eyes were the color of the giant octopus I had photographed—bright golden orbs. The look it gave me was evil, an evil I could never have imagined. I trembled, and was unable to move closer. I was afraid and could not save the woman I loved. The monster growled and slid into the water disappearing into the blackness with Emma still clutched to its chest.

I ran to the end of the dock and hoped that Emma had been released and I would find her, clinging to the dock. The water swirled where they had made their descent, but, except for a barely discernible trail of bubbles, there was nothing but black water. Emma was gone.

"Emma--" Nothing. Hot tears stung my cheeks. I could do nothing but turn circles on the end of the dock. I tried to think, to find a way to bring her back. I was lost, and then I remembered that the Sisterhood would probably conduct one of their age-old rituals.

I called Lois's house from a pay phone at the head of the dock and told Mary that my plane to Belize was leaving in two hours, and I would catch the next ferry to town. "Please give everyone my regards."

Maybe there was still a chance. Maybe if I hurried, I could save Emma.

Chapter 27

The broch was energized. Black-robed women chanted a litany,
which had been passed on through generations of the Sisterhood.
The altar was cleansed with saltwater and gleamed in the steamy
environs of the cavern. The women knelt on the stone floor
around the altar, hands held. They turned their heads upward and
the chant echoed off the stone walls.

  This would be a night of rapture, and the participants
would partake of human flesh, to help preserve the way of life for
these women of the sea. They sang a dirge that mourned the
death of all the sisters of the past. It was low and sorrowful and
tears stained the women's cheeks. Catherine stood and dropped
her arms. Quiet filled the cavern.

  She walked to the center, rested a hand on the altar and
said, "My sisters; tonight we shall feed on the flesh of our
enemy." She pushed her hood back and shook out her hair.
"Tonight we shall become stronger by consuming our enemy's
soul." She gazed upon each uplifted face. "The flesh you devour
tonight will enhance your birthright to remain a member of the
sisterhood." She pulled her hood back on and began to intone the
prayer of the sisterhood in a low melodious voice and the sisters
repeated the invocation. The celebration would continue until

Catherine signaled for the feasting to begin.

Emma's hands were tied to a ring embedded in a stone column. Her feet barely touched the floor. Her hood had been abandoned, and no tears stained her cheeks. There would be no escape. This time it was hopeless, and a quick death would be her only hope of release.

As I surfaced in the pool of black water, a chant filled the cavern and overwhelmed my senses. I remembered Catherine's taunt, "You need to work on your stealth." I took her at her word and eased out of the water with hardly a ripple, removed my gear and crawled slowly to a hiding place behind a boulder and waited. I left Emma's equipment floating on the surface of the pool. The requiem continued as I slid on my belly to the far side of the cavern. I was able to see the sisters, yet I hoped the dark recess of this side of the enclosure would conceal me.

The floor beneath me sloped into a depression. I turned and slid feet first until I touched the bottom and discovered a basin or a drain that culminated in a pool. This trough encircled the entire perimeter of the cavern. Stooped over, I made my way around the enclosure until I was directly behind the column to which Emma was bound. As I began to exit the depression, my foot entangled in something and sent me sliding right back. I held my breath and listened. The dirge continued. <u>Goddammit, don't be so clumsy</u>, I chided myself. I pointed a tiny dive light, with a red lens cover, at my feet. I jumped back, repulsed. At the bottom of the ditch, bones lay helter-skelter, scattered as far as my light beam was able to illuminate. Human skulls looked up at me through vacant eye sockets, Halloween apparitions in a horror movie. My foot was tangled in the strap of a buoyancy compensator. <u>The missing scuba divers</u>! My stomach heaved with the taste of vomit in my throat and I gasped for air. I held my breath as my light glinted off something else at the water's edge.

I bent down, picked up a pocket watch, opened it and read the inside cover. <u>To John from Abigail</u>. It was the watch that Dr. Griffin consulted on our visit. I laid the watch back down to untangle my foot. Sweat cascaded into my eyes. I wiped them clear, and eased back up the incline. I lay flat, a few feet away, behind where Emma was secured.

I stood up behind the column and glanced around the corner. I couldn't see the altar or the women through the fog. I heard children's voices mimic their elders and was saddened. I didn't expect the children to be present.

***

The women assumed that Gil was well on his way to Belize and now Catherine would take pleasure in making Emma's vigil long and painful. The killing of the captain was inexcusable, and Catherine looked forward to devouring the flesh of the woman who had seduced her new soldier. Part of her flesh would be taken to the babies and used in their baptismal ceremony to welcome them to the Sisterhood.

The women stood and then dropped their robes and lay on the warm floor to begin their transformation. Their sharp claws and needle teeth would be necessary to rip the flesh from their host. However, there was no need to hurry, besides, the transformation in slow motion was likened to a prolonged and wondrous sexual climax; a pleasure the Sisterhood treasured.

* * *

The fog lifted for a moment as I watched the women writhe in rapture. I was repulsed by the degradation that was to surround Emma's death. The fog closed in again. I rounded the column and whispered.

"Emma, I'm here." She smiled. Her eyes were closed and I called to her again.

"Emma, wake up." She blinked and closed her eyes again. I stood in front of her and tried to loosen her bonds. I prayed the fog would continue to conceal us.

"Emma, wake up and help me." She clenched her eyes even more tightly. I cradled her face in my hands and shook. Her eyes popped open and a look of anger emerged.

"Wh--?" She cried.

"Shush." I covered her mouth with a kiss, held her by the waist and cut the ropes. She folded into me. I bent, slung her over my shoulder, gingerly made my way to the pool and sat down with her cradled on my lap.

"Here we go again, Kiddo. Hang on. It's liable to get rough unless we get out of here before they finish turning into fish."

"I don't know what to say, Gil, I--"

I kissed her nose. "No time, we gotta rock and roll."

I was better organized this time and was able to gear up in a hurry, zipped Emma into her drysuit and strapped a tank on her back. She was unresponsive and we lost precious time readying for the descent. I knew my way through the cave and pushed Emma hard to the sandy bottom. Once there, we had only to navigate the caves before we'd ascend to the boat anchored offshore. I could almost feel the claws of the Sisterhood raking down my back and I knew that if we were caught, we'd both be torn to pieces.

We surfaced about ten yards from the boat, with a rainstorm in progress. I unhooked our tank assemblies and pushed them away from us. Time was precious.

"Are you alright?" I called out to her.

She raised her arms in a big circle over her head; an okay sign for divers and called out, "Let's get out of here."

Gale force winds knocked the tips off the swells and waves slammed at us from every direction as we swam desperately for the boat, I looked behind us for signs of the Sisterhood, but I couldn't see more than ten yards.

The small boat bobbed crazily on its anchor. It pitched and rolled on its anchor and nearly capsized as we swam toward it. Emma arrived first, as she pulled herself up. I pushed her over the gunwale. I hauled myself halfway up and Emma dragged me the rest of the way. When I dropped into the boat, I splashed into twelve inches of water.

"Start bailing." I yelled, and pointed to the blue plastic bucket hooked to the side.

Emma lurched to her feet and looked back to where we'd surfaced. "Let's go!"

I held onto the windshield as the small boat tried to pitch me out. The engine started on the first try, a loud booming clamor of pistons and valves resonated in the harbor above the cacophony of the storm. I leaped over the windshield and holding on for dear life, severed the anchor line with my dive knife. The boat slid downwind like a racehorse in the direction I least wanted to go.

Emma screamed, "Turn the boat around, they're surfacing! Hurry Gil, we've got to get out of here now!"

Her voice cut through the noise of the storm. I slammed the boat into gear and pushed the throttle handle all the way forward. The engine sputtered and died. The boat lay broadside into the wind and was near to blowing over sideways.

"She's going to broach," Emma shrieked.

"Shit, shit!" I pushed the starter again. It coughed and died again.

"Jesus Christ, they're right on top of us! Gil, get the boat out of here!" Emma held an oar over her head and stood at the side of the boat.

It was now or never, I crossed my fingers and pushed the button. The engine coughed then started. It belched blue smoke into the wind and screamed out in protest. I eased the throttle forward and the little boat came to life and jumped into the waves. I heard an earsplitting shriek swell to a deafening roar as we left the island far behind.

"Emma, come on, start bailing," I bellowed. She tried to bail the water with one hand on the bucket and the other clenched on the rail of the boat. The boat slugged through the waves. "There's too much water in the boat, Emma, you have to bail faster."

"I can't Gil. It's too rough." She tugged off her hood and let it sail into the wind.

"Then come up here and steer." I held my hand out to her and helped her sit behind the steering wheel while I took her place in the stern. "Head east to Seattle, and don't let up on the throttle."

The water was two feet deep behind the steering station and deeper near the outboard motor. The boat wallowed in the high seas and threatened to dive into a wave and sink at any second. Rain slanted sideways as we left the relative protection of the harbor. The motor groaned as the propeller plunged into the water and tried to lift the boat up onto a plane. I dug the bucket deep and threw the water overboard as fast as I could. I finally felt the boat lift up and begin to ride higher in the water.

I looked at Emma, gave her the thumbs up and thought that by tomorrow we would be back in Belize on a white sandy beach. I stared at her in shock.

"Bring her left, Emma. We're heading in the wrong direction." I stopped bailing and pointed.

She looked back at me and smiled.

"Left," I stood and waved my arm like a traffic cop. "Head the boat left, for Seattle."

She ignored me. My back and shoulders ached but I managed to pull myself forward and fall into the seat next to her. She steered the boat south and it hit me, Emma was heading to Lois's home, to the babies and the un-hatched egg. She sped the boat around a red buoy, looked at me quickly and winked. Her jaw was set and her eyes fixed straight ahead.

I grabbed the wheel and pulled. The boat lurched. "Are you out of your mind, Lady?"

"We're not finished here, Gil." She jerked the wheel back.

The boat bounced wildly. I cupped my hand over her ear, "This is crazy, Emma. We'll never pull it off. Let's get the hell out of here, now."

"I didn't come all the way back from Belize to give up. You knew that." Water whipped over the windscreen trying to pull her words from my ears. "We can do this." She stood up and the wind blew her hair back and with one hand on the wheel and the other waving to the sky, she whooped like a cowboy riding a bull. "If we hurry, their bodies won't have had time to change back."

I sat back against the seat and groaned. The pool house

came into view and Emma slowed the boat. A pungent odor of gasoline assaulted our noses. I stood up and looked at the property thinking I might see the beach crowded with members of the sisterhood, it was empty.

She cut the engine and the boat glided into shallow water and touched bottom. We were directly behind the pool house. Emma jumped into the knee-deep water and said quietly. "Come on, Gil. Let's just get this done and get out of here."

We pulled the boat up onto the beach as far as we could and I tied the bowline to a log ten feet from the lawn. Emma ran to the side of the pool house and spied around the side toward the main house. She signaled to me and I joined her.

"What now?" I whispered. "You have a plan?"

"Yeah, I have a plan. We have to get rid of those babies and the remaining egg." She grabbed me by the zipper on my drysuit and pushed her face into mine. I saw tears in her eyes. "Look, I don't like this any more than you do, Gil. You have to remember that these babies will grow up to become monsters. We have no choice." She pushed me against the side of the pool house. "Just show me where the nest is, Gil. I'll--" She took a deep breath. "I'll do the rest."

We ran up the lawn and to the door that led to the basement and then stopped. I tried the handle. The door was locked. I looked at Emma and touched her elbow. "Let's get out of here."

"Bullshit!" She smashed the glass in the top of the door with the butt of her dive knife, reached through and turned the handle. The door swung open silently. She pushed in ahead of me and then turned. "Which way?"

"To the left," I said and shook my head. At any moment a dozen creatures could descend upon us. Emma disappeared beyond the turn into darkness. On shaky legs, I hurried to catch up, turned the corner and saw her next to the trough where a single egg remained. The brick stairs to her right led up and into the main house. I lifted my finger to my lips and she nodded. I joined her as she lifted her knife to drive it into the egg.

"Wait," I whispered. "I don't see the babies." The lights cast meager rays into the enclosure and we were unable to see into the chambers to the right. "Let's check over there first."

Emma looked at me sadly. "Just turn your head, Gil. It will be over quickly."

A light flashed from the top of the stairs and then extinguished. Footsteps descended the staircase. We melted into the blackness beyond the trough.

"Who's down there?" The strident voice of the housekeeper called down the stairs. "Catherine, is that you?" The voice became louder and the woman descended. "Hello?" It was the housekeeper-cook.

When she appeared halfway down the stairs, I stepped into the dim light. "Hi, it's just me," I called out shakily.

"Gil, is that you?" She remained where she was. "What are you doing here? I thought you were supposed to catch a plane today?" She backed up a step. "The sisters won't be back for some time and you're not supposed to be down here without one of them present."

"I've just come to see the babies, but I don't see them down here." I walked to the base of the steps and looked up at her. She shifted her weight like a wrestler. Her right hand held a rolling pin still dusted with flour and her left was behind her back.

She stepped down one step and said, "The babies stay in the nursery over by Hidden Cove. I thought you knew that, Gil.

What's going on here?"

She flipped the light switch on at the bottom of the stairs and when she saw who was with me, her rolling pin clattered to the concrete floor. "You bitch," she cried out. "I thought something was fishy here."

Emma froze like a deer in a headlight. In that second, I watched in horror as the housekeeper snapped her left hand from behind her back and threw a kitchen knife into Emma's shoulder. Two inches to the left would have impaled her heart. Emma coughed once and then slid to the stone floor.

"Now, you," the woman thundered, and turned toward me.

I quickly grabbed the egg from the trough and tossed it high into the air above the housekeepers head. She gasped, and made a try for it. The egg was too high; she stretched and catapulted headlong across the floor. Having caught the egg mid-air, she smiled but then a scream echoed off the stone as she hit the ground with a wicked thud. A gasp of air was expelled from her lungs though her arms still cradled the egg. A crack developed and the egg began to open and spit red juice along the side of the housekeepers sleeve; the stench of sulfur turned my stomach. The housekeeper's eyes fluttered closed and she drifted into unconsciousness.

I turned around to Emma on the stone floor. She panted and grasped at the knife. I knelt beside her. "It's okay, Babe. I'm here." I gently moved her hands away from the knife. The knife was imbedded in her shoulder muscle. Blood leaked from the wound and spilled across the arm of the rubber suit. "It's not bad, Girl, but you're going to need a doctor."

"No time, Gil. Just pull it out, or were going to need more than a doctor to put us back together when the sisters return.

She was right. I placed my hand on her chest and then

yanked out the knife. She cried out and then was quiet. The wound still bled, but did not spurt and I knew the blade had not hit an artery. She tried to sit up so I pulled her up and leaned her against the brick wall. From a basket of folded laundry by the bottom of the stairs I grabbed a small hand towel, dashed back to Emma and shoved it inside her suit against the wound.

"Break that egg apart, Gil. Hurry and we can get out of here."

I looked back to where the housekeeper lay but she was gone, and with her the egg. I heard something shuffle in the dark recesses of the basement and I had to make a choice. I picked up an unconscious Emma in my arms and then placed her over my shoulder and jogged out of the house and down the lawn to where the boat was still tied. With a sigh of relief I stepped in and lay Emma on the floorboards between the front seats. A few inches of water still swirled around the seat fastenings but not enough to worry about. Our worry right now was getting the hell out of here.

The storm still raged and pitched the little boat like a cork in the ocean, while the wind drove the stinging saltwater into my eyes. Emma groaned. "Hang on, Girl," I called out.

I untied the boat, crossed my fingers and pushed the starter. The engine purred without so much as a cough, and I swung the boat around, gunned the engine and headed for Seattle.

"Did you do it, Gil? Did you smash that egg?" Emma's voice was weak and tired.

"Don't worry, Girl, I took care of everything."

* * *

Two days later I awoke to the laughter of young children.

The bright Caribbean sun filtered through the veiled curtains and patterned the bed with rosebud shadows. The ceiling fan re-circulated the warm air and as it whirred dust motes glinted in the sunlight. Our clothes were in a pile near the door where we had dropped them, in our hurry to warm ourselves under the sheets. Caught in a Caribbean downpour, we docked the small skiff and ran for our room. Thinking the bed sheets would warm us, we soon discovered that friction does a much better job.

Emma still slept, curled like a fetus, her hands balled into fists, jammed beneath her chin. She was naked, except for crude bandage on her shoulder. Her body crawled with goose bumps; her wrists bruised the color of ripe plums. I slid off the side of the bed, retrieved the sheet, and covered her. She pulled it tightly around her shoulders and continued to sleep. I tiptoed around the end of the bed and sorted through the damp clothes, found my shorts and pulled them on. I turned to look at Emma again, then left the room and gently closed the door.

White cumulous clouds floated like lazy sheep in the azure blue sky. The deck on the balcony was already hot from the morning sun, and steam rose from leftover puddles. I looked over the railing and discovered the source of the laughing children. Steve's girls sat on the dock and trailed their toes in the water, giggled and slurped juice from plastic tumblers. They looked up, saw me, and squealed.

"Uncle Gil! Uncle Gil!" I shushed them with a finger and hurried down the stairs.

"Hey kids, what's happening?" They leaped into my arms and overwhelmed me with kisses.

"Uncle Gil, we thought you'd never wake up. Dad says we can't go diving until you and Emma are ready. Are you ready? Come on, let's go!" Marnie tugged at my arm.

Steve came to my rescue. "Whoa, Kids, let Uncle Gil have some coffee and breakfast. He looks like he had a rough night."

"I'll bet he did." Melissa and shook her finger at me. She was two years older than Marnie.

"Sit down, Uncle Gil, we'll get your coffee." The girls bounced into the dining room.

I sat down at the white plastic table and stared across at Dave and Steve who smiled at me like Cheshire cats. I ignored them. While the girls brought my coffee, I watched a black woman rake palm fronds into a pile at the edge of the water.

I took a sip of weak Caribbean coffee, unlike like the northwestern brew I had grown accustomed to.

"Well?" Steve grinned.

"Well what?" I sat back and sipped the coffee.

"Well, hell." Steve said. "We haven't heard from you in a week. Didn't know if you were alive or dead and here you show up in the middle of the night with Emma in tow, injured, and act as if nothing happened? And for the record, the photos you wired were phenomenal. Tell us all about it." Steve's glasses lay on the table and he scooped them up and wiped at them with his shirt.

"We had to get out of town in a hurry," I began as I replayed my trip that ended with the rescue of Emma. Dave and Steve sat transfixed and breathless, as I recounted the death of the captain and the near death of Emma. "And so, here we are."

I watched as the two girls cavorted on the beach and I imagined them as young mermaids, so similar on the outside and yet so different within. Marnie waved at me, screeched then splashed her sister.

"Unbelievable." Steve adjusted his glasses. He stood

slowly and carried his coffee cup into the kitchen.

"What about the babies, Gil?" Dave asked. "You can't just, you know, abandon them to those women, can you?" He looked at me, his head cocked like a spaniel.

"I don't know what to do, Dave, I've been thinking about it, but what else can I do?" He opened his mouth and then closed it as I continued. "I called the Bainbridge police once we were safe."

"And, what did they—uh—you know do?" Dave fidgeted for the correct words. "I mean, like did they investigate?"

"No, Dave, they thought I was a nut, and I can't blame them." I finished my coffee. "I didn't even give them my name. When they started laughing at the idea of killer mermaids on their little island, well—you know?"

Steve returned, sat and propped his elbows on the table. He removed his glasses again and tossed them on the table as if he were displaying a winning hand. "Look, Partner, I know you love this woman, but--"

"You mean Emma, right?" I leaned back in my chair.

"Right, Emma, but how do you know she wasn't the one who shot the captain?" He picked up the glasses and tapped them on the table.

"Well, because she--"

"She admitted she was there, Partner. God knows she had motive, if you believe her story about her brother." He leaned back and folded his hands. "I mean, well, how do you know for sure?"

I sipped my coffee and looked at Steve for a moment. "Steve, we've known each other a long time." He nodded. "Have I ever lied to you?"

Steve sat up straight. "Gil, I'm not talking about you lying to me. That's not the--"

"Emma never lied to me. I wasn't totally convinced myself until I found the pocket watch and the pile of bones. God knows I would have tried to save her anyway because I honestly do love her." I looked down at my hands and then into Steve's eyes. "Those women are killing and probably eating human beings and Emma knew about it and wanted my help to stop it."

Steve absentmindedly rubbed his glasses against his tank top. "So you think it was Lois that was the killer? You think she…" He let that thought trail off as if he couldn't say the words.

"Yes and no." I tipped my chair back against the rail. "I believe that they are all killers, even Catherine. Sometimes the prettiest packages come with the biggest surprises. But there's some kind of power-play between Catherine and Lois that I don't, and will probably never understand." I shrugged and shook my head. "I don't even want to know about it."

Dave cleared his throat and scratched his stomach. "What I'd like to know is who sunk the boat? I mean, what was the point in that?"

I thought a moment and smiled. "You know, Dave, I believe that the Spirit and the captain were so inextricably connected, that when he died, the boat just couldn't live without him." I wiped at something in my eye. "I believe the Spirit died of a broken heart. As simple as that."

Dave smiled and nodded his head. "Yeah, I kinda like that, and it makes as much sense as the rest of the story." He stood. "Come on, let's get in some diving today, have some fun. We can tell horror stories tonight around a beach fire."

I looked at Steve, thinking I'd had enough horror already

to last a lifetime.

Steve slapped me on the back. "Let's get you in this nice warm Caribbean water and I'll help you wash the scales off your--"

"Yeah, you would just love to wash me off," I interrupted. "We need to find you some young Belizean filly to fix you up." I slapped him on the belly. "Come on, I'll race you to the dive shop."

* * *

The water was black beneath us as we watched the late February sun touch down on the horizon. The seas turned to fire in the distance and then the sun was extinguished. They say if one listens closely, you can hear the hiss of fire and water mixing as the sun touches down on the horizon. Emma and I floated in the warm, calm water beside our skiff as the vast field of stars that filled the tropical night became unveiled. We were naked and let the tropical waters heal our bodies and quiet our souls. I reached out and traced the jagged scar on her shoulder. Emma took my hand and pulled me to her. She kissed me and held me close. Then she laid her head on my shoulder and closed her eyes. Her breaths came in long and even whispers.

From the corner of my eye, I saw movement. When I turned around, I saw a young woman lying in the shallows. She had long hair and her skin was so light that it glowed luminescent under the light of the full moon. Her face jerked up. She stared at me through eyes that immobilized me. Emma moaned and slid from my arms. I pulled her back and kissed her cheek. "Emma?" I whispered. No response.

I remembered Dave's words, "No one is booked until

273

next week, Gil. So you have the whole damn ocean to yourself. You and your pretty, of course."

I turned my head back to where I had seen the woman. She was gone, replaced by the faintest of ripples on the dark water as if a fish had surfaced. I shivered.

"Gil?" Emma whispered into my ear so quietly I thought it was a breeze that tickled my eardrum. "Tell me we're safe here." She breathed deeply, asleep once more.

"I don't think I can." I held her tight against my breast and wept in silence.

THE END

Epilogue

The air inside the broch was hot and steamy, the temperament of its inhabitants melancholy. Kerosene lanterns flung shadows across seven women who lay on the floor. Catherine and Lois talked in sign language and at the same time exerted pressure to break the membrane that held their human legs prisoner. The crackling was audible throughout the broch and the smell of decay was pervasive as the shed membranes accumulated around the women and dissolved into liquid.

Two women sat in the black pool at the far side of the broch and cleansed each other's bodies. They whispered and smiled, content with their partner's intimate ministrations.

The steam drifted, as if unable to decide whom to hide and where to move next. It muffled the sounds the women made, as their voices took on human intonation, which was garbled with hisses and growls, until the metamorphosis was complete.

Catherine's angry voice could be heard above the rest and was directed at the young girls who were huddled together near the column where Emma had been held prisoner two weeks earlier.

"Grab some buckets and wash this floor down." Her muscles were in spasm; a puppet being manipulated by an inexperienced puppeteer.

Lois stood and stroked her, "It's all right, Catherine. It'll be okay." She held Catherine in an embrace and whispered, "They're long gone, forget about them."

"Forget about them? Forget about them?" Catherine screamed. "Never! Not until she's dead and I can't remember the taste of her blood in my mouth, like we savored the sweet blood of her idiot brother." Her voice was hoarse as she gasped for breath between words. "How could we have been so stupid to lose Emma and Gil?" Catherine slid out of Lois' arms and knelt on the floor. She bent forward and cried silent tears of frustration. As Lois watched; a smile touched her lips.

The little girls finished their chore and the rest of the women gathered their robes and prepared to leave. Catherine remained on the stone floor, prostrate; bits of membrane still adhered to her skin.

As the door to the broch closed, Catherine wept again for the loss of the Captain, and for the loss of her soldier. She would need some time to contemplate her mistakes and time to plan for the future. Lois rubbed her leader's shoulders and hummed tunelessly.